Please... Call Me Derek

Mac Black

U P Publications
2012

Please... Call Me Derek

Derek travels from child to confused adult, from reporter for the local paper to any job available, doing everything he thinks he should, but doing it his way. Pursuing life and employment leads Derek to fling himself into the sort of sticky situations he won't want to have to explain to his friends or his family. With determination, gritting his teeth, doing everything for the best, how could anything go wrong?

Mac Black

Current occupation: a writer of humorous fiction.

Previous working background: shipbuilding on the River Clyde, tyre manufacturing in Dundee and working in the food industry in Fife (in jobs which didn't make his hands too dirty...).

He was born in Glasgow and lived there for about half a life, then he moved to Carnoustie and then to Cupar, his present home. He has been married for a *long* time...

The Complete Derek Series by Mac Black

Please... Call Me Derek
Derek's In Trouble
Derek's Revenge
Derek's Good Relations
Derek in Action

Please check the publisher's website, www.uppbooks.com for more information or follow Mac on www.macblack.info to see more about the new series that starts with Lofty Issues.

First published in Great Britain in 2012 by U P Publications Ltd
Eco Innovation Centre PetersCourt, City Road Peterborough PE1 1SA UK

Cover design based on designs by Mike Peers
Copyright © U P Publications Ltd

A CIP Catalogue record of this book is available from the British Library

ISBN 978-1-908135-10-0 Paperback
ISBN 978-1-908135-21-6 eBook

9 3 5 7 0 8 6 4 2

Printed in England by The Lightning Source Group

www.uppublications.ltd.uk
www.macblack.info

1

What is a gang? A gang can be described as:

'A group of young people who spend time together for social reasons and may engage in delinquent behaviour'. Sometimes its members can be vicious and cruel. Selfishness and self-aggrandisement can also be prevalent in the group. Very often they form a distinct threat to the surrounding community.

In contrast, there was 'Derek's Gang'. It should not really have been called that because their leader was the last to join, the youngest and the smallest of the group and wore glasses – oh, and was called Sweaty...

It was Wally who found out first, but didn't know he had. He'd heard his mum and dad mention it one night after the local news had been on, but at the time for him, it didn't even register.

"That'll be nice," his mum had said. "Having a big supermarket is just what the town needs."

"What?" said her husband who hadn't been paying attention and was also slightly deaf, so she repeated it.

Twinkletoes lived along the road from Wally. Twinkletoes' dad had a little sweet shop in Newingsworth High Street. His reaction was quite different from that of Wally's mother.

"Oh my goodness... That is terrible... I can shut up shop right away. I can't possibly compete," he moaned.

"You'll manage, love," said his very supportive wife, although she had a horrible feeling that he could be correct, as usual.

"At least it would be a good use for that vacant ground," was the comment by Eck's mum, who lived at the end of the road. "It's nothing but rubbish that's been gathering there for years and goodness knows what happens in there at night..."

"You are right, Mother," said his father.

Jacko was round the corner. Jacko was just like the rest of the little gang but his mum liked to think of herself as a cut above all the others who lived locally.

"How common," she muttered, "A supermarket – huh..." Her husband just gave her a funny look – he was used to this. Jacko learned nothing of it from his mum or dad.

As the youngest members of the little gang, Sweaty and Curly were the least likely to know about the world outside. As usual, they were oblivious to this exciting news or any news in fact. At six-years-old they were only concerned about the important things in life, like being at school on time, being fed, and playing their favourite games with the gang.

There were six in the Blytheton gang – Jacko, Twinkletoes, Wally, Eck, Curly and Sweaty (who was just beginning to understand what his nickname meant). At school, the other four were in the class above Sweaty and Curly, which meant they knew so much more than the two most junior members, in fact they knew everything.

One day, twenty-four years ago, the comments they'd overheard three months earlier took on meaning.

They all lived close to each other and played together. Their young adventures took place on a piece of land that had lain unoccupied for a long time, long before they came into the world. It was midway between their homes and school, close enough to be acceptable to the parents if they knew they were there, which wasn't often, and far enough away to be daring to visit. There they could imagine anything they wanted.

This was where they used an old metal tray to practice for the toboggan races in the Olympics, even though there wasn't any snow. It could be a jungle when they wished, and they would be wild animals being chased by the natives – who were being chased by a man with a big gun. It could be the desert and they'd be lost under a raging sun searching for water. If they couldn't find any, and there wasn't any there anyway, they'd eat their sandwiches and drink their lemonade instead. Trees couldn't be climbed because there weren't any but there were lots of shrubs that had grown wild over the years to hide in and that was good enough for them. It was their land... ...until, one day in early spring, they came along and there was a big sign that said, 'This site has been acquired by BISKO and CO. LTD. for future development – KEEP OUT'.

Being at school and able to read proved itself useful at times, although exactly what the words really meant might have been uncertain, but today, their collective little brains agreed that this looked threatening. How *dare* they put up this sign telling them to keep out of *their* territory... Six pairs of hands grabbed the board and heaved and pushed and, unceremoniously, that annoying piece of wood was pulled from the ground and thrown into the shrubs. They'd shown Bisko's what they thought of that sign – and on they went with their games.

Two days later, the sign was back, but this time it was in a concrete base. They tried and they tried but they couldn't move the blooming thing. So, they just had to ignore it.

One week later and things began to get serious. A wire mesh fence was being erected. It was a big job for the men who had to put it up, so for a while these children were content to sit hidden in the shrubs and watch, mesmerised, as the muscled adults struggled and sweated away with their hammers and machines, digging holes and mixing concrete for the large posts, and unrolling the massive rolls of wire for attaching to the posts. Then the little gang of watchers became bored and, to occupy themselves, threw stones at the hot and irritable team, and hid again in the bushes. The workers shouted at them to go away, or else, but they didn't and some more stones were thrown. The men rapidly became annoyed and started shouting louder and then ran towards them, so they left quickly – but they would return, they vowed. They wouldn't be kept out. They'd been here first.

The following week, when the gang returned to the site, the fence had been completed and encircled the whole area but no-one could be seen, no workmen and no watchman, only warning signs dotted around the perimeter saying 'KEEP OUT'. So, they went in – well Sweaty did. He was the smallest and the only one easily able to squeeze under the fence. Several huts had been erected in the field now. In Sweaty went and had a look about and reported back that the new huts were locked. He was too small to be able to see what was inside and anyway they couldn't do anything this time even if they'd wanted to, but they couldn't just let these minor obstacles be allowed to keep them out, could they? They didn't know what they could do, nor could they understand why these people were stopping them playing there.

So, the collective decision was that they would have to go away home and have a long and serious 'gang think' and rise to this challenge.

Sweaty loved Superman and had a lot of the comics. Twinkletoes was a fan too, but didn't have the comics, so the two of them would do deals. Twinkletoes could get sweets from his dad's shop and Sweaty liked sweets. That day there had been a big swap. Twinkletoes got a Superman Comic and Sweaty got a big bag of Aniseed Balls. Sweaty wasn't selfish and so each gang member was sucking an aniseed ball as they went back for another visit to 'their land'.

Again they could see no-one about, and Sweaty once more had to be the one to squeeze under the wire. He wriggled through. The others were starting to make the gap bigger for the rest of them to follow when Eck noticed the sign had been changed. Eck was not the world's best reader and was slow to inform them that the sign said 'BEWARE – GUARD DOG'.

They all started shouting to Sweaty at the same time but the panic-stricken noises they were making weren't understood by Sweaty. He waved back and carried on towards the huts. That's when they saw the huge dog for the first time, and so did poor

Sweaty. The aforementioned creature had spied him, and started barking fiercely as it ran towards him. Sweaty stood transfixed. The others sensibly stayed on the safe side of the fence. This large Alsatian looked a killer – until it stopped beside Sweaty and started to wag its tail. Sweaty just stood – frozen to the spot. The dog sat down and gave Sweaty a puzzled look. That's when it nudged up to him and sniffed at his pocket with the sweets. The rest of the gang all knew what Sweaty should do. They were on the other side of the fence, so it was easy for them to make decisions in a calm and rational way, but Sweaty remained absolutely petrified.

"Give it a sweet," they all yelled, *"Give it a sweet,"* and eventually the volume of the combined voices pierced his numbed brain and he gingerly reached into his pocket. The dog sat looking expectantly and Sweaty held out his hand and the dog was rewarded with an aniseed ball – and Sweaty had gained a friend for life. Another sweet was given and the dog was delighted, but Sweaty was still nervous and decided that leaving the site by the way he'd entered would be wise. The little watchers had all been silenced in awe of his bravery and glad it was him inside the fence and not them. Sweaty handed over yet another sweet and the dog licked his hand. He backed away and quickly squeezed under the fence. The rest of them heaved a sigh of relief, and were happy to leave until they saw the Alsatian had wriggled out exactly the same way as Sweaty, and was standing behind him. Sweaty wasn't much bigger than the dog, now breathing down his neck, but it looked a little less fearsome wagging its tail.

"Let's go home" was the general opinion. But the dog went too, following closely behind his new friend Sweaty. As one by one they reached their own door, each member of the gang was pleased to have the excuse to abandon Sweaty and the dog, and the pair of them continued along Blytheton Road to Sweaty's own door. He knocked and, when his gran answered the door, she nearly laid kittens on the doorstep to join her grandson and this very large dog.

His request to let his new friend enter the house was met with a firm, *No*. Sweaty said if the dog couldn't get in, he wasn't coming in either, but then he recognised that 'don't you dare' look in his gran's eyes and changed his mind. He parted with yet another aniseed ball and told the dog to, *Sit*, and it did, as his gran grabbed him and pulled him inside, and the dog was left behind. It didn't go away. It sat patiently for a while then began howling – now whether this was through losing its little friend, or because it felt it deserved more aniseed balls, could be debateable. When the police dog-handler arrived it changed from being Sweaty's docile big friend into a very aggressive animal.

Of course, questions had to be asked hadn't they? Gang loyalty prevented Sweaty telling the whole truth and involving them all. The sceptical policeman who called next day was only told that this big dog had followed him home and that Sweaty didn't know who was the owner, which had a little bit of truth in there somewhere. It was disclosed though that both Sweaty and the dog loved aniseed balls.

The little gang decided to find another place to play after that episode, but didn't forgive or forget about Bisko's and the loss of their territory. Within the gang, Sweaty from then on was recognised as a hero. He'd dealt with both a big dog, and a big policeman, just like an expert – and he was only little.

During the next months they watched from outside the wire fence as work progressed with this new and very large building. It was surprising how quickly the concrete base was laid and the new supermarket structure, mainly glass, was put together and eventually ready for opening. For their special day the media had been organised by Bisko's and were there in force including the local television company and a large crowd of onlookers. However, what was shown on screens later was not really what had been intended by Bisko's.

The Press and TV people attending were delighted to discover they could use a different approach for the opening of this particular store. Thanks to a gang of young boys, they chose to concentrate their efforts on the six small marching figures parading in a circle at the front entrance, with the hand-held banners.

Jacko's said, 'Bisko's don't care for kids'

Curly's said, 'Only the streets to play in now'

Twinkletoes', 'No park now – no fun'

Wally's, 'Unloved by Bisko's'

Eck , 'They stole our play park'

Five of them had been given help by Twinkletoes' dad in preparing the placards. He was disgruntled about probably having to shut up his sweetshop and vented his frustration by helping the children. The banners were made from hardboard attached to little poles. Twinkletoes' dad had gloss-painted the board for them but they'd hand-painted the words themselves with gloss paint too, so the words looked a little bit messy but were legible. Sweaty had decided to make his own and he'd used cardboard and his own water-paints.

As they marched around they chanted, "Go, go, Bisko's, go, go away... Go, go, Bisko's, go, go away..." over and over, encouraged by the TV cameraman, until it suddenly started to rain heavily.

Everyone ran for cover, except the little gang – they kept marching until Sweaty's banner started to go floppy and the water-paint started to run down his arm, so they gave up their protest. The onlookers were clapping and laughing and cheering them on as they were filmed, except for the New Store Manager who would have happily strangled each individually if the cameramen hadn't been there. The Store Manager must have had to think fast and probably had made a few hurried phone calls, because he recaptured the Press and TV attention by announcing that Bisko's were going to donate a large sum to improve the playing facilities for the children of Newingsworth.

Behind the scenes, that Manager had suddenly become well known to the Bisko Company Directors, and had proceeded to blot his copy-book. He had been reminded – *Bisko's do not do Charity* – but seeing little alternative, he insisted it was the only way, and in consequence identified himself as potentially disposable. Although Bisko's did pay for a lot of new swings and roundabouts and slides to go into the town park, this little group of protestors never played there – they found it to be much more fun to play in the streets from then on.

That evening, the star of the show was Sweaty, because the television news announcer, and the newspapers next day, referred to their little mob as "DEREK'S GANG". He was proud as Punch watching the footage even though, at the end, it showed him bedraggled and his hair, face and glasses streaked by his paint. Oh, and it should be said, the protest words that were on Sweaty's floppy placard, they read in spindly printing –

'PLEASE... CALL ME DEREK'.

2

Bisko's was a much changed building from the one that began in the days of the young Blytheton Gang. Twenty-four years ago it had been opened. Extension after extension had been added since, and whereas it began as a little Supermarket serving the *town*, over the years it had developed to become a Superstore serving the *Region*. Nowadays it sold almost everything anyone could want. All the usual foodstuffs, fresh and tinned, electrical goods, and clothing, and it had a pharmacy. Its size had increased and the name above the front entrance had pretentious six-foot high letters that declared to the world it was *BISKO'S SUPERSTORE* – but it was still referred to as *The Supermarket* by all who used it.

Many of the smaller shops around town had thrown in the towel, unable to compete as the growth had continued, and of course, the large free parking area encouraged more and more people in to buy, often at discount prices.

Twinkletoes' dad's predictions had been correct in his having to close his little sweet shop because of this, but at least he'd come out of the business *almost* of his own choice. Four years ago, Bisko's Ltd. had required some additional land to create an access from the High Street, a pedestrian footpath, and where his sweetshop was situated was the perfect position and the perfect width. He'd argued long and hard over the money this international company had offered him, but not so long as to chase them off elsewhere and in the end had sold his little shop and the land it stood on for an exorbitant price. When he closed the door of the shop for the last time, and heard the little doorbell that had tinkled for all his working life, he was a happy man.

The Bisko's Manager, who'd nearly burst a blood vessel during the Supermarket's opening ceremony all those years ago, and had caused uproar in the Director's boardroom, had actually done a wonderful job in the stores development. Surprisingly, he'd been forgiven for spending the money on the Children's Play-park, had moved upwards in Bisko's organisation, and had been replaced about five years ago. The security had been upgraded to suit. Bisko's had a good reputation in the industry for caring about its staff, and the staff in turn caring about the business. The original supermarket had a night watchman who had patrolled around the store during the closed period. The most recent superstore contained a great deal of high value items such as the latest televisions and fancy electronic gadgets including laptops and phones, which had excellent street value for thieves, and in consequence was monitored constantly by a barrage of CCTV cameras to record all action during both open and closed times for the store. This hi-tech system churned away for every single day of the year, or nearly...

The working day for the store's most recent manager had become a ritual, a ritual associated with the CCTV monitors. They were positioned in a special locked room which was accessed every four hours to ensure that they were all functioning correctly and also for spot checking the various areas covered. Occasionally the manager made a point of doing unplanned spot-checks if he had a suspicion that something underhand might be happening. He was exceedingly trusting as a manager, but would have hated to be made a fool of by his staff by them taking advantage of that trust, and landing him 'in it', as they say.

His current suspicion was that the back-shop group, and the vehicle unloading teams, were having extended breaks, but not *all* the time, which made it difficult to pinpoint and give justification for action. He was going to speak to the Supervisor for that area anyway, when he had a moment. Obviously re-motivation was called for. What technique should he use this time, he wondered? Threaten to fire him? Would that bring the whole store to a grinding halt? Very probably, so don't go there. No, gently, gently would be wise, and it could wait until the end of the week.

Every morning, recently when he went in to view the monitors, he'd had a slight twinge of guilt himself, but only very slight.

He was beginning to see himself as a voyeur, and was actually enjoying it.

When going through his start of day routine one morning, which was checking that each camera was rotating and recording correctly, he'd noticed a habit that his Office Supervisor had.

She obviously came to work each day on her bicycle, and wore special clothes for travelling and she changed into other clothes when she arrived. One morning he noticed one of the cameras could focus to a corner of the office where she could be seen changing her blouse and her cycling shorts for trousers. She was middle aged, probably similar age to him, but she looked fit and slim and nice, particularly in a state of partial undress, her trim appearance probably linked with the cycling he presumed. And he had become addicted. Every morning he hurriedly went into the monitoring room, making sure he was in plenty time, and enjoyed the moment. He'd do all the other checks then with a happy smile on his face.

Of course, when he had to speak to her about anything, which was at least daily, he'd have a little smirk on his face to accompany the slight increase in the colour of his cheeks, and tended to avoid eye contact. She noticed this and thought he was either a very shy person, or that he fancied her, but she said nothing.

This morning, he hurried in as usual, and there she was, phew... but the picture, it went blank for about three seconds, and returned, and about a minute later it did the same again. It rather spoiled the moment for him and a bad omen for the day, he thought.

He had a horrid feeling that she'd seen the camera moving

and was on to him and had covered it over to hide the view. Oh dear... but the camera was a long way away from her and out of her reach. Then he suddenly realised that the camera or the circuit could be mal-functioning – and nothing to do with the person he'd become well acquainted with. He lifted the phone and dialled the Security Company's number. It was essential for the cameras to be always operational...

3

The rain trickled down the panes of glass, partially obscuring her view and forcing her thoughts to become self-centred once more, painful thoughts, grey dismal thoughts to match the grey dismal day outside. She was lonely, but had brought it all on herself. She'd been headstrong and independent, totally rejecting any advice or guidance offered all those years ago by her parents, and oh how she detested her twin brother, her rich, happily married twin brother. The hate for him was deep and bitter.

With her parents now departed to another world which she cruelly hoped was not a better world because she did not consider they deserved it, she was now suffering the consequences of the type of person she had become – and she was all alone.

In her view, no matter how she'd behaved towards them, it should have been her parent's responsibility to have supported her and cherished her, bitch though she'd been.

If she'd been the parent herself, she'd have crushed all resistance out of her scraggy little body at the right time. They'd left it too late to tackle the problem and the result was entirely due to their failure.

She refused to accept any responsibility whatever but no matter how she considered it, she couldn't see herself as being Miss Wonderful.

Money had not been of any consequence to her until they'd cut off the allowance. She'd never had to think about not having it before, had she? It had always been there to use freely, a twin daughter in a wealthy family who'd been spoiled all her formative years.

Those years since that savage awakening had been tough but she'd managed in her own way, taking advantage of many people to achieve her goals as time passed. Of course, it was not surprising that these chosen friends had eventually realised how they were being used and had severed the relationship, in many cases with difficulty, and often with embarrassment and pain for them only. To her the associations had been unfeeling and they had quickly become just faded memories with no sense of loss to her. Her letters to her brother had been a failure, a big mistake – her mistake.

Her father had obliterated her from his will. She'd refused to believe it at the time, all the money and the large house, all left to her twin brother, the snivelling, whimpering, crawling wimp... It had hurt her father deeply that his wife had died broken-hearted several years after the acrimonious parting of the ways with her teenage daughter. Her mother had always been the sympathetic one when arguments and disagreements had blown up between father and daughter.

Refusing to attend her mother's funeral was the final cause and became his reason to forget she existed. Her father could never forgive her and never saw or spoke to her after that time. The Will had specified everything to be left to her twin brother, that snivelling, whimpering, crawling wimp, *though the Will had not stated it in those precise words.*

It had been wrong of her to send the letters.

In retrospect, they had given the appearance of her softening towards her twin, which was certainly not the case, but it had seemed a necessity at the time. The first attempt had been meant to be seen as reconciliation, beginning with a get-together for a coffee, and she'd said it would be simply to *talk* about everything, though her motives had been totally mercenary. At least he'd written back, but only to say, "No".

Disappointment at that response had turned to annoyance at not getting her way, and after a few months became a bitterness which would only worsen with time.

The second letter, through necessity, had been begging for a little financial help, at least until she could sort herself out, she'd said this time. Again he'd replied by letter, but by what he'd written he'd almost brought a death-wish on himself; he'd used the phrase, *"Well, you've made your bed..."*

Her tone and her composition of the words in the third letter had not been difficult, in fact, she told herself, he should have expected it – he'd rejected her, hadn't he.

She didn't encourage any reply this time. She gave him no clues of her whereabouts with this correspondence. It had been *intended* as one way only.

Having had to move into a shabby flat that she could barely afford, she'd sent the letter without an address. This was deliberate, partially due to the embarrassment of her poverty, but more so because the letter was hate-filled and threatening to him, his wife and their newly born baby. She didn't want him seeking her out afterwards, he could become vicious if roused, she knew, and that letter was sure to rouse him.

She'd survived those years in between but it had been hard. Finding a job, menial tasks at first, general cleaning, cafe and bar work, had been necessary to keep her going. Gradually she'd established that she could do other types of work, in fact, she'd discovered she had a brain. She had been lucky to have an opportunity and moved into office work and quickly progressed from the basic clerking routines into supervision and management.

She was a tough taskmaster, driving her staff harshly and getting a great deal of satisfaction out of just being nasty. Boy, did she enjoy that? She'd pondered the possibility of this being due to her genes and presumed her dear brother could be of a similar temperament if that was the case. She held on to each of her jobs, because she had the knack of forcing success out of the people having to do the tasks. Yes, definitely a bitch – but a successful one.

Any contact with her brother had been long ago, but maybe now was the time to renew the acquaintance. Could she make this her retribution? Some more mature thought would be given to this next action. *This time Thelma would be aiming to win...*

4

Derek lived with the name – well he'd really no choice, of course. 'Sweaty' followed him through college and then to working life, a working life, incidentally, which had ended relatively recently.

Up until about three months ago he had been a reporter for the local paper, "The Slatterfoot Evening News". He'd always done anything and everything he was asked to do and at some point had been involved with reporting the local court cases; sometimes, it was a spread about large houses for sale and the people who had lived in them. He'd done articles recommending recipes for summer barbecues and regular reports of the local football team, both home and away matches.

He had also written criticisms of the shows performed by the local Slatterfoot Am-Dram Group. These criticisms had to be carefully constructed. He'd always tried to be kind to the performers and attempted to somehow make them feel good about themselves, even though they were dreadfully inadequate and amateurish.

He was almost certainly a jack of all trades on that newspaper team. But he had ambition.

Derek wanted to be a *real* writer.

Over the years that he'd been working, his head had been filled with so many ideas. Eventually, that had led him to the decision that he'd only succeed in becoming a *real* writer if he concentrated totally on his musings and developed them into a good saleable story line. That was how he was going to make his fortune. He would earn his living using the true talent he now believed he'd been born with – *and so he gave up his day job*. It had seemed right at the time...

When he mentioned his intentions to his workmates, these practical folk – who'd always preferred having money in the pocket – said, "Don't be so effing stupid." But he was...

And so, on a whim, he'd handed in his resignation eleven weeks ago. His boss had been livid because Derek refused to work his notice and wanted to leave immediately, "...because I have to *catch the mood and write*." Unfortunately, his home computer, which had given him faithful service for nearly three years, suffered a terminal illness and expired two weeks after he stopped the day-job. Even more unfortunately, the computer's demise had been co-incidental with his developing writer's block, the total drying up of ideas, call it what you like, he suffered monumental failure – *at writing.*

So his mindset became, "Why has the world turned against me?" Yes, oh yes, it did seem a bit like that... However, Derek's confidence had always tended to fluctuate from being almost super-human to cringe-worthy hide-in-a-corner. Another week passed without any new ideas surfacing and during that week he'd regretted having recorded all those original ideas, his own very special thoughts, on his dead computer. All the information was totally inaccessible and he could remember only few of the ideas, never mind the detail.

What should he do? What choices did he have?

He could sit it out and wait for the ideas to flow again and suffer for his art? What were the chances of that succeeding? Slim... Buy a new computer? No spare cash, but he'd need one anyway if he was going to write, wouldn't he? How did writers cope before computers? They used typewriters, or wrote longhand on hundreds of sheets of paper, didn't they? No, he didn't fancy that. *Next?* Go back to his old job? No chance there either – his boss wouldn't even *speak* to him, never mind give him a job again.

Any more he could choose from?

What about finding a *new* job? Yes, *that's* the answer. Find a new job, earn money and buy a new computer, and sit down *in the evenings* and write a fantastic novel. It was suddenly so obvious. His mind went back to the discussions and suggestions that had been offered by his ex-work colleagues before he'd left them. "Hold on to this job," they'd implored, "...and write *in the evenings.*" *Oooops...*

He'd have to find a new job then, but having found his previous job with the aid of the College Work Placement Team and having worked in that one job for all those years since leaving college, he had not had a lot of experience at the unenviable task of job-search. In fact he'd had none. But he told himself he'd find something and the Job Centre would be the place. He tried there with no success – not many organisations were looking for his skills it seemed. He watched the newspaper adverts with the same lack of success. So, a change of tack, why stick with journalism? He'd go for anything. When he did attempt employment with the local builder, he found countless others who were experienced in that type of work and *they* couldn't even get the job. It was a depressing situation – until one week ago.

The advert for a new post at 'The Newingsworth Weekly Gazette' caught his eye and suddenly he knew this had to be the job for him, the one he felt he'd been waiting for all those weeks – his speciality. Disappointingly for Derek, the exact same thought had gone through the heads of another thirty-two persons who frequented the Job Centre. He discovered this when he asked for an application form and, of course, this caused his confidence to plummet. It soared though when the letter arrived requesting his presence for an interview at the Job Centre offices – to whittle down the applicant numbers. His spirits tumbled again when he found he was the last of twelve candidates being interviewed. Though lacking in confidence at that first interview, he presumed he must have done alright because he was delighted to be recalled for a second interview. *This time he would excel.*

For this second interrogation, the total had been reduced. This was now a competition involving three people only and he was third to be interviewed on the day. That day was yesterday. He'd already found out and been disappointed to discover that the organisation was small, tiny in fact, and that the money being offered was nothing like he'd been earning, but on the positive side, there had been a special attraction, Mr Sheldon's Personal Assistant. He'd have been happy to let her get personal with him at any time. She was lovely...

Yesterday, he had been sitting nervously at the downstairs front entrance to the office building. His mind had a diversion watching the Main Receptionist set up a new display of pots of everlasting flowers. This was something she intended would not have to be done again for a long time, she'd told him. She'd given the new layout considerable thought and was now rather proud of the end result. Derek had assisted her by holding a few items in position, glad to be of help, but he lost all interest in her and her project the moment Mr Sheldon's Personal Assistant appeared at the top of the stairs. He felt a little miffed sitting at home later thinking about her – he didn't even know her name.

The interview had been a blur to him after that. He'd walked up the stairs behind her to the first floor, to the Newspaper Office – and that had been a lovely experience in itself and he'd have appreciated more stairs to climb. The meeting had been in Mr Sheldon's office and the door had been closed for privacy, but it seemed to Derek afterwards that he had been directing all his answers and thoughts towards the young lady sitting outside, even though she appeared to be totally oblivious of his presence.

This morning, as his thoughts went back to the previous day, he reckoned he'd done himself proud. He'd made up a little about himself when it suited the occasion, obviously not being totally honest, but he told himself that was allowable. Is anyone ever totally truthful at an interview? Deep down he'd been desperate to impress the young lady sitting outside.

The interview had ended with the promise that he would be informed during the following day, one way or the other. He narrowly averted making a right fool of himself when leaving. Gazing lovingly at the young lady, who sadly seemed to have forgotten his existence, he almost walked into a cupboard, next to the door, before quickly realising and shouting, "Bye, see you later..." and exiting the correct way.

Today he'd been nervously twiddling his thumbs. How do you occupy your thoughts when you're on tenterhooks about a job – and about a girl?

He had a claustrophobic feeling when inside the house today. He'd taken himself outside – well almost. He was sitting in the wooden shed in the back garden, the sun was shining and it was beautiful. The shed door was standing open and he was ensconced in an old but comfortable armchair, an armchair which would have looked just as good at its original intended destination – the local skip... but he was suffering pangs of guilt by just sitting there. He wanted to do something to occupy himself but couldn't quite summon up the willpower. So he just sat.

It was a sizeable shed with a large side window. It was the home for a variety of gardening tools, hung and stacked at the far end and not disturbed too often, which pleased the spiders. Surrounding the shed, there was a modest garden, desperate to be cared for, grass that needed cutting again, although the hedging was neat having been trimmed last week, a few shrubs, which had proved they were survivors but nothing too exciting in the way of flowers. He wasn't really a gardening person but he did cut the grass to keep it respectable, and he was the one who'd trimmed the hedge.

Gran and Grandad had gradually lost interest in the garden as the years had passed.

When he'd been younger, he'd known this garden as being a place where he and his pals could kick a ball around for hours, and play the usual stupid games for ages, or until someone took the hump and stormed off. He could also clearly remember the rollicking he used to get from his grandad for creating multiple skid-marks on the grass. Everyone in the gang didn't have a little two wheeler but they'd make do with four bikes and take shots each at racing round the circuit like they did at the real speedway. It didn't half churn up the grass and in those days his grandad took more pride in the garden. If that happened now, would his grandad notice, he wondered?

For him, those nostalgic thoughts couldn't engender any original story ideas – the creation of a special story being his current reason for being alive of course. As he'd sat there on this particular morning, he determined to be more creative than the last few days, nothing physical though, just a more productive thinking process. In truth he was just desperate to receive that telephone call, but alone and comfortable in the chair, his mind swung back guiltily to gardening. Maybe he should do something practical with the ground, like creating a vegetable patch. It was probably too late to start growing vegetables at this time of the year, but he could dig over the ground. It was a good idea, and very enjoyable to imagine, but not for today. The digging could wait until tomorrow.

If he didn't get this job – he'd have plenty spare time to do it.

5

Steve fingered the piece of paper. He shouldn't have it, he knew. Thelma had warned him not to write anything down, but he couldn't trust his memory...

When he'd returned the other night he'd had to take notes, there had been too much detail, and anyway he'd destroy it shortly. The final decision of the destination had been a surprise. He put the slip of paper into his shirt pocket, knowing full well it could be incriminating evidence if found and used later. He went over the list in his head, once again.

Contact telephone numbers

He was good with numbers, for telephones, for the bank, credit cards, and key pads. It was one of the few things he felt confident about. He didn't know who the other drivers were to be, and didn't want to know...

Time of arrival – 3.45pm

All actions had to be precise, she was demanding that. It was her plan after all. *"Do precisely what I say"* her exact words *"...or else..."* He was regretting having agreed to do the job but couldn't stop now...

Maddie had been irritable all day, which wasn't like her. She was usually the strong resolute one but this was different, a bit more serious than just playing a joke on a friend. Of course this time their friends were involved too. Steve hoped they weren't feeling as rough as he did. They'd make a great team if they were, all nervous and bad tempered, getting on each other's nerves, but what did he expect under the circumstances?

"Pick up the ignition key from under the stone on the waste

ground near the school"

He'd been shown the exact spot – it was turning out a bit like an old spy movie – how corny could it get? Except it was very serious – if it all went wrong. The vehicle to be used would be sitting at the end of the road and the registration number would be on the key ring. He hadn't been told what type of vehicle they'd be using.

The home address.

That planned visit to the house was something he was dead against – he'd agreed to do it but... they'd see who was right on the day, wouldn't they?

Clothing?

They'd be wearing workplace overalls, gloves, and masks – had to make sure nothing could fall out of the pockets that could be traceable – these details were not all finalised yet but would be sorted out shortly. The bag of possible bits and pieces was sitting in the other room. He should have a look at it, shouldn't he? He wanted to remain untainted just a little longer, if he could.

Mobile phones.

Make sure they are charged and have some credits. He was in the habit of remembering when he ran out and usually topped-up in a panic. He didn't want panics on this job. It had been well thought through and he'd had clear instructions. Nothing could go wrong...

Weapons?

He'd stood firm on that one – *no* weapons. He'd accepted this job but not for the gang to be seriously hurt in the process.

These were his friends.

He'd done some boxing at school and could handle himself in an emergency and that should be enough – same for Michael. Anyway the police react much more fiercely if there are weapons involved; marksmen and shooting to kill had been in the news recently. It was not the way he wanted to leave the world, though to be honest he hadn't any intention of leaving the world anyway. They would bluff their way and pretend they had guns if needed.

He was sure that was usually enough to get the right reaction anyway.

Plan the route.

Yes this had been done, and he hoped thoroughly enough to bamboozle anyone who might try to follow, but unfortunately you never know for certain. As a non-driver himself, he'd always had difficulty navigating, particularly if he was in a vehicle where the driver hadn't a clue either. None of them came from the targeted area, but he was relying on their driver being good. No – *perfect*... Well, he had to hope that, hadn't he?

Was there anything else? What had he missed? It was very important to assess the risks – much more important than when it was a real job of work. This was self-preservation, remember. Would there be enough fuel in the vehicle? Now that would be a laugh – sending for the RAC in the middle of the job...

Mustn't become paranoid... The biggest fear was maybe not meeting *her* expectations and having to face her afterwards. They could all land in jail, of course, if it all went wrong. No – *they* could land in jail. *She* was calling the shots and would become vicious if she was linked in any way with what they were doing. Anonymity had been demanded by her, with the usual, *"...or else"*.

Madeline was lying there asleep, his Maddie.

She looked lovely, all curves and enticing.

To hell with worrying about the job – he was beginning to feel randy.

Was it thinking about the formidable task ahead, their first attempt at crime, or was it just Maddie's warm body making him feel like this? Silly question...

He slipped off his clothes and slid in beside her.

Her back was to him. His hands moved gently around her body, feeling the softness of the curves, and his body took up her body shape...

"NO – *gerroff*," and suddenly she was awake and... and *nothing* ...other than frustration!

So, he lay and worried about the job instead.

He had to believe it could be more successful than *he'd* just been...

He must be able to get something right, and he must remember to destroy that piece of paper...

6

Today it was Derek's turn to do the shopping but he'd get round to that later. He had ample time, and as twenty-four hour shopping was possible, there was really no need to rush – so he didn't. It wasn't that he was totally lazy. No, he usually had a jog of a few miles each day. He just hadn't reached the jogging stage for today, yet. But he knew how easy it could be to do absolutely nothing.

However there had been no gestation of a brilliant story line though he was trying very hard. The surrounding tranquillity wasn't doing him any good either. It only seemed to be contributing to his self-reproach and minor depression. If only the phone would ring...

His mind returned to yesterday... and negative thinking kicked in. "Oh, but..." and for him there was always an 'Oh but...' What if the editor follows up on the name he gave as the reference – his previous boss? Maybe that gent didn't think as much of Derek as Derek did of himself... In reality, Derek wouldn't have to worry, though he didn't know that. When the phone call had been made enquiring about him, there had been reluctance to admit it at first, but he had been recognised as willing and capable by his ex-boss, although that gent would never have admitted it to Derek.

The warmth of the sunshine began to affect his wakefulness, as he slipped farther down the chair. He entered his state of 'Frantic Inactivity' and began to have some very pleasurable thoughts. He'd started daydreaming about the Editor's PA, the long, dark hair and the deep, brown eyes and the lovely smile, and wouldn't it be nice to work beside her and...

"Derek – telephone. It's your mobile."

The shout came from inside the house. It would have been sensible to have brought the mobile with him, wouldn't it?

Granny Smith had looked after him for most of his life. He'd never managed to find out why though... every time he'd asked her about his parents, she'd told him something different.

"Your mum ran off with a sailor and your dad's still chasing them – somewhere," was one of many. So he'd stopped asking. There was little point as he'd been perfectly happy with her caring for him. She took very good care of him – in fact he was spoiled – oh, him and his grandad, Hector, he lived there too.

His grandad's name was Hector. That was a fact, but to his cronies at the Old Folks Club, he was known as Sinbad, Sinbad the Tailor, from the old days. That had been established by his pals years ago when he'd begun as a boy to work in 'Jackson – The Fifty Shilling Tailor'. So, Derek was not the first in the family to acquire a nickname, oh no, but although, all his life, Derek had known his grandad had this nickname he'd never used it, even in fun. He would tease the old fellow about lots of things, but not that. When he'd been young, his gran had told him that his grandad had always been a bit touchy about it. So each time that Derek was called Sweaty by someone, he'd tell himself it was a family trait – *touchiness* – and that made him feel so much better.

Derek's mother's maiden name was Smith and she'd married very young. It was his dad who had landed him with 'Toozlethwaite' – and then run off, and left him with it, so he'd had two grudges against his old man most of his life. He could almost accept his father vanishing, but couldn't forgive him leaving the name behind...

Where *Toozlethwaite* came from he had really no idea.

He'd searched and found that 'Toozle' could mean 'tousled'. He'd also found 'Thwaite' could be Danish for 'a small coin' or in Norse meant 'to hurl'. It also seemed to mean 'forest land cleared for agriculture'. From that he'd made a guess that his ancestor could have had 'curly hair and paid a small coin for some land' – but he couldn't imagine how 'hurling' fitted in.

Of course, another possibility that he didn't want to think about too much was that maybe his mother had become pregnant, didn't know who the father was, and had made up a name to prevent him feeling bad about not having one. No... That was just being silly. *It must have been a 'curly haired ancestor'.*

One of these days, he often told himself, I'll change my name by deed poll. The obvious choice currently was his mother's – SMITH. What could be simpler? He could be happy with a nickname like 'Smiffy'...

"Derek... Where in heck are you?" Granny Smith yelled this time. Granny was in the hall, standing holding his phone in one hand and a washing basket under her other arm.

"Coming – sorry," as he galloped in. He met her going back into the kitchen with the basket, now full of dirty washing – she'd left his phone on the hall table. It had stopped ringing.

"Who is it? Is it about the job?" he called in to her.

"Oh, I don't know. I didn't answer it... You can call back anyway," came from the kitchen and his phone started ringing again.

A deep breath – don't get over anxious, he said to himself – it's got to be good news – it's got to be.

"Hello..."

"Don't talk," instructed the female voice *"Just listen. Be in the park at the bench beside the Memorial at three o'clock. Be on time or you won't get the money."*

"Oh, right... and what about...?"

Then he found himself standing with a silly grin on his face, holding a telephone that was not connected to anyone.

"She's hung up."

A bit brief, he thought and it didn't tell me much either, certainly not what I wanted to hear. Did she say he'd got the job? No – only *'meet in the park'*. She sounded, sort of – uptight. It was *her*, wasn't it? Today she was tense and irritated, he thought... Didn't seem the same gorgeous beauty he'd seen yesterday – the one he's been...

Surely this wasn't to be yet another interview was it?

"Good news?" asked Granny, being really curious and caring, but trying to appear only half-interested, as she popped her head back out of the kitchen.

"I dunno," replied Derek.

"What do you mean? Don't know...? Didn't she tell you? It was the newspaper office, wasn't it?"

"I think so. Yes, it must have been – I recognised her voice... I think," he replied, with his recurring loss of confidence.

"Well, ring her back and ask her to repeat it – slowly..." she said with a sigh.

"I'd rather not. She'd probably think me a bit of a dumbo."

"Hard to hide that sometimes, Derek," she said softly but lovingly. "At least you could check the phone number, couldn't you?" He wished he'd thought of that first. He was glad when the check confirmed it was the number he'd rung for the interview.

"I knew that all along" he told her, but she'd returned to the loading of the washing machine and didn't hear him.

There would be no clean clothes, very little cooked food, and probably a dirty house, if Granny Smith stopped doing all her chores, but for her it was what she was born to do. She tended to go into automatic mode when doing them – a bit like the washing machine. This household would probably grind to a halt if she wasn't there. Derek and Grandad took full benefit of her always being present and neither dared consider what it could be like if she weren't.

A ten second phone call – must be a record. That was the length of the conversation – between him and the young lady he'd become infatuated with, and he hadn't even said a word. Not exactly romantic, was it? The news hadn't given him the pleasure he'd hoped for. In fact, it hadn't really told him much, and the *money?* What was that about? But on the bright side it was to be a chance to meet her again – in the park and just the two of them – *he might as well enjoy the daydream.*

But, wait a moment – it might not be her he had to meet.

That thought was immediately wiped from the brain cells – in case it was true and he'd be really disappointed – so he returned to his daydream – much more pleasant.

Anyway what time was it?

"Meet at three o'clock – don't be late," he'd been instructed.

So, what to wear? Suit and tie – no thank you – going to be casual. Shave or not? Stubble it shall be, he decided, with a splash of aftershave. I must try to impress this young lady from the word go, was his decision.

But he also didn't want to forget about the book he was intending to write. He could do that as well as the new job, couldn't he? Yes, of course he could. No problem, he told himself, with another splash of confidence. Pity he was still devoid of ideas, but a good story could take time. It had only been eleven weeks... He'd have to get a move on – mustn't be late. The world seemed a brighter place now... It had been a long time since he started humming his favourite song out loud... of course, as usual, it was tuneless.

Oh no, his grandad's in the loo, perfect timing.

"Grandad – are you going to be long?"

Why was it every time he wanted to use the bathroom, it seemed that Grandad had barricaded himself inside?

"D-d-don't rush me. I'm at a crucial m-m-moment."

Conversations with his grandad could be slow affairs. Derek always had to hold himself back from prompting when he stuttered because that got him annoyed and meant it took even longer to get the information out. Yes, he did hold himself back but he couldn't stop himself altogether – he did it for devilment...

"I'm having t-t-trouble with c-c-con..."

"Constipation?"

"N-no, it's a th-th-thirteen letter w-word. C-c-constipation is only t-twelve"

"Grandad, are you doing the crossword in there again?"

Grandad Hector Smith was under pressure and it was to a certain extent of his own making, and it wasn't to do with a bowel movement. At the newsagent he worked for, he had access to unsold copies of lady's magazines which normally would be returned to the supplier, but as a favour to his wife, he'd brought her several every week for a long time which she'd read from cover to cover, even though they were out of date back numbers and now sitting in the front room in a large stack. One day, an article on *'mental degeneration in the elderly'* had caught her imagination...

Gran had no doubt of her own current or future sanity, but decided that her husband, Hector, would have to be watched and although she had been suspicious for a long time that old age was making him a little eccentric, she'd rarely seen any actual signs of brain deterioration. Gran hadn't been to university and this had been her great regret. When younger she'd convinced herself that she had the brain power to have achieved a degree – if only the opportunity had been there. So, four months ago, she decided that she could still do it, and that she would prove it by completing her own personal dissertation in her spare time, at home.

What spare time? She'd just have to do the other work quicker. She didn't even consider off-loading jobs to her husband or her out-of-work grandson. Immediately a theme had formed in her mind, and her chosen subject would be *'The effect of crosswords on an ageing grandad',* and guess who the grandad was to be...

Every magazine in the stack was scoured to find all that related to preventing someone elderly going scatty, batty, or bonkers. She was surprised to find that in almost every one there was an article, or a question with an expert's answer, or a cross reference to a book for further reading, about her selected studies. So, the magazines were searched once again but this time with each relevant piece of information being cut out and placed in her scrap book. In a very short time the book was full and required indexing, which she did. She found a dusty copy of the Family Medical Dictionary for additional reference.

Generally, the advice seemed to be 'don't let an elderly person's brain vegetate' and 'keep both the body and the brain active'. It was also stated in print time and time again, that there appeared to be little success in curing the condition and so therefore it was best to *prevent* rather than attempt to cure.

In late spring, the project had been explained to Hector. That *he* had been chosen didn't appeal to him, but when his wife explained that all he would have to do for his 'brain training' was to complete some crosswords every day, he reluctantly accepted. Grandad had always found enjoyment in attempting the odd crossword. The 'body activity' he agreed to initially as nothing out of the ordinary, because she wanted him to continue cycling, which he did every day anyway, though not energetically. Less pleasing was the exercise regime she eventually devised, to be added to his afternoon activities, only half an hour she said. It was half an hour more than he'd ever done, but he gave in and said, "yes". That was way in the future, wasn't it? It would all peter out very quickly, he told himself confidently. Just go along with her for a peaceful life.

It began easily enough. During that first week, he'd done the daily crossword, she checked that it was complete and correct, and the result recorded, but each day after, it became tougher. Next stage, and he was onto being timed for each puzzle, but it was no longer one per day. He had to do more and more crosswords as each day passed. Now he was doing his paper-round in the morning, his exercises during the afternoon, and when he'd finished the exercises, he was doing more crosswords.

At least he was allowed to sleep in the chair in the evenings while watching television, like a normal grandad. He was proud when she added his first 'gold star' to his chart, but this then added pressure for him *always* to achieve a 'gold star'. Music playing in the background helped when he was doing his crossword, but if there was no music it had to be solitude. He couldn't concentrate when his wife was rattling pans or talking to him, or herself, or doing all these things she constantly was doing.

In the beginning, the garden shed had become his domain – his safe haven. That was – until Derek had ended work and then *he'd* commandeered it, each day, before Hector returned from his paper-round. Hence the bathroom had become the alternative refuge.

For Hector, there was a major flaw in his wife's approach to her whole thesis, and he hadn't the heart to tell her. He was failing to cope. He felt the pressure she was putting him under was driving him over the edge. He felt he was rapidly becoming – *scatty* – *batty* – or *bonkers* – maybe even all three...

"It's the only p-p-place I can get p-peace and qu-qu-qu-qu-quiet away from your g-g-gran to c-c-c-c-c-complete this," he shouted from the other side of the locked door. "It's the l-last c-c-clue. I've got it. It's c-c-*configuration*."

"Don't write in what you've just said, Grandad – that's fifteen letters."

"Ha-*b-b-bloody-ha*."

But at least the toilet's been flushed, hands have been washed, the door's opened and he's out.

"Thanks Grandad. Oh Grandad, would you mind doing a favour for me and taking my turn for the shopping? If I give you this list – she only needs a few things for tea."

"G-g-give it here. I wouldn't do this for every ch-ch-cheeky young p-p-p-p-pup."

"You're a great g-g-g-g-g-grandad," were Derek's parting words as he rapidly dived inside and locked the door.

The swipe from his grandad's paper just missed, but his grandad smiled. At least, this afternoon, the shopping would give him a legitimate excuse to dodge some crosswords.

7

Derek shouted, "I'm off now Granny."

"Just a minute, just a minute... Let me look at you," and she stopped bustling about the kitchen and came to the front door. "You haven't shaved."

"No, I..."

"But at least you smell all right. Although...?"

"It's the stuff you bought me last year for my birthday – the blue stuff – smells good doesn't it?"

"It's maybe wise that you're going to the park for your meeting. Did you have a bath in it? Don't go indoors – everyone'll suffocate."

He didn't want to admit to her that he'd dropped the bottle, last year's birthday present, 'Very Irresistible Givenchy for Men, Eau de Toilette' for which his grandmother had paid a small fortune – and most of it had finished up on the floor. By mistake, he then stood in the puddle so most of the aroma was coming straight from his socks. It was powerful stuff.

"Just don't forget the food or we'll all starve tonight," she instructed.

He was going to say that he'd sub-contracted his turn for shopping and that Grandad was doing it, but didn't due to a sudden pang of conscience. His poor old grandad – he was taking advantage. Then he decided Grandad would go on his bike anyway, so it wouldn't be any bother to him at all – so he happily cancelled his 'pang'.

"But aren't we looking a bit casual – 'smart but casual' I think is the way they say it, isn't it? You look as if you are going out on a date. Remember you are looking for a job," she said.

"Yes, yes..." Was she trying to make him late?

"I think you should have had a haircut."

"Gran, I've washed my hair and I can see out. That'll do me."

His haircut was not modern and probably would have benefited from a good hairdresser. He made do with the local barber. Some quality time spent by a specialist on his head was more than his expenses could cope with currently. He was also undecided on whether he preferred the shaved head look or the modern hippie, but probably neither would have suited him anyway.

"Have you a clean hankie?"

"Granny I'm nearly thirty... Will you stop treating me like a four-year-old," and he opened the front door. "I'm going off then – bye for now. Wish me luck."

"Derek, are you forgetting something?"

"Sor-ry..." ...and before he leaves, the good old kiss-my-cheek routine has to be completed. It's been the same ritual for a long time, even when he was just going out to play. The little gang used to stand giggling outside the open door and then have fun embarrassing him afterwards, when they were kids.

And it still happened when they were older. If Curly was waiting for him, he'd look away and tended to be the one who'd get embarrassed, but Derek carried it on dutifully and still does – at nearly thirty... Strange – he'd become immune to it and is not in the least embarrassed nowadays. At least he was his own man, not necessarily a fully matured adult he'd probably admit, but he had his own ideals. The environment he cared about, and voted for any green candidate that stood for the council, though he felt very often that not enough people were with him on that when he looked around him.

Both his gran and his grandad had retired, but Grandad Hector was still fit enough to do a paper-round on his bike every morning, including Sunday's, and Gran? Well, she's aiming to become a guru in 'Perpetual Motion for Grandads' or something like that...

Inspection over, however, for Derek it was onward to the park. His gran was pleased he'd gone out for the afternoon – that after-shave; it was a strong smell...

The central park wasn't too far away and he'd fifteen minutes to get there. Plenty time. He had to remind himself it is for a job and not a date, as Granny had so rightly pointed out. That fact didn't stop his imagination working. But he felt uncomfortable about not knowing the girl's name. What should he call her? At least he could picture what she'd looked like and that was nice... He knew nothing about the young lady but she somehow seemed inspirational and he could tell she would have a positive effect on his creative powers... There was a tale waiting to be had but for the moment it was just beyond his reach...

BEEEEEEP.........

"All right – keep your hair on, you ruddy road-hog," he yelled at the side, then the rear of the vehicle.

If Gran had seen *that*... He'd nearly stepped out in front of a furniture removal van. His own fault entirely but he wouldn't admit that – would he? Gran would have clipped his ear if she'd been out with him. He was crossing a busy road, maybe not the best time to be day-dreaming, and although it may be a good trait for a budding author, this way would establish the end of his story – *before* a beginning. And still he hadn't found something that he could use.

Wouldn't it would be better to sharpen his thinking for this meeting? Everything could pivot on it. Guaranteeing that this job was to be his would mean concentrating on the matter in hand. He must secure this job. Shouldn't he try to portray the intrepid reporter that he'd claimed at the interview? He'd generously imagined himself to be a boy wonder... Some boy...

His thoughts went back to one of his childhood heroes – Superman. Clark Kent had been a newspaper man too, hadn't he, but he never did get off with the girl he fancied, Lois Lane. It had been tough for him. He had the world's problems on his shoulders, had to change his pants in a phone booth, couldn't share his secrets with anyone, and worse still, his girlfriend thought he was a sap. Derek had always left the cinema feeling really sorry for Clark – but Superman didn't have it *all* bad – he could fly...

It had remained a sunny and balmy summer's day, a perfect day for a visit to the park, and the park was being well used. He could see an informal game of cricket in progress at the far end, and children playing under the watchful eyes of parents on the swings and roundabouts. Generally the children were screaming and shouting happily. Of course there had to be the tumbles and the tears in there as well, but that tended to be the parents.

The children's play area had recently been upgraded and looked bright and cheerful, with a new 'bounce your head off it without getting hurt' surface, added to meet the usual obligatory 'must make it safe even if it spoils the fun' bylaws.

On the pond where he used to fish for minnows there were a few model yachts sailing lazily about, but the scene was spoiled a little by the summer's day carelessness of visitors, which had caused used crisp packets, and aluminium drink cans to float around like little islands. As the aluminium cans moved gently in the breeze, they glinted in the sun – almost artistically – but it was still rubbish; not that Derek noticed, of course, his brain was now tuned to homing-in on 'The Target'.

It was a nice park and well maintained even though there was constant criticism of park staff and the state of the park. This was one of the public's many regular subjects to grumble about in the *Letters to the Editor*, he'd had to edit them sometimes. The less than complimentary ones and downright abusive often had names and addresses withheld.

Some people seemed to have been born grumpy. How well he knew this from the various interviews and reports he'd done in his time. What a pleasant change when he talked to someone who had nice things to say. For the newspaper, it was always easier to satisfy a story-hungry editor by finding and talking to people with grumbles he could scribble down, than to get the happy news stories published – and that was sad. Unfortunately his happy tales often seemed weak once they'd been typed out and therefore tended to be ignored. Of course, it could be that he was just a lousy journalist.

The War Memorial flower beds always had a nice display of colour, either annuals, bulbs, or pretty patterns of succulents, subject to the time of year. Flowers were currently blooming beautifully. And who would believe that this park was being successfully and lovingly cared for by quite a small team? And it was a team which worked hard through all seasons.

This small group cared about the job, but of course, didn't let that care get in the way of them having their own grumbles and grouses. Give them the chance and they'd eagerly bellyache to anyone using the park, that is anyone that would be willing to listen, and even sometimes to those who weren't willing to listen, but who were too kind to just walk on.

A spade or brush would be used to lean on, if one was being carried, but if not, something to lean against would be favoured before starting. To the visitor these should be warning signals. They would then discourse on – the weather being too hot or too cold or too dry or too wet, all the leaves falling from the trees that they had to clear up, hoses that were burst or too short, seeds that failed to germinate, vandalism and footprints in the flower beds, their low pay, dog poo on boots and not having enough staff to do all the jobs... Oh, and the fact that they achieved such perfection even with a bloody awful boss. Otherwise they were a happy bunch.

Those park users who knew better and had experienced 'the chat' would be wary of getting too close to them, and would shout a cheery, "Hello," from a distance. Derek, as a regular visitor over the years, had been on the lookout, and, so far today, had seen none of the park staff to have to dodge.

The bench beside the Memorial was shaded from the sun by some large oak trees. He thought this would have been a well occupied spot on a day like today, but no. He was pleased to see that it was not being used. This was the bench where he hoped that he would be meeting her...

A glance at his watch – he prided himself that it was always exactly at Greenwich Mean Time, and he confirmed he was two minutes and twenty-five seconds early. Excellent timing, Toozlethwaite, and he gave himself bonus points for that. But he saw no sign of anyone waiting for him. Or was there?

Was he mistaken or did someone dodge behind that tree? It was a female.

Yes, it was.

He pretended not to see her but was delighted that it was the girl that he'd hoped it would be. Hide and seek wasn't mentioned in the phone call, was it?

He nonchalantly sauntered over to the defined bench and hesitated. Would two people be able to sit on it without being on top of bird poo? Only with difficulty, he concluded, and being a gentleman, hoping to impress, he sat on some to ensure a clear space for her next to him.

Keep calm, he said to himself, knowing full well that his heart had already kicked onto a faster pace. His future depended on this.

Where is she now?

Don't look round. Relax...

"What are *you* doing here?" The voice was at his left ear and he jumped, startled.

"I..." he just about managed to splutter out.

"I said, what are *you* doing here?" and she sounded aggressive.

"I... What do you think I'm doing here? You asked me to come didn't you?"

He was a little unnerved to say the least as she stood looking down at him.

In his daydream she'd fancied him – instantly... I'm getting a lot of things wrong these days, he told himself.

"Don't get smart with me. You are the one who came for the interview yesterday aren't you?"

"Yes and if I'd known this was how I would be welcomed into the company I wouldn't have been here today," was his irritated response, and he immediately regretted it.

What had he done wrong? Was this another test? Had he burned his bridges already?

"I didn't expect it to be you. You are not one of *them*, are you?" she said giving him a really haughty down the nose stare. "If you are, you have *really* disappointed me."

"One of *whom?*" he replied making sure his grammar was perfect, because nothing else appeared to be.

"You're here for the money?"

"Of course I am. Isn't that why we all work?" He was uncomfortable and he knew he was sounding edgy. "...And that's why I was at the interview obviously..." He was verging on sarcastic. "...and I didn't ask or expect to be paid beforehand if that's what you were intending. Is that your normal way?" He must remain calm and not say too much. "I'm not sure I even want the money or the job now" and then he bit his tongue as he turned his head away. That's not what he'd wanted to say... He should be saying less, rather than digging a deep hole...

"Wait a minute – you... what? You are confusing me," and she sat down beside him and just stared straight at him.

"I'm confusing *you?*" was his response.

And it was his turn to stand – totally forgetting that a moment before his policy was going to be 'to say less'. No, he seemed unable to prevent himself from figuratively jumping into the figuratively previously dug deep hole – and pulling the soil down on top of him. So he continued... "Could we maybe start all over again? I'm here because you phoned me and I thought hopefully that you were going to be the one who'd confirm that I was to start working for your company. I may have presumed wrongly. I'm here on time and at the right place, as requested, but I'm receiving strange messages in my head and it's not good."

"Oh no... Oh no..." she gasped.

Blast... Yes, he'd definitely made things worse...

"Dear me, no... I've made a terrible mistake," she gulped, looking up at him in a sort of cowed way that made him feel he was starting to bully her, which was obviously a bad move.

"I didn't get the job then," he said disappointedly, and the happy breeze that had earlier been merrily blowing through his sails suddenly went very calm.

"No, I mean, yes. It's not your fault. Oh, my goodness. This could cost me my job," and she started sobbing.

Now at this point he really appreciated Granny Smith's attention to detail, because like a magician, he whipped his handkerchief out of his pocket and... *damn*... "I should have checked and changed it when she asked me" he muttered. He couldn't give anyone that. He slipped it back into his pocket quickly – she didn't notice... Phew...

"Oh no... *No, no, no*... I've been incredibly *stupid*," she sobbed.

It seemed wise not to respond to that – certainly not to agree. She was genuinely upset. Should he try the sympathetic approach – giving her a shoulder to cry on would be the manly thing to do – maybe. But these were real tears and his jacket could be ruined.

"Can I help you?" he said "Sometimes it's good to talk to someone about a problem. I'm a good listener," and he sat down again and tried to look sympathetic, but thought he probably just looked silly with the expression he'd chosen.

She stopped sobbing and looked at him, and his daydream floated in again... *Ooooooh*... I think she sees the real me shining through for the first time – a beautiful moment... was the clear thought in his head.

"I thought I'd recognised you," she said.

He wanted to wipe the tear from her eye. "You did? I would hope so. I was the one at the interview yesterday – remember?"

He rapidly did a memory bank search – if she meant she'd seen him before yesterday, had he met her in a previous life?

"Yes... I remember now," she exclaimed. "You're *Sweaty* – Sweaty – from two years above me at school. You were a senior... *Sweaty*... We all used to think that was a really sad nickname for someone to have. *Poor you.*"

"No, I'm – I'm *Derek*..." he protested.

Instead of him offering the sympathy, he was receiving it.

This was not how he felt the conversation should be progressing.

"Sweaty, Sweaty, *Sweaty*... Oh it's good to see you again. I'm so glad it's you. I always thought you were too nice for that name."

I wish she'd stop calling me that... And why can't I remember her, bounced around his brain.

"Did...eh...Did I know you then?" he enquired.

"Oh no, I just admired you from a distance. Sorry, I should have introduced myself. I'm Sally. Sally Donaldson, but I've made a real mess of this."

"I'm very pleased to meet you Sally but can you tell me what is going on?"

"I've messed up – badly. I've mixed up two telephone numbers and I've given someone else your job."

"Oh..." was his saddened response. "That's nice"

"No it's not and I wish I felt as calm as you. *You* were the one we wanted."

"Well wasn't this other person surprised? Being offered a job over the phone... one that wasn't even applied for? Did they want it? What did they say?"

"I don't know – it was an answering machine. I just left a message."

"So you were going to give me money instead then?"

"No silly... *That was for the bribe*... Oh, I shouldn't have said that," and she blushed – and it made her look even nicer, he thought.

"I shouldn't be talking to you this way but I'm feeling really guilty about messing up your chances. But maybe it's better if you are not involved now anyway."

"Wait a minute – surely you realised that I'm an eager and extremely proficient newspaper reporter and wouldn't want to miss out on a story? I can't let this go."

He'd lied, but it was only a white lie because at least he dearly wanted to be proficient ...and this was sounding like a story that demanded a follow-up. He had to hold on to the situation.

"When was I supposed to start?"

"Tomorrow at nine o'clock."

"Then why don't I appear as I was supposed to and no-one else will know about the phone mix-up and then I'd be around to help you in the future and poke in my investigative nose. When bribes are being paid, someone's up to no good."

"But the message I've left...?"

"I am *convinced* that I'll be the only one who arrives tomorrow," he declared with fake confidence. "But you said you'd left the wrong message. Shouldn't you get back to that person and rearrange something to cover your tracks. Was that who was to be given the money?"

"Yes," she replied meekly.

"So, if you tried phoning again maybe you could still pass the money over tonight and keep yourself out of trouble."

At last, he felt he was winning her over, he really liked her – *and he wanted the job.*

"Look, I don't know what this money is really for, and I'm guessing it's a bribe but I'm almost certain it's illegal," she said. "I'm his PA but he doesn't tell me everything – just special instructions – which I mess up..."

He then moved into control mode and suggested she should immediately call the 'other' number again and re-arrange the money collection for four o'clock. He was back in charge and Sally was grateful to be led. It now felt as if he was doing a useful job. This was more like what he was used to – working unpaid overtime in advance – but if it could get him the job – and Sally – he'd be happy. She took his advice and it wasn't the answering machine this time. There was a relieved smile on her face.

"Thanks Sweaty. I may just keep my job. He'll be here at four. We might make a good team..."

"Please don't call me *Swea...*" he started to say ...Oh, what does it matter? All's well that ends well, but deep down he hoped this was just the beginning – of him and her.

"I'll see you tomorrow – Sally. Better get a move on. Lot's to do. I'll have to get back to writing my book. You've given me some ideas and I think I might make you the heroine."

A nice touch there, Sweaty – he could maybe have seriously impressed her now.

"I have never been that before," she said, "I'd like that – but Sweaty, perhaps you shouldn't use quite so much after-shave. See you then – tomorrow." She smiled.

8

Down at Saddanbroke's Betting Shop, it was Spider who answered the phone. He always did. He was the voice – and the brain behind the voice – and he worked there.

He had a low opinion of most of the punters who came in day after day to make their fortunes. He had tried it and failed himself so he was able to claim to be an expert loser, but he had a gift for prediction – a gift he couldn't use for himself for some strange inexplicable reason. He could tell which horse to put your money on, at good odds, taking account of the course, the weather forecasted, the jockey, and the competition, all based on an unerring instinct. He could tell you which to go for and your chances of winning would be very good usually, but for some reason he daren't actually place a bet himself. That had never worked.

He was destined to be a loser if he indulged himself. This made him a good bloke to know... Not necessarily a good bloke to be, but he lived with it.

He had to be careful how he used his talent though, because his boss would have done him serious injury, never mind kicking him out of the job, if he'd thought fiddling was happening on his own doorstep – particularly if Spider's friends were helping reduce the profits of this cosy little betting organisation.

So Spider's capabilities were not public knowledge, he was loyal to his boss, and generally his talent he kept to himself. You would have to be a *very* trusted friend to be offered the benefit of Spider's undoubted skill and you would have to place your bet at another bookmaker's.

But it didn't stop Spider playing his own fantasy betting game. He was doing well currently – worth millions – fantasy millions, of course... but today he was confused, well, confused and excited. He'd answered the phone in the Bookie's this morning and discovered he'd been headhunted.

It didn't half brighten up his day for him. He'd been told to start the following day at a new job. Although he continued doing all his duties in his usual efficient manner, he'd also been deciding the wording of his resignation speech, a rather unusual duty for a long-serving employee. Therefore, at three o'clock, just before he was due to end his working day, he knocked on his boss's door and walked in confidently.

"Sorry boss, but I won't be in tomorrow. I've now got a prior engagement – I've been 'ead 'unted."

At first his boss thought he was moving to another bookmaker's, pinched from under his nose, which was against all the rules, and made him very unhappy. Spider hurriedly told him it wasn't a job in another bookmaker's and his boss became less unhappy. Spider explained that he was joining a newspaper team.

His boss just about did himself a serious injury – laughing his head off. He liked Spider but found this tale a bit far-fetched. He asked him to explain how he'd got this job. He knew Spider well and it did not seem all that likely.

"The phone message was left fanking me for bein' at the interview and telling me to be at the office at nine-o'clock to start the job, an' 'at."

His boss asked when he'd been at the interview but Spider couldn't remember. He thought it could have been a while ago. However, since taking the phone call he'd convinced himself that he *had* attended an interview somewhere, at some time, for some job – must have been this one, mustn't it?

This was accepted doubtfully by the boss but he was happy that Spider could be making some progress, however unlikely it seemed. He was decent enough to tell him that if it didn't work out to give him a ring and he'd have him back in a shot. Reacting in this soft-hearted manner was way out of character for his boss, who for some reason had always felt kindly towards Spider. He looked on him to be more a part of his family than his own kith and kin. Spider had given him good service and was extremely trustworthy – a valuable thing in his business – a thing his family members were shaky on.

So, Spider was leaving on good terms – with the added bonus that he'd been *'ead'unted*.

Before opening the front door, he looked around. He saw all the well-known faces dotted about the betting shop, faces that were all anxiously watching the viewing screens as a race approached its completion. He shook his head sadly. No one noticed his departure. The energies in the room were directed at the flickering screen and the many desires of winning. For the last time he hoped, Spider closed the door behind him.

He stepped outside and didn't hear the shrill ring of the office phone, the phone that had brought him his good news.

This time, his ex-boss answered it.

9

Derek didn't leave the park.

He was curious about who was putting the pressure on Sally and decided he wanted a glimpse of the individual who would be coming to collect the money. Now he hadn't actually seen any money and didn't know how much was involved but he guessed it would be more than a tenner.

Sally had a large shoulder-bag with her. The money must have been in that. She didn't seem to truly know what the money was for. Was someone really being bribed or had Sally let her imagination run away with her?

His imagination was going into overdrive – about her and him. He thought it wise not to build up too much hope but deep down he felt happy that she liked him too. He couldn't let Sally know he was still around and watching her. It wouldn't help the trust would it? Is she still standing there, he wondered? If I can't see her, she shouldn't be able to see me. A park can be a great place for hide and seek, as had been obvious earlier. He decided it was his turn, so, slipping into the bushes, he worked his way farther round, putting himself into a good viewing position. Yes, now he could see what was happening and he couldn't be seen. Just get comfortable...

"And what are we doing 'ere then, might I ask?"

"*What the...*" exclaimed Derek.

"Startled were you sir?" the constable continued.

"I eh... I'm just looking for the ball, Officer, it was a bad bounce and..." he stammered, as he scrabbled around the base of a thorny bush, scratching his hand in the process.

When viewed from his crouching position, this policeman was tall and slightly menacing and stirred old memories. Ever since he was six-years-old, after the dog incident at Bisko's when he'd had to *lie* to that giant of a policeman, which he'd never been able to clear fully from his conscience, he'd felt traumatised by *any* policeman. This one certainly played the situation to his advantage. It was an unfortunate coincidence for Derek that this bored policeman, who was nearing the end of his shift, had noticed him vanishing into the shrubbery. Being allocated the park duties for a full day to some constables was a doddle, but this one had joined the force because he, "just 'ad to get some action".

With the sun shining today, everyone was happy and being annoyingly well-behaved in the park but that meant he'd had nothing worth reporting in his little black notebook to satisfy Sarge. Seeing Derek leave the formal path showed some promise, and it could be his last chance today to act on a potential misdemeanour. So off into the bushes he'd traipsed too, deciding, "If this bloke's gone in for a piddle, a widdle, or a leak, or whatever 'e chooses to call it, I could 'ave 'im for Indecent Exposure or Lewd Be'aviour, or maybe even for Creating a Public Nuisance." He couldn't make up his mind which would gain him the biggest credits in his sergeant's eyes. Anyway, this bloke hadn't actually done anything yet, "...but I'll give 'im time," he decided. "I'll get 'im for something..."

So he had crept up on Derek.

"We wouldn't like to think that we were getting up to mischief, now would we? ...what with all those pretty girls about and the young children playing and you, sort of, hmm, 'iding in the bushes? Peeping Tom, is it? We don't take kindly to that sort of thing, y'know. When we come across these types of people we usually tend to treat 'em rough-like – if they 'ave to be dealt with. Just making sure you are aware, *Sir*. We wouldn't like that now would we, *Sir*?" He stopped his lecture and sniffed, and sniffed again, and gave Derek a very funny look. "We like strong perfumes, do we, *Sir*?"

"I beg your pardon. I said I was looking for my ball."

"Yes sir – and you 'eard me. We've 'ad a lot of your sort recently and I 'ate repeating myself but if..."

"I can't see the ball, Officer. I'll... err... I will just have to buy another I guess."

"Good idea, I'd say – *Sir*."

And the constable very obviously sniffed the air once more as Derek passed him sheepishly. Much as he wanted to explain his aftershave accident, this seemed neither the time nor the place. He wisely concluded that getting a sympathetic hearing of his earlier ablution mishap, from this policeman, was well beyond the realms of possibility.

Derek therefore, to his shame, had to make a hasty exit from his intended hiding place, followed by the gentleman in blue, who was disappointed that Derek hadn't even become a little obstreperous and given him some excuse to act.

Derek was thankful that he couldn't see Sally because, hopefully, she could not then have seen him in the hiding place nor his confrontation with the law, nor glimpsed him slinking back out of the shrubbery.

"What sort of a bloke did he think I was?" he muttered to himself. "What a cheek. I wish he'd stop looking at me like that – he's making me feel guilty."

He was irritated. "I'll walk away briskly. Aw look at *that*... There's mud on my knees. *Bugger!* My good jeans..." Derek's day was starting to go downhill again. He sensed rather than heard the measured step that was continuing behind him. Big feet on a big policeman but with rubber soles can be surprisingly quiet.

Why doesn't he walk the other way? He's obviously got nothing else to do. He's still following. Should I run? No, don't panic. Must find another place to watch from but I'll have to shake off Constable Plod. I'll make for the far park entrance and lose him outside the park – I've time to spare.

So he kept walking steadily, then a little faster, and chanced a quick glance round. Thankfully the frustrated constable had given him up as a lost opportunity and had gone off desperately looking for the worst in someone else – his shift hadn't long to go.

For Derek, a swift turn on the heel and back along the path he went, feeling marginally happier again. He'd met Sally and he was glad now they knew each other, and then there had been that nice policeman – yes, Derek was forcing himself to generate a positive attitude to the proceedings – but it wasn't easy.

To observe from another position was called for and, from somewhere this side of the pond, there was still a view of the Memorial – for example by climbing one of the big trees. What a choice he had too. These were magnificent specimens that had been standing for three or four times his age. Look at the height – *enormous*... Stop. Behave yourself. New jeans, remember ...and then he realised he couldn't possibly in a month of Sundays get up a tree. There must be somewhere else where he could see but still be hidden.

"Hmm," he pondered, "I could be a little out of practice at this surveillance lark I guess." Good surveillance should be from the car, with binoculars and a camera and a telephoto lens at the ready, and a flask of hot coffee to keep the brain alert – but he had none of these. Ah well... but there was a big shed which looked like the Park Attendants domain, and intruders were unwelcome – obviously. 'No entry without authorisation' it stated on a large red and white sign nailed to the side of the building.

That's it, yes... the shed – and he was already visualising getting on the roof so he'd be well above the bushes and be able to see across the pond. All that was required was for him to climb up the drainpipe, get a foothold at the top of the window, and grab the roof ridge and hold on tight, but what next? Ah, swing his left leg onto that outlet – oh, oh, and now he was *stuck*... Now he was dangling and daren't look down, and his arms were getting weak, he couldn't hold on much longer... Don't panic... He needed a foothold – *but he couldn't find any... Help...* He was in a cold sweat as he actually stood flat on the ground, looking up, both feet rooted to the spot and his body rigid in terror.

If he couldn't cope in his imagination, it might be wise not to proceed in reality, he reasoned, and then he noticed the ladder. It was hanging on hooks on the side of the shed and was crying out to be used. That would get him easily onto the roof and, with the trees at his back, he wouldn't be glaringly obvious to anyone and the Memorial would be in full view then. And anyway the policeman's gone. Nothing ventured... just lift the ladder...

"Oh, it's heavier than I thought. Careful, get the balance right and gently turn it round," he told himself.

"Whatcha doin' wif our ladder," came from a man in working overalls who'd appeared from inside the shed.

"Sorry, I didn't see you there," Derek stopped in mid-swing.

"Whatcha doin' wif our ladder, I said?"

"I was just going to..."

"S'our ladder."

"I wouldn't dream of suggesting that it isn't, although technically it belongs to the Council and, as you should know, the Council are the representatives of the public so therefore..." Derek sounded really annoying when he spoke condescendingly. Luckily for him this gent hadn't a clue as to what he was actually saying, or he might have thumped him.

"Whatcha on about?" the guardian of the ladder demanded.

"I was just explaining in simple terms that..." but, Derek should have realised that this was a conversation that could go nowhere.

"*CHAR-LEE.*"

"Wot's wrong Arfur?" shouted Charlie, a voice from inside the shed. Oh God, thought Derek, how many of them are there? Maybe I shouldn't have started this. He stood there balancing this heavy extending ladder with difficulty and wondered how long his arms could support it.

"*Iss berks pinchin' our ladder.*"

"No, you've got it wrong – I was just about to..." Derek squeaked, as the ladder began to slip lower.

"Shurrup, Smartass. *Makin' us out t' be stoopid, Charlee.*"

"*We aint stoopid, Arfur – you tell 'im 'at.*"

"Well, we aint stoopid, Smartass," said Arthur, "*I told 'im, Charlee.*"

"*Charlie,*" shouted Derek trying a different approach, "*I am trying to explain to Arthur that...*"

But Charlie had left the comfort of the shed and was standing behind him and reached out for Derek's shoulder with a large hand. Derek's hold of the ladder gave, and it clattered to the ground smacking Derek's shin on the way down.

"*Ouch. My leg. Oh. Oooooh – you are hurting.*" Derek realised he would have liked Charlie better if he had remained in the shed and the whole affair hadn't become physical...

"I don' like smar' asses *ever.*" Charlie squeezed Derek's shoulder in a vice-like grip. "Member las' week – 'at geezzer oo took our value-able forks an' spades?" asked Arthur "D'ye fink zisses 'im again?"

"I think that suggesting that your forks and spades are valuable is exaggerating a little..." Derek ventured. "...*OUCH.*" Derek squeaked again.

"You fink ee could be 'im, Arfur?" said Charlie.

"Lemme look a' 'im again. Yea – absolutely, Charlie. This is maybe *deff*-inately 'im. Sure as daisies 'ave roots."

"Wheresa' copper oo comes into the park? 'e saw 'im too din't 'e – when 'e stole 'em?" said Charlie.

"Yea," said Arthur. "An' 'e would... ehm... whatsa' legal frase, Charlie?"

"*He'd corroborate your statement...*" Derek just felt he *had* to help, a habit associated with Grandad. His shoulder was squeezed tighter.

"EE... AST... ME... Smartass," snarled Charlie and continued "Arfur, listen, the frase yer searching for is – *yer wantin' 'im t' corroborate yer statement,* ok?"

"Fanks Charlie. Ah'll go get 'im 'en... eez just passed," said Arthur. So off Arthur went, leaving Derek gazing lovingly into the eyes of Charlie. There was a long silence.

Charlie's grip could be described as like a gorilla's and Derek was unhappy but couldn't think of any way that would help other than talking nicely to Charlie. What do you talk about in a situation like this, thought Derek? He hadn't experienced anything like this before.

"Charlie... Mate..." Derek ventured.

"*Shurrup*. Arfur's my mate."

That approach hadn't been too successful but a mobile phone starting to sound from somewhere on Charlie's person. The ringtone was 'Love me tender'. "How sweet," thought Derek... "Elvis would be pleased..."

Charlie fumbled out the phone with his free hand. "Allo..." he said, "Yea, but... but... but... awrigh' Muvver. 'ow much? Dunno... but... lemme check..." While he was talking he removed his apelike grip to feel in his trouser pocket for money, and Derek stood patiently – until he suddenly realised this could be his only chance – now – *GO*. He ran as he'd never run before, leaping over the ladder, which thankfully Charlie managed to fall over while apologising to his mother for ending the conversation abruptly.

Meanwhile, Arthur had found Derek's other friend PC Plod and they were running along the path towards him too. Into the bushes he went and doubled back, aiming for the gate. He hoped if he could get out of the park he'd lose them at the main road or even farther along at the supermarket.

This was not the way his day was supposed to turn out. How he longed to be back in his old armchair in the shed. He looked back. He was well ahead but they'd spotted him again. Derek had to keep running, but a little faster... As he covered the ground in large bounds, he began to question why he was running – he hadn't done anything – he was innocent – but those facts didn't stop him.

It just seemed wiser to keep moving – *fast*.

He'd come out of the park now but the road was busy. In the circumstance he decided to chance playing dodgems with the traffic and hoped his pursuers wouldn't be as stupid.

BEEEEEEEEEP......

"*Bloody hell.* Is that the same furniture van? That's the second time. Is *he* out to get me as well? This road never used to be this busy. *Whoops.* Made it. Phew. They've chickened out – gives me a bigger lead"

He was running in the direction of Bisko's. This twenty-four hour shopping facility always appeared busy, especially the car park. The perfect place to 'vanish'... It gave the impression of constant, though inessential, activity. The target for all car-shoppers of course was to find a parking space closest to the store entrance with the minimum walking distance, and vehicles were circling around in the search for these valuable spaces which were rapidly refilled. One came out – one went in – perpetually...

Should be easy to lose them here – surely?

Derek slowed down to a fast walking pace in the hope he would draw less attention and imagined he was on his way to do today's shopping, as he should have been anyway.

As he crossed between the cars, he stopped behind a very large vehicle and had a look back. Damn – they'd followed him in but he didn't think they'd seen him there. Anyway, he thought, that policeman should be chasing real criminals. Derek considered entering the store itself but decided it would be wiser remaining in the car park, out in the open air. He appreciated being able to hide behind this giant car, a large Range Rover, but at the same time had a guilty conscience just being so close to this environmental hazard. Deep down he criticised the owner for the car's existence – it was a real gas guzzler, but it was high sided, he was unseen, and he was able to sidle casually round the far side, so it had its uses. If he could stay hidden they'd pass him by.

"Hey, look who's here... It's Stinky. What are you looking guilty about, eh?" said the voice accusingly...

10

Derek didn't have to see the face. The memory of that voice made him uncomfortable. Please no – not today, thank you – especially not now – but yes, and right beside him. He didn't want to look, but it was who he thought – Freddie Watt. He remembered him and his elder brother for the chaos they'd caused back at school. They were both still up to no good he'd heard.

They knew him but Derek didn't look on them as friends.

Freddie appeared to be loitering with intent as usual – the intent right at this moment seemed to be to chat to Derek, who didn't want to listen. "Are you not talking, Stinky?" he prodded. "Is your old pal not good enough for you nowadays?"

"You're no pal Freddy – and it's Sweaty, not Stinky, I'll remind you – *I mean it's Derek.*" It suddenly occurred to him that if he continued talking to someone he'd be less obvious to the fan club chasing him. "What are you doing here anyway?" he enquired with his mouth only – his eyes and brain were on other matters.

"Oh, this and that," said Freddie slyly, "Ye know..." with his well known nod-nod-wink-wink look.

"No I don't know." Derek was already regretting having asked.

He continued to watch PC Plod, Arthur and Charlie out of the corner of his eye, and tried to make himself as small as possible.

"Me and my brother are just having a little fun this afternoon," continued Freddie. "D'you fancy a run in the country with us?"

"Sorry – haven't brought my running shorts, Freddie," was the witty reply, well, Derek thought it witty...

"Very funny, but I bet you've never driven a four-wheel-drive."

"You're right, I haven't and you were going to give me a chance to drive yours, I suppose," he said, hoping Freddie wasn't too thick to appreciate a little sarcasm.

"No, of course not, but Bill will have this one going in just a few more moments," Freddie grinned. And as he said that the engine of the vehicle Derek was hiding behind, sprang into life and there at the wheel was – oh no – the elder brother, Bill...

Freddie opened the passenger door. Bill shouted, "Get in quick. Are you coming too, Stinky? Go on – live dangerously – jump in."

"No thank you – *and I'm not Stinky* – I'm Derek," he yelled back as the door closed and the two of them roared off leaving him exposed to a cloud of exhaust – and then totally exposed.

"*Stop them. Somebody stop them. That's my car they're stealing.*" The voice came from behind a filled trolley coming at breakneck speed – towards Derek.

Derek panicked as he realised that this was a life and death moment, or at least severe injury if that trolley hit him. He jumped aside just in time, as the trolley and its driver tried to do an emergency stop – and failed – and it toppled into the side of the new Mini-Cooper parked beyond...

"Got you." Derek was grabbed. "*Officer, Officer, come quickly – I've caught one of them. Help me. Help.*"

Now what annoyed Derek was not that he had been caught, but that he was being manhandled by the owner of that threat to the environment, which had just been driven off. He felt this fellow holding him needed a good talking-to about all the damage he was doing to the world around – Derek's world. Then he suddenly appreciated that the bad-guy to anyone observing the current scenario was actually him.

In the distance, running towards him, was his friendly

policeman, with Arthur, and Charlie, still pounding along too. They were actually running to help someone yelling for assistance rather than because it was Derek, but Derek didn't know that. He just felt he had fallen in very deep water and had forgotten how to swim. He was being held by a big man but, fortunately for Derek, a man who was flabby and not very strong, which Derek instinctively could tell was due to his sitting behind the wheel of his big four x four most of the time. The feeling of being an innocent victim, sinking, gave Derek extra strength and impetus and with a rapid shrug he was free – but for how long?

A bike! How convenient.

Someone had been careless enough to leave a bike leaning against the side of the trolley shed and Derek could ride a bike (even though he'd forgotten how to swim). He jumped into the saddle and pedalled like mad away from the developing chaos.

He wasn't really caring what the owner of the Mini-Cooper was going to say to the owner of the four x four, or to feel guilty about not helping reload the spilled contents of the trolley, sadly lying on its side, with tins of beans, soup, vegetables, soap powder and rice, etc, etc, in a colourful pattern around the Mini-Cooper – it would give PC Plod something to do for the remainder of his shift and, if he completed all the detail properly, it could fill his notebook.

Derek zoomed along one lane then weaved in and out of the gaps in the parking areas into another lane, surprising several caring and cautious shoppers reversing their cars into spaces he'd chosen to charge through.

BEEEEEEEEEEEEP...

"What the...?"

It was that ruddy furniture removal van again. Nearly knocked Derek off the bike this time...

"It can't be my fault every time. He's really starting to get up my nose. And anyway, he was wearing a balaclava, I think – blinded by sweat probably." He hoped the policeman and his pals would give up the chase. He could go faster than they could on foot but what if a squad car joined in? The furniture van had stopped at the lights. He determined to give the driver one of his serious stares.

"That'll make him feel bad."

That's when he noticed he was starting to talk out loud. Not a good sign he thought. What he also noticed – the bike *squeaked*.

He reached the cab of the van and looked at the driver moments before the lights changed to green. If the driver had been wearing a balaclava moments before, that certainly wasn't the case now. She was putting on her spectacles.

SHE?

Yes, it had been a female – with short, bright-red hair.

Maybe Derek needed *his* eyes tested again. He'd been so sure it was a male driver – a failure of his observational skills? His confidence was in question yet again. Maybe with her glasses on now there would be less chance of him being hit. She probably couldn't even see me before, he thought, and she'd totally ignored his infamous threatening glare. The van had pulled away far quicker than he had and was well ahead before he'd even cleared the traffic lights. So he gave up any hope of vengeance.

He also gave up on observing Sally in the park. Well, he tried but with no success. He'd gone around on the bike and managed to view the memorial from a distance but there was no-one to be seen. She'd obviously done the business and left, he had to presume. It was well after four now and he didn't want any more trouble. He'd see Sally tomorrow anyway, provided there were no more incidents.

He did feel a little guilty though for having 'borrowed' this bike. He'd take it back tomorrow after his work, he decided, once the dust had settled. He'd leave a 'Sorry' note with it.

So, homeward he went.

He hoped Grandad had been to the shops for him and bought everything on the Granny Smith list. Derek was always sent back if he'd forgotten anything and no excuses permitted. So, if Grandad had failed to buy something on his behalf? Who'd go back? Derek suspected the return journey, if necessary, would be subject to negotiation.

He hurried up the path and placed the bike out of sight, behind the shed.

"I'm back Gran."

"How did you get on then? Got the job?"

"Of course – no problem," he lied, "...starting tomorrow."

"That's good. You haven't seen Grandad on your travels have you? He should have been back by now, more crosswords to be done."

"Why, isn't he back yet? He said he'd do the shopping for me."

"What happened to your trousers?" she asked. "They're covered in mud." She immediately went into the hall cupboard, brought out a clothes brush and started brushing him down.

"I...um...I went for a run in the park and slipped." Well, that was nearly true.

"You should have been at the supermarket," she said.

"I know, but Grandad said he'd..."

"There was a lot of excitement there today." How come you know, he thought anxiously? "It was on the local radio news, just before you came in," she continued.

Oh no, they recognised me... Surely not a description of me on the radio... They'll be coming to get me... No torture please... I'll confess everything. *Just a minute* – what I did wasn't *that* serious. Calm down...

"Yes, because there was a robbery. Thieves got away with a lot of money and took one of Bisko's supervisors as a hostage. Do you know your trouble Derek?"

"No Gran but you're going to tell me..."

"You are never in the right place at the right time are you? A newspaper reporter you call yourself. And you miss all the excitement."

Ding-dong. Ding-dong.

Oh no – they're here already... I'll hide in the attic...

His gran went to the door. "It's just Grandad." Phew ...and he'd thought... "What took you so long?" Gran asked him, "Derek and I are desperate for some food. Are you not hungry yourself, Hector, and why are you looking so grumpy?"

"I've c-c-carried the shopping all the way from the supermarket on f-f-f-foot," said Grandad.

"Oh, hard lines, love. Did you have a puncture?" she sympathised.

"No I d-d-didn't. Some b-b-bugger stole my ruddy b-b-b-*bike*," he exploded.

Ah well, at least Derek wouldn't have to go back to the supermarket the next day.

11

The Co-operative Bank, Slatterfoot Branch, had been located in Slatterfoot High Street for thirty-five years. Not a long time in banking history maybe, but the local manager was proud that, as far as his customers were concerned, very little had apparently altered in all that time.

The bank sat comfortably between 'Simms – The Best Bakers in Town', and 'Ye Olde Book Shoppe', which, a year ago, had become The Red Cross Charity Shop.

The owner of the bookshop had retired due to ill health but the ending of his book sales had been influenced largely by the success of the large supermarket in the middle of the nearby town of Newingsworth – *Bisko's Ltd*. There you could find an enormous variety and cheaper range of books than his small independent bookshop could possibly carry. Although it was no longer 'Ye Olde Book Shoppe', The Red Cross had decided it would be to their benefit to retain the name because the frontage was so distinctive and well known. This had proved correct, and they were successful at a time when other charities in the town were struggling. Of course, they'd emblazoned their own name as well across the windows.

Since it had been opened by the local mayor, the Co-operative Bank frontage had been kept the same, except for, bi-annually, the addition of fresh coats of the same colours of paint. Inside there was none of your modern open plan layouts, neither was there a 'make you feel very comfortable' sort of decor. No, it was the good old standard, solid-wood counter with the glass division for the full length. Staff worked on one side in calm control with the customers on the other side being shepherded to the counter clerk – when instructed – and dealt with, provided they had completed the correct form. An appointment was required if you wanted to speak to the Manager, and you gained access from the main area through the locked door into his office, ceremonially, at the pre-arranged time. Proper behaviour in this bank was top priority for the manager.

Mr Alexander Donaldson considered these premises to be his second home. He felt comfortable here and so he should. He had been in residence since the opening and had grown from the Counter Clerk of his youth to become, as he would willingly inform you himself, the highly respected Manager in this building. It was with pride and affection when he referred to it as 'My Branch'.

Banks and bankers had not been having a very good press. Government loans for banks, low interest rates to investors, and the converse for loans if you could get them, coupled with suggestions of corruption in high places in the stock market organisations, all dominated the daily headlines.

He liked to think that his customers looked at him and his branch as being different from all that and that they were not involved with the nasty bits, and he was probably correct. Other than the low interest rates being paid, over which he had no control of course, he could probably emerge squeaky clean in this modern 'blame' society.

Long before the current practice of refusing loans and mortgages and playing hard to get with the bank's money became fashionable, he was being criticised by his peers and his directors for being too restrictive with his lending to Slatterfoot local businessmen, but his interviews with local employers wanting to expand, or with prospective house buyers, were actually appreciated by them. Each individual would leave his office, after a tough grilling, feeling that if Mr Donaldson had agreed their request then they were making the right move. They'd made their case, and by accepting it, he had added the stamp of approval. It had to be admitted that in the high debt-ridden society we'd become, his approach was different.

Other than his reluctance to part with money, very little criticism had been directed his way. The annual bank audits and inspections revealed nothing untoward in the finances. The computerised systems introduced over the years and the other bits and pieces of new technology had all been capably slotted into working procedures, thanks to his own and his staff's dedication to the cause.

In fact the only adverse comment made by one of the bank inspectors, after the audit last week, had been personal and that had been stated confidentially and not recorded on any paperwork.

"You have lipstick on your collar, Alexander," she'd said suggestively. This blonde inspector thought she'd recognised a naughty boy underneath this highly polished exterior – and that attracted her. She may have guessed at the reason for the lipstick but it was unlikely to have been the correct one. It went no further than that.

He was tall and quite good-looking, and as people say, surprising for his years, partly due to his keep-fit regime. He didn't see it as a deliberate attempt to keep fit – it was simply that he enjoyed cycling. Each day he'd pedal back and forward between home and work. This had been his routine for many years. His Newingsworth home was about ten miles away from Slatterfoot and on roads without too many demanding hills, so for him it was not hard graft. Traffic had increased both in volume and speed since he'd started as a young man but he'd negotiated the journey safely each time. He would arrive at the bank in his 'dayglo' cycling outfit and change into one of his more sombre suits for the working day. The one hazard he'd had to face was having to dirty his hands if he suffered a puncture and had to repair an inner tube. Thankfully punctures had been rare.

The use of a taxi was becoming a little more regular these days for various reasons and he felt slightly guilty about that. Although he'd found it could affect his muscles sometimes, so far, that routine hadn't caused his waist, or weight to have increased to any extent.

His downfall could be on his doorstep though – directly next door in fact.

He knew he should be more careful with his food. He had the start of an ulcer he thought, but this didn't spoil what was fast becoming a tradition, each morning and afternoon, of the junior clerk nipping into Simms to collect a fresh cream cake for his coffee breaks. He hadn't indulged when he was younger – he hadn't needed these little pleasures then. Now the day wouldn't be the same without them. It was left to the baker's staff to select which was to be 'cake of the day' and his anticipation had kept this little excitement going for several years. He wasn't the skinny figure he'd been when he'd started in this bank, he'd filled out a bit, but it *was* fairly recently he'd begun this cake addiction. So, it could be just a matter of time... This morning it was a cream slice. Hmmm...

He really shouldn't be reading all this upsetting news in the Financial Times while eating. It spoiled his enjoyment of the cake a little and encouraged the indigestion. He read of the current accusations of banking corruption, stockbroker's insider dealings, a worsening value of the pound against the euro, the latest bank raid using a bulldozer, the bank security guard killed in USA while doing his job – and sighed.

He knew there were easier ways of getting big money successfully, without the attendant publicity. At least he *thought* he knew. Recently he'd been puzzling over a few new possibilities himself because he was beginning to look forward to being able to retire comfortably with a small fortune, or maybe even a large one, which would be all his.

But how would he pass his time if he wasn't working? Life at home was dull these days. It never used to be that way.

Having their daughter and watching her grow up had been a great time for both him and his wife. They had been a happy team, even though Muriel did most of the donkey work. His back-up and support had been important too, he liked to think.

However, mother and daughter had grown closer over the

years. The relationship his daughter had with her mother nowadays was much stronger and more comfortable than it was with him. Previously, he'd put this down to the rebelliousness of youth, but she was no longer youthful and the divide was now even greater. It was probably due more to her disapproval of some of his activities, and he would have to admit, he'd done little to try and change the situation.

His daughter still lived with them but had her own life and pursuits and these days he saw very little of her. She had her own work and had become an opinionated young adult who could irritate him, oh so easily. He wished she'd find the right fellow and go off with him and give him a rest from the criticism.

When his daughter had started working, Muriel, his wife, had decided that she too wanted to do something to fill her day and found herself a job, but the novelty of that had worn off for her a while ago, although she didn't stop working. Now, at nights, she'd come home tired and the pair of them would sit and do very little. Maybe they'd have a drink together but inevitably he'd start to overindulge. He'd then doze off in his armchair. Muriel would sit and usually watch some television, very often repeats of one of the many fictitious detective series, then she'd switch off and tip-toe off to bed, alone.

As a diversion, he at least had 'The Club'.

12

Beep-beep, beep-beep, beep-beep, beep-*THUMP.*

Derek felt that he had only just fallen asleep.

Bad habits can creep up on you so very easily. Waking naturally, and rising *eventually* for a leisurely nothing-to-rush-for breakfast had become Derek's habit over the last eleven weeks and today he would have slept on happily once again.

The persistent noise of his electric alarm was essential to waken him this morning – the first time it had been used in eleven weeks – and he'd forgotten the great pleasure it had always given him to silence it with more than essential force back in those difficult to remember days, when he'd had a job.

It would be nice to return to some sort of normal working pattern. This would be the first day for the new job and he didn't want to be late for that, but before he left today, he had to deal with something borrowed. Grandad's bike needed to be moved. He'd have to get into the bathroom before Grandad, and it was fortunate he rose when he did. He won the bathroom race – but only just. He had started washing and shaving when the door handle moved.

"Are you g-g-g-going to be l-l-l-long? I'm d-d-d-*desperate.* I d-d-d-d-didn't get up in the m-m-m-middle of the night," was Grandad's plaintive cry.

"Just two more clues to get, Grandad," he shouted back to tease and to make Grandad more desperate, then, *"Damn."* He realised he shouldn't be talking when he's shaving with a safety razor. He gave a rueful smile at his reflection.

"Serves me right for... *Ouch."* and another cut appeared.

He felt wide awake now – shaving had brought out the new man – and drawn blood. He would have to remember to look in the mirror and remove all the toilet paper before leaving the house. A new job – a new boss – and seeing Sally again – all this called for this fresh and clean new image – and he was ready ...but first – the bike...

He went out quietly and moved it to his Grandad's normal parking place at the back door. That sorted, he tip-toed back inside again gently closing the door, though Grandad was in the bathroom and he couldn't possibly hear. Gran was still in bed. He'd go and have some cornflakes...

"Breakfast, Derek. Are you ready?" a call from the kitchen.

Goodness, his gran was up too. He hoped she hadn't seen or heard him, and she hadn't.

"Now sit down and eat up. I want you doing well in this job but don't expect a cooked breakfast every morning. This is a very special day," she fussed, "...now, where's your grandad?"

"*Hector. Your breakfast is on the table. Remember that you've no bike. You are going to have to leave earlier today,*" she shouted up the stairs.

Oh, oh. Grandad came in wearing his dressing gown and slippers and looked more than normally grumpy. At a guess he hadn't slept well. That could be unfortunate for anyone he happened to fall out with today, thought Derek. "If I find the b-b-b-bugger that p-p-p-pinched my b-b-bike I'll-I'll-I'll..."

"Eat your breakfast," Gran told him.

Grandad sat down as Gran poured out a cup of freshly-made tea. He poured in some milk. Two sugars were then added, and it was stirred – *anti-clockwise* – it was *that* type of morning.... He was hoping a nice drink of tea would improve his mood and waken him properly. It usually helped. He lifted the cup.

"Are you sure you've lost your bike, Grandad?" Derek enquired innocently.

"Of course I have, you cheeky b-b-b-blighter. I should kn-kn-kn-know. It was me that w-w-w-walked all the way from the s-s-s-supermarket l-l-last night."

He raised the cup again, this time he was desperate for a mouthful of tea.

"Well, there's a bike sitting outside – in the usual place..." Derek munched away enjoying this one-off bacon and egg experience.

"What? C-c-*can't* b-be," spluttered his grandad, as the calming, tea-drinking routine failed to be completed. He jumped up and out he went to check – and returned looking a little sheepish.

"I d-d-d-did take it with me when I went to the s-s-s-supermarket, d-d-d-didn't I?" he asked his wife, shakily.

"Don't ask me," said Gran, "I was upstairs. I didn't see you."

"And I'd already gone," Derek cheerfully chipped in.

"Oh..." was all that his grandad said.

He looked so sad that Derek almost had to tell him the truth, but, as he guessed correctly, that could have been suicidal. Derek kept silent. At least his grandad's paper-round could be done in the usual way and that salved Derek's conscience – a little. He decided, as compensation, and if he remembered, he'd oil whatever was squeaking...

It was time to go. With a quick look in the mirror, he removed bits of toilet paper, cleaned spectacles, and checked zip was up on trousers. It felt a bit odd wearing a tie, he would rather have done without – but it was the first day. He'd soon learn their dress code and settle gently into the office routines over the next few days.

"I'm off Gran." Mandatory kisses dutifully given and received.

No bus for him today. It would be the healthy option. He felt he was doing the right thing by walking. A walking routine is good for your constitution, Granny kept telling him. Derek was mighty grateful that his gran had picked on his grandad, and not him, to be the 'voluntary' subject of her thesis, but having this job could mean additional pressure on both him and Grandad. How long would it be before Gran twigged that, since he'd stopped his last job, he, Derek, had been doing a lot of the crosswords for his grandad? It was lucky their printing was very similar – and that Gran's sight wasn't quite perfect, but she was putting a lot of pressure on the old guy, he thought.

It was a beautiful morning. The sun was shining, the birds were twittering, little fluffy clouds were slowly drifting by. On a day like this, could there possibly be a nicer place to live than Newingsworth? Derek would probably have asked himself that question if it hadn't been for the noise of the vehicles rushing passed, and the smell of the fumes lingering in his nostrils...

He'd started off feeling bright and cheerful, unusual for him so early in the morning, but the surroundings were already starting to be irritating and taking the shine off the day. He'd not walked along this stretch of road before at peak time. He knew his destination, and his way about town, and this was the shortest route, but it occurred to him that he'd plenty time and didn't have to go this way. It could be much nicer going through Cloverton.

Cloverton Estate was not one of your 'just built yesterday and thrown up overnight' sort of places, with fancy plastic doors and windows, narrow gaps separating houses, and postcard size gardens. Oh no. If you were well heeled, this was the area in town you'd choose. Maybe they weren't all mansions but they were substantial buildings all the same and had been standing since early last century. The name for the estate had come from the land having been owned by the wealthy Cloverton Family, a long time ago...

It was then he remembered he'd intended starting his book last night – but after the way the day had developed, he hadn't. He missed the simplicity of typing away on the computer, and for him, hand-writing was such a chore.

"You'll be my heroine, Sally" he'd said...

He had been full of good intentions, but... What if Sally remembers and asks about it? Should he lie to her? No, he would tell her he can't divulge the plot yet as it would spoil the surprise. Another reason of course was that he hadn't yet thought up a plot. Nothing more he could do anyway other than keep thinking...

It was pleasant being able to use this route, well away from the busy traffic roads. This part of town was probably as up-market as Newingsworth could be. Only rarely would outsiders manage to acquire one of these old houses because when the occupants died, the ownership was normally retained within the family. Rarely did someone move away from the area through choice. Unfortunately, if you were a company director whose business had folded with enormous debt, which did happen, you would slip quietly away and hide, and your treasured property would *have* to be sold. And if there was to be a sale, estate agents then fought for the opportunity to handle the business. In those isolated cases, the house sold quickly and for a small fortune. The combination of a business collapse and the prized house sale couldn't fail to appear as a favourite local news story. He knew...

A choice area to live and to pass through, as Derek was doing, and the tranquillity had encouraged a calm, receptive and surprisingly observant mood, in him. He actually noticed how nice the gardens were. Of course, this was just the time of year for the best displays, so it should be hard to miss. He was totally relaxed as he looked at the many different colours of flowers, all neat and cared for, but he wondered how many of the people who lived here did the work themselves. Very few, he concluded, these people would probably all employ gardeners and wouldn't get their own hands dirty. He was relaxed and enjoying the day, but behaving as cynically as most involved with newspapers do.

It surely deserved the reputation of a high-class neighbourhood though. It was so quiet and peaceful. This road was totally lacking in the normal rubbish of paper, cigarette packets, and coke cans. There wasn't even a plastic supermarket bag blowing like a wind-sock in the trees, which was unusual these days.

Does someone come out first thing and clear these, and dust everything down at the same time, he wondered? No, more likely that there was never anyone around to make the mess in the first place. Unusual to see so few cars parked on the roads. This seemed to contribute to the tidy effect. Every house had a driveway and garages and the road was almost totally clear – except for a furniture van. He supposed if he had been moving house this would be a super day for it.

Just a minute...

It's not just *a furniture van* it is *THE* Furniture Van, the one that nearly knocked him down – three times. The one which was being driven by a maniac with a personal hatred for him – or so it seemed.

He might as well have a sarcastic moment with the driver, he thought bravely. A woman driver, wasn't it? Was her last job driving a bulldozer with her eyes closed, he'd ask? Maybe even question why she was wearing a balaclava in the middle of summer – unless he'd been mistaken. Was she from a hot country perhaps and felt the cold? She'd have a problem here in the winter, if that was the case, because it wouldn't be getting much warmer than yesterday. This is Britain, he'd tell her...

The driver must be inside the house though, for she wasn't to be seen. He couldn't see any other people about the van either. There would normally be more than one person if household goods were being moved. The door of the house wasn't open – the furniture movers could be inside of course doing packing. The people who lived in these houses wouldn't do their own packing.

He suddenly realised how big an inverse snob he was being and didn't like the feeling, but it wouldn't go away.

Maybe the driver's asleep in the cab, he thought, wasn't that what they did sometimes on 'overnighters'. He peered in – no, there was no sign of anyone in the cab. Derek looked at what it said on the side of the van and it clearly wasn't local. It was a company from down south.

He heard a thumping from inside. There was somebody moving about and he guessed it could be the driver. He decided to be a wee devil and bang on the back door – and be ready to run... Strange – this rear door could only be opened from the outside? If the driver was resting inside, or even working, she wouldn't be able to get out again without someone's help. He heard the thumping again.

"Hello," he called, "Is there someone there?"

No answer – but the thumping continued.

Surely it couldn't be an animal...?

The door wasn't locked. In fact, it wasn't even properly closed. He decided to be really nosey. Firstly, a furtive glance along the avenue and at the surrounding houses – and there was no-one to be seen. What if it was an animal – trapped – and fierce? He'd have to be very cautious, in case ...and then it occurred to him it would be even worse if he opened the door and the driver had been sleeping and was standing in her bra and pants – she'd probably be fiercer – might be worth it though.

The handle was warped – probably why it was only partially closed – it couldn't *be* closed properly. He grasped and pulled. Movement of the handle only came with difficulty. It took a fair effort but with a grinding sound it gave – and the door was open. Nothing leapt out. He peered in. There was only some stuff lying on the floor, but as his eyes became more accustomed to the gloom in the van he saw it wasn't *something* lying there – no – it was *somebody* – on the floor...

"Are you all right? Can I help you?"

His voice echoed in this large space but there was no reply. Was that a rope he could see tied round...? The person was tied up ...and it was a girl. She'd been blindfolded and gagged and she'd been kicking at the van sides.

What was going on?

He climbed into the van. And bent down over the body...

"What the...?" he exclaimed. "*It's Sally.*"

"Sally, Sally – are you all right? It's me – Derek. Let me get this stuff off your face"

The blindfold was easily removed. She blinked and obviously found the sudden light painful. He felt bad pulling the tape off her mouth but there was no easy way. He thought she was being really brave – well, she tried to be – but the pain obviously brought tears to her eyes.

Untying her was awkward. He'd no knife and the knots were very difficult to loosen and hurt his fingers. He had to try hard not to cry too. Yes, he was a big softy... but he managed eventually.

"Sweaty... How did you find me? Oh Sweaty, am I glad to see you again?" and she gave him a big hug and held on, and he wasn't complaining. "Where am I? I've been blindfolded for ages and couldn't see what was happening," she was sobbing, with relief he reckoned rather than pain. "I could only hear and imagine what was going on."

"I should have stayed with you in the park," he said gallantly "Was this the person who came for the money?"

"No, it wasn't like that... Mum – oh no – where is she?"

"She'll be at home surely and she'll have been worried about you, I'd say" Derek replied.

"No, no, *no*. You don't understand. *They took her.*"

He'd helped her onto her feet. She was a little unsteady at first. It seemed wise to get out of the van. Sally was blinded as they stepped into the sunshine and then she struggled to take in what she saw. "But... but... we're outside my home!" she exclaimed. "The curtains are closed – have they taken her inside?"

Derek still hadn't a clue what was going on. Deep down he was afraid he was going to have to be brave again, which went against his nature. "Maybe we should call the police," he suggested and then thought that maybe getting involved with policemen after his own little escapade yesterday wouldn't be so smart, but Sally's problem was more serious – so that's what would have to be done. He reached into his pocket and found his habit of leaving his mobile on the hall table at home hadn't been broken – he'd left it there. Some hero... "Where's your mobile Sally?"

"It's in my bag – but they snatched the bag from me, last night."

"What? Have you been in that van all night? And anyway who are 'they'? Were there many of them? Were they big?" he gingerly enquired. At least Sally had stopped crying and shaking and seemed a little more confident. Derek was anything but confident and nervously kept looking around. Is this what a potential hero should feel like, he wondered? Sally seemed to need to talk – it could be shock, decided Derek. She should be wrapped up in a blanket and have a cup of strong tea with two sugars – me too, he thought, chivalrously.

"There were four of them. After you left, I went across to the Supermarket to chat to my mum. I felt down in the dumps. Speaking to Mum always helps me. She was in the office on her own – she's a supervisor in Bisko's – but while we were talking these four men came in the back way and grabbed us. They were all wearing balaclavas with their faces hidden and…"

All this information just tumbled out.

"They must have been awfully hot – it was roasting yesterday – I know because I was running about in it," Derek reminisced. "…And did you know yesterday was the warmest day of …?"

"Sweaty, are you listening to *me?* I told you we were put in that van early last evening because they attacked us and made my mum open the safe and she looks after the wages and money and I think they had guns," and then she needed a deep breath…

"*Guns,*" he gulped. "Yes, I'm definitely listening."

"They tied up our arms and put on blind-folds and made Mum and me walk into this van. They tied our legs and drove off with us. I don't know what happened to the people who work at the back of the store – no-one interfered to help us."

"Where's your mobile? Oh, yes, it's in your bag. We must phone the police now." It had become a very decisive Derek – a man of action.

"The bag might be in the van. I was still wearing it – they took it off me when they tied my feet." There didn't seem to be any activity in Sally's home that could be seen so he leapt back into the van and, yes, he found her bag in the corner.

"Surprise, Surprise…" she muttered when she looked in it.

Don't bother with the Cilla Black impressions, he thought.

"They've taken my phone… *Oh* – but they haven't taken the

money from the bag."

"How much is there?" he asked. "Obviously chicken-feed to them if they've left it."

"Three thousand pounds," she replied.

"Three *thousand?*" he gasped, "And you've been carrying that about with you and they missed it?"

"It's my boss's money – but he's almost certainly about to become my ex-boss. But my mum...? I'm worried about her. They opened the doors and took her out when they stopped but just left me. Then I heard a car drive off. It sounded really fast. Oh, where is she? I hope she's in the house and safe."

"Well, you don't have a phone and I don't have a phone so let's look and see, shall we?" He said it bravely and felt anything but brave. But I'm doing this for Sally... oh... and maybe her mum.

There was nothing obvious at the front of the house. All the curtains were closed or blinds pulled down. The house was large and detached, and looked to him from the front as if it had at least four bedrooms, a living room, a dining room, two bathrooms, a fully fitted kitchen, an integral double garage, with large well-kept garden, and could be appearing on the market at... Hey – that's what I could do – I should sell houses. No, maybe not – but he hadn't totally forgotten that a very short time ago he had been on the way, hopefully and happily, to start a new job.

What would have happened to Sally if he hadn't been passing? As he stood there the fantasy developed in his head of the knight in shiny armour, him of course, in a modern-day setting tackling the equivalent of the flaming dragon ...and the damsel, that would be Sally, with long flowing locks ...and he'd... A storyline was appearing in moving pictures ...at long last... *Yippee...*

"Sweaty... Are you all right?" asked Sally. "You've a stupid look on your face."

Pop.

The idea had vanished...

Nothing obvious could be seen from the back of the house. All the curtains were closed.

It was then that they both remembered the easiest way into a house is usually through the door. The position of the front door in this house was slightly unconventional in that it wasn't actually at the front. It sat at on the corner of the building, and looked imposing because directly above, sitting like a crown, was an attractive little windowless turret. Derek wouldn't have been surprised if there had been a flagpole and flag flying but there wasn't. There was another door at the back of the house leading into the garden, and that one looked really solid, the kind that could hold out to a battering ram. A conservatory jutted out into the garden space but it had closed venetian blinds and patio doors. Derek tried these doors but they were secure.

Of course, ringing the doorbell was not an option – if there were people inside who shouldn't be, it would warn them. Stealth and surprise were the methods to be applied – maybe?

"Do you have your house keys, Sally?" which sensibly should have been a question asked earlier.

Sally's search of the large handbag unfortunately revealed no keys but did expose the usual amazing amount of rubbish that a female can accumulate in a handbag, particularly if it is large. Equivalent to the contents of his shed, Derek estimated, but had to admit he could be prone to exaggeration.

And of course in the bag was the money – three thousand pounds... though it was wrapped up and looked like a parcel.

A peek through the letterbox and it was apparent that there had been visitors. Doors were lying open and some loose carpets were out of place. Some ornaments had been knocked over as well but no current movement could be seen from the limited panoramic view through the letterbox flap.

"Can any of the windows be opened, Sally?"

"Possibly upstairs, I suppose," she replied.

Derek looked around. There were a lot of long-established trees in the extensive garden but none with overhanging branches that could give him access to a balcony or window. He would have created these for his hero to crawl along, if he'd been writing a story about an adventure like this, he decided. It would have been just a single leap for Superman.

"Is there a ladder I could use – safely?" By 'safely' he meant without being attacked by someone who claimed the sole rights to its use.

"Yes. There's one in the shed at the back. It's not locked," ...an aluminium extending ladder that he was capable of lifting.

Although the ladder was aluminium it was still heavy and he staggered as he carried it out of the shed towards the rear of the house. Careful – he already had a bad experience with a ladder, and he didn't want to break a window. Sally pointed out her bedroom and said that her window was rarely locked. He crossed his fingers that this was not to be the rare occasion.

Although Sally was obviously worried for her mother she still had the presence of mind to warn Derek not to stand on the dahlias. They were prize ones. He also had to be careful not to damage the sweet peas, her mother's pride and joy, and watch out for that rose – it's a very thorny type – too late. He didn't want to look at his trousers, and doubted his own intelligence – choosing to wear his best ones again? He was concentrating so hard on all the things he was being warned about that he almost stepped into a fishpond that he hadn't even realised existed – but thankfully, he didn't.

Steady... Get the ladder upright... He placed it against the sill and climbed up carefully. Success – the window opened and in he went. Unfortunately, they hadn't taken account of the local neighbourhood-watch, next door.

13

Muriel Donaldson had been hoping for a little excitement to enter her life. Recently she had led a fairly humdrum existence. She had her own work that she had been doing for many years and she enjoyed it. But now she could perform those duties without any panics, she didn't have to make many major decisions, and generally, hardly had to even think about the daily routines.

The days just seemed to trundle on. She had no money worries. She was married, had a bank manager for a husband, had her own earnings, and worked because she *chose* to do so. Married life had been fun and new when Sally had been younger. Where did all that go, she wondered, but then again maybe this was the natural way it just developed as you grew older. She could still remember meeting Alexander Donaldson for the first time at her cousin's wedding. He had been a good pal of the groom, and full of fun. They'd danced together and they'd become a pair immediately. He had been tall and good-looking, still was, but with a little less hair. He'd changed more so when Sally went to College. Personality clashes all the time with Sally.

"Looking not too bad myself..." she'd think wistfully when she glanced at her reflection nowadays, except for a few more lines, and the odd grey hair which thankfully was controllable, her hairdresser made sure of that. The regular cycling had help maintain her figure. She could still squeeze into her wedding dress, she told herself, if it hadn't been used by Sally for playing dressing–up games. Anyway, maybe it wouldn't have been wise to put it to the test. That's how self-confidence is crushed.

Sally, her daughter, worked hard and enjoyed her job, and was good at it. That fact had been recognised. She was a PA at the local newspaper and she liked her boss. Her earnings were excellent, having been there for a long time, and she happily contributed to the household costs, although it wasn't really necessary. Muriel was eager to see Sally married. Lots of boyfriends came and went, but the right one had never appeared – yet. The downside would be that the house would seem empty without her in it.

Three regular salaries meant a high family-income and allowed them the luxury of a comfortable life in a large house in a fairly exclusive neighbourhood.

But Muriel didn't live the high life.

Didn't do much other than work, eat and sleep these days – and that had been largely her own choice she realised. So, was she happy? Yes, but... maybe a little bit of excitement? ...and it had come to her last evening.

Didn't it just...

It had been pleasant talking to Sally. It always was. It was comforting to Muriel that Sally felt she could approach her mum and talk about any trouble she was having. She'd sometimes ask advice – and accept it graciously. They could even just sit contentedly and have a woman to woman chat, and girlish giggling wasn't at all unusual.

Sally had slipped into Bisko's cash office late yesterday afternoon, clearly upset. It had been obvious she had dropped a large clanger by stupidly mixing up telephone numbers – but having to boost a daughter's confidence was not unusual for a mother. Her mother had reassured her that the new plan was sensible and Sally was about to leave feeling considerably calmer – and then the robbery kerfuffle had occurred.

Four people had rushed in, all wearing balaclavas hiding their faces. The suddenness of it all had been shocking. She had been frightened, petrified in fact, but her first thoughts had been to protect Sally. The gang seemed to have been expecting her to be alone in the office and became flustered by Sally's presence.

Sitting here on what had been determined as *her* bed, feeling calmer and a little more in control of her emotions, she supposed now that these people would have made themselves aware of her working routines beforehand. As an addict of television detectives programmes, who must have seen all the variations of a crime scenario, and the repeats, surely she should know what the next actions would be. It would be surprising if she *wasn't* correctly able to predict the outcome to expect from the pattern so far of this particular incident. What were they likely to have planned for her? Then again, would it make her feel any better to guess correctly? Possibly not...

It had been obvious that they had come to rob the place. Mrs Muriel Donaldson's heart had begun to thump at an unusually high rate for her – was this to be the excitement she'd hoped for? Did she have any choice? At that precise moment, Muriel's brain had begun functioning sharper than it had been for months, maybe years.

Last night, had she reacted instinctively or had she wanted to become a heroine, she pondered...? She'd made to go for the panic alarm button but one of the gang had been too quick for her. Her reaching the button would have made all the difference. The alarm would have gone off in the Manager's Office and at the Police Station and it is unlikely that the robbery would have been successful. And she would have felt considerably better about the whole affair than she did now. Sally would have been safe. Oh, and she, Muriel, wouldn't be sitting here on this bed feeling sorry for herself.

She'd failed...

She'd thought at the time that at least the CCTV was recording all of it but – oh no, it hadn't. The office camera had needed to be replaced earlier, but the security engineer hadn't had a spare with him and worse still, the local fault had disabled the whole system. Parts were to be flown in from France. The engineer was to be back in the evening.

The whole system had been out of action – *kaput*.

At the time, don't panic, she'd told herself, another employee will appear any minute, someone always does, and they'll raise the alarm, except then she had remembered – it was Thursday.

"Please don't bother me on Thursday afternoon when I'm sorting out your wages sheets," she had regularly pleaded with them, and for once they'd heeded her plea – *damn*.

As the incident repeated in her mind later, she had a feeling of guilt that she'd given in too willingly in response to the threats. She'd let them have access to the safe. She had been responsible for them succeeding, but she balanced this with what could have happened if she had refused. She gave an involuntary shudder. She'd had to protect Sally, as well as herself.

Sally... Oh, where was she?

Muriel knew both of them had been in the gang's escape vehicle, whatever that had been. When they'd escaped, had it been a Bisko lorry they'd used? Would they have been so brazen? Often, there were some empty lorries and vans sitting on the bays, having been unloaded, or available to begin.

It had been a very uncomfortable ride bouncing around the floor of *whatever* it was. When she was shoved in the car she'd appreciated the soft, leather seat – but would have preferred nicer circumstances. The first vehicle seemed to travel a long distance – then in the car it had been much the same – she had been judging the time they'd been moving. Her being blindfolded didn't permit enjoyment of the scenery unfortunately.

Where was she now? She'd absolutely no idea, only that she must be many, many miles from Newingsworth and her home.

She couldn't complain too much of the treatment they'd given her after she'd been taken from the car. They had been kinder to her than she had been to them, but they had brought it on themselves. Cussedness had never been a fault she'd been accused of, ever before, but the moment the tape had been ripped from her mouth, she had given them a fine tirade of invective. In the middle of her unprepared and venomous yelling, the pressure of the situation had caused other very important words to be said.

"TOILET... Must go... right now." she'd screamed.

And they had reacted remarkably quickly.

Muriel had been rapidly untied, although they'd left on the blindfold, meaning she had to be led to the loo. And that had been an early discovery about the gang – at least one of them was a female and realising it was female had felt a little less embarrassing, but she was immediately trussed up again after.

However, with the toilet break over, a somewhat more comfortable Muriel was able to continue to release pent up emotions and to expand her abusive language with renewed energy. Even now, her cheeks coloured thinking of the language she'd used last night – that had been swearing of a very high quality and she'd even been using words she didn't realise she'd known.

Surprisingly, her captors had been somewhat cowed by this behaviour. They reacted as if it was only what was expected and what they deserved – as if they were truly sorry and were glad it was her and not them suffering these indignities... That they reacted so calmly to her raving caused her a mixture of frustration and embarrassment. She presumed at least the female gang-member had understood her anxieties and had sympathised. Were the other three males? She couldn't tell. In Bisko's it had been grunts and gestures as communication, in the car it had been silence. What surprised her more was, after her letting off steam in that loudmouthed manner, they *hadn't* immediately taped her mouth again.

The removal of the tape and the blindfold had been done a little later inside the house so she had no idea what the outside of this house was like. She managed to see out of a couple of windows but all she'd glimpsed was a large garden with a high hedge and a few strategically placed shrubs, before they pulled down blackout blinds and the room became quite dark. She couldn't see too much of the gang in the dim light.

Initially they had kept her tied to the kitchen chair, in front of a large television set with the sound turned up, obviously to prevent her hearing any of their discussion.

She did overhear one comment.

"I'll have to take off this bloody balaclava or I'll melt," and that was a male voice.

"Tough... Wait till we move her. You can't afford to be recognised," was the reply, and that was another male identified.

It had been, and still was, a very warm day but for some reason she didn't care if they suffered a bit too. In fact, it seemed to her to be justice if they melted.

So, the current count was one female, two males, and one unknown.

She felt bruised and filthy from bouncing around the floor of that first vehicle and hoped she'd have access to a bath or a shower soon, provided nothing more serious than keeping her here was planned. For certain, being tied to the wooden kitchen chair didn't make her bruises any more comfortable and sitting in front of a large and noisy television set wasn't the most pleasant experience either.

Watching television was normally a pleasant pastime for her but why had they selected *CBeebies*? She reasoned that it was probably because there was no news or current information. Initially she was a bit peeved, expecting to be viewing all the programmes that she'd watched when Sally had been very young, but she hadn't seen any these programmes before. A lot had changed... A novelty initially, and interesting though they no doubt were to children under five, to an adult, like her, dumped unceremoniously and uncomfortably in front of a large-screen TV which was out with her control, they began to become very annoying.

To pass the time, and keep herself as amused as anyone could be while tied to a chair, she closed her eyes and decided to try and give the gang some pet names. What foursomes could she think of? The Beatles came to mind first, but no, John, Paul, etc didn't seem right. Abba? But what were their names? Was one Ingrid? No, can't remember. Never mind. Keep thinking... Modern groups were not familiar to her either so she thought back to her younger days. She eventually settled for Dave Dee's backing group – Dozy, Beakie, Mick and Tich. Yes, those names had a sort of bisexual ring to them that would suit.

One of this gang was obviously female, and anyway she wasn't going to be telling them the names she'd allocated, and unsuitable names could be more satisfying. The Dave Dee pop group were favourites from way back – and she had always thought them cute – like this gang... She could be ironic when she wanted to – and she didn't think that Dave Dee would object.

Being passive in her behaviour, she decided would be the most sensible option at the moment. If she portrayed a quiet and frightened little old lady who wasn't any threat to them, they might drop their guard and she could escape, even though she was not little, and hadn't felt old until today (and would be annoyed if anyone were to suggest that she was), and had proved herself definitely *not* a lady with her earlier language. However, she didn't have to pretend the 'frightened' bit and she wasn't over-confident about any escape plan.

Last night for tea they'd had pizzas, a phoned order which was delivered a short time later, but she was not happy that the other four had already made a choice and that she'd had to take what was left. It had been the plain and simple Margarita. That wouldn't have been her choice – she liked spicy, and she would have preferred to have been asked. Even in her grumpy displeasure though, she'd actually eaten it all and enjoyed it – for her it had been a point of principle. She could see she would have to be a bit firmer and put her foot down and pull this lot into line – her line. The alternative would have been to refuse to eat it, but that would have been stupid – she had been *starving*.

Then she reminded herself, *I'm their prisoner*.

When the food had been delivered, she'd wondered how they would manage to eat without her seeing their faces. Would they eat while wearing these stupid balaclavas?

They didn't.

In fact they had erected a curtain barrier between her and them so she dined almost alone. Her hands were released only long enough to eat. At first she thought they were starting to play psychological games with her. When CBeebies ended for the day they switched to one of the cartoon channels. How did they know she hated these? It had now become torture, and she was convinced there must be a law somewhere prohibiting this sort of thing. If there wasn't, she'd be contacting her Euro MP, as soon as she escaped, to demand that one be created. This had succeeded in getting her into a foul mood when they decided to release her from the chair.

Beakie, she'd given this name to her female captor, was the one who had been allocated the task of transferring Muriel elsewhere. She'd had to don her balaclava once more while the others relaxed behind the curtain. The blindfold was reapplied and Muriel's arms and legs were untied. She stood up stiffly. Beakie held her arm and led her out of that room. "You are hurting me," Muriel grumbled, even though it wasn't true.

"Sorry..." Beakie responded and sounded as if she meant it.

It appeared that she was crossing a large hall. A door was opened and in they went, and the blindfold was removed.

Now she was in a bedroom, *her* bedroom.

There was a single bed, a chair, a small table with a bedside lamp, a clock, and a stack of paperbacks. There was also a shower and WC en-suite, she was pleased to note. The house could have been used as a 'Bed and Breakfast' before they'd fitted the bars. This was the minimum you'd expect as a B and B customer – but a luxury for this hostage.

It was not yet dark when she became the sole resident of this new prison. At least she had her freedom within the confines of the room, but there were bars on the outside of the one window. She suspected these had been specially fitted recently, so there could be no escape that way. Through this window there was a similar scene to the others – a view over the grass to a high hedge only. She could not see any large trees which, in a garden as large as this seemed to be, was unusual she thought, and there were no buildings overlooking the property, apparently. She was disappointed that there were no flowers to be seen in this garden either, to brighten up her day.

She turned down the bed-sheets. "These sheets aren't clean. I'm *not* lying on that bed with dirty sheets." and she stood with folded arms, again just to be difficult...

"Look... We changed..." Beakie started to say, but in a resigned voice said, "Right..." and went away. Muriel was surprised to have elicited that reaction. It gave her a feeling of being a little less of a prisoner but she was pragmatic and realised that it was only in her mind. She, Beakie, returned with clean ones and left Muriel to do the swap, which she happily did. Muriel smiled inwardly. The applying of the nicknames could be a satisfying diversion. She was curious to learn more of this group and that curiosity was helping her relax and easing a little of her fear. She was worried about the fate of Sally but was unlikely to find out any more tonight. She lay down on the bed, exhausted, and dropped off to sleep immediately. She'd hoped earlier for some excitement to enter her life – now she wasn't so sure...

14

He wasn't exactly an expert at house-breaking but at least he was inside and without doing any damage. If he could make his way downstairs he would open the front door and let Sally in, but he didn't know anything of the house layout. He did remind himself that the house could be occupied and it might be by a gang of thugs, so he would have to go carefully.

Another thought occurred, that Sally's mum might have been given a lift home by someone in the furniture van who deep down really did care that she reached home safely – or maybe just wanted rid of her. She may even be sitting downstairs right this moment, unharmed and having breakfast.

If *he* suddenly appeared, she'd have the fright of her life.

No – the curtains would have been open somewhere, wouldn't they? At least that was the first thing Gran did at his house when she got up. Derek presumed 'getting rid of the night demons and letting the daylight in' to be a common trait of all females, but this house was all dark... So, forget that one. Mrs Donaldson couldn't be here – he'd just think *thugs*...

He stayed perfectly still and listened. He could hear no noises, but that meant little. The bedroom door was closed and he'd no idea how sound might carry in this house.

It was bright daylight outside but the room curtains were still closed and didn't let in much light. He decided to open them to see better in the room. He didn't want to inform this group of ruffians of his presence by knocking something over or falling over the stuff that was all around the floor.

With light streaming in, the room could be seen properly –

and *it was a mess*.

There were blouses and skirts and trousers over chairs and the bed, shoes tumbling out of the open wardrobe, jewellery strewn about the tops of surfaces, and drawers sitting half-open exposing the contents.

Sally would not be pleased.

He made his way to the door, opened it gently, and looked out to a large landing. The stairs were at the far end. Were these stairs like those in his house? If they were, he knew the moment he tried to creep down them silently, it was guaranteed each step would creak – never at any other time, but he was surprised. The carpeting was thick and if there were any squeaks, he didn't hear them. What he did hear, when halfway down as he trod on the silly cat that was asleep on the stair, was a horrendous *screech*. The animal didn't make too much noise – it was Derek's own voice as his leg was seized by the claws of a very upset cat. And if there was anyone else in the house, they certainly didn't rush out to help him.

By the time he'd succeeded in detaching the cat, he'd concluded the gang hadn't stayed. His nerves were on edge.

The voice behind him, that asked, "Are you all right?" didn't help his emotional stability either. Sally thought he'd had a heart attack as she tried to comfort the shivering wreck that had collapsed beside her on the stairs.

"I was going to let you in the front door..." Derek gasped out.

"I came up the ladder after you," said Sally "I was worried that you wouldn't be all right."

"I'm not..." Derek whimpered. He felt a little self-pity was appropriate, under the circumstances.

Sally helped him to his feet. Although Derek was moving with some difficulty and with more caution than her, as a team they descended the remainder of the stairs.

"If Mum's here she might still be tied up – as I was," said Sally.

She seemed to love that large handbag of hers. It had been brought with her, and she'd had it slung across her shoulder as she climbed the ladder. She placed it on the hall table and moved to look in the various rooms.

That's when they realised that the ladder at the back window had become a busy thoroughfare – as two policemen came clattering down the stairs towards them. One of them Derek immediately recognised from yesterday... and he recognised Derek.

Early this morning an irate resident had phoned to complain about a common furniture removal van having been parked overnight cluttering up this exclusive neighbourhood and near her driveway. Worse still, it had been observed that a rear door was now swinging dangerously in the breeze and no-one was doing anything about it.

Initially this call was thought to be of secondary importance and was decided not serious enough to warrant immediate action by the local station.

"We'll be with you as quickly as we can Madam. We're extremely busy but I'll allocate someone immediately," were the words the caller heard.

"You'll be lucky, Ducky" were the Desk Sergeant's exact words as he replaced the receiver, but it had been closely followed by another call from the same complainant. This time she had reported 'undesirables' climbing in a window of the house next door.

Now this could be more fun, the nearest foot-patrol decided when contacted, and had hurried to investigate and, by coincidence, they had been in nice time to see Sally's bottom vanishing through the window. As the bottom had been an attractive one the two-man patrol had decided to follow it – by the same entry – up the ladder.

"Just stay where you are please," seems pleasant enough when written down, but when said by a policeman staring you straight in the eyes and standing at a higher level, it can feel very uncomfortable, especially when he is holding a baton threateningly, and has a mate standing just behind him with a similarly menacing expression on his face. Maybe if this

happened often enough I'd grow a little more used to it and start to enjoy confrontations with policemen, thought Derek, and then decided 'bad idea'.

"So this is where you've come for a new ball then, *and* you 'ave an accomplice now, 'ave you? A bit brave attempting 'ouse-breaking in broad daylight I'd say," stated Number One policeman, who hadn't actually introduced himself yesterday to Derek but who seemed so familiar.

Was this policeman really trying to be funny? A new ball... Ha-ha-ha-ho-ho-ho... Derek decided – *no*.

"Officer, you don't understand..." he started to say.

"No sir, of course we don't – we never do," said Number Two.

"I was trying to..."

"I think you could save your breath for the moment. You'll 'ave plenty opportunity to talk at the station – sir..."

"Officer, I live here," said Sally firmly.

Sudden silence...

"Yes, yes indeed," said Number Two trying to ignore the comment. "Let's be getting on with it then and no struggling please. My friend is very short tempered."

"It would have been Mrs Masterton next door who will have phoned you. She's very observant but she obviously hasn't seen me, just my friend who was helping me get back in without keys."

"Yes, yes madam – without keys... No need to state the obvious. Now, let's just get on with it please. Don't make our job any more difficult than it 'as to be," said Number One, but with a little less conviction now.

"Mrs Masterton has lived next door to us all my life, Officer. I'm sure she'll recognise my voice if I could speak to her. Now please – may I use the family phone?" Sally sounded really calm and in control – and insistent.

Good girl, thought Derek, but don't forget I'm here too – don't let them drag me off – *please*...

"Well...?" mused Number One.

"Get it over with, Alf. Ask the old dear to come round for a minute. Go through the motions so this pair can't complain about their 'Human Rights' afterwards – though their kind always do," Number Two decided.

So the 'old dear' dutifully appeared and identified Sally and went away again, happy that by phoning she'd, "done the right thing for her community". As she'd left, she'd offered to have everyone round to her house for an early morning cup of tea and a biscuit because she'd, "*caused so much bother – and was making a pot anyway*".

No-one went.

So, it was accepted reluctantly that Sally did in fact live there, but the coppers didn't give up on Derek.

"Now, about yesterday... There was a little matter of an attempted theft of a ladder, sir..."

"Officer, my mother is *missing*... What are you doing about it?" Sally interjected, "and this house has obviously had a *real* burglary," she continued, "...and you are just standing around wrongly accusing someone of the theft of a ladder that wasn't even stolen. What's this to do with the robbery at the supermarket? Derek has been helping me, and he's obviously as innocent as the driven snow. Just look at him..."

Derek stood feeling very uncomfortable as they *looked at him*.

Don't push it Sally, please, he thought, and I wouldn't have added the last part of that sentence – they might want to prove it wrong, but they didn't, thank goodness for him.

They were a little subdued after Sally's rebuke and started to look around the house.

"Has she been reported as a missing person?" Number Two asked. "Nothing will happen until she's been reported missing."

"Don't you know there was a robbery? My mother was taken from the Supermarket yesterday and could be in great danger. Has that not been reported yet?" Sally continued the attack. "Don't you policemen know anything?"

"No need to be nasty, Miss. We have feelings too, you know. Obviously everyone knows there was a robbery. We're all very busy looking for the thieves."

"Didn't you know this is where my mother lives?" Sally kept prodding.

"I –eh– I... Of course we did – and we're here, aren't we?" was Number Two's hesitant response.

Never be misled by the attraction of a well shaped bottom, went through his head. This one is no *bimbo*...

"We're here to search for clues, obviously. And anyway, we don't know that you two weren't involved in the robbery, now do we?"

And that 'policeman's stare' had Derek feeling guilty again...

"Don't either of you touch anything. You might disturb evidence," instructed Alf. (We could call him Alf seeing we know him so well, couldn't we? It's so much nicer than Number One).

"At least my bedroom wasn't disturbed by the gang, Sweaty" shouted Sally from the front room.

"Yes, that is good, thank heavens," Derek shouted back. *What?* So who'd made the mess, he wondered? *Then the coin dropped...* Oh...

"Did she call you *Sweaty?*" It was Alf, who had popped his head back into the hall.

"Yes, but it's really Derek and I'd prefer if you'd refer to me as..."

"Because the name 'Stinky' was used at the Supermarket yesterday when a car was pinched," continued Alf. "Do you ever go under the pseudonym of *Stinky?*"

Pseudonym – *wow*. Police College had done a good job there. Derek was surprised. "Wouldn't you think Sweaty was bad enough, Alfie. You don't mind me calling you Alfie, do you?" Derek responded.

"Watch it Sonny. It's constable to you." Alfie made his point as his scowl went deeper.

Sally's shoulder bag on the hall table was noticed by *Constable* Alfie and he picked it up.

Derek was inclined to quote back the instructions he'd given them a moment ago about evidence – "Don't touch anything," but wisely, he didn't.

And then Constable Alfie emptied out the contents. Of course, all Sally's personal rubbish came tumbling out, confirming Derek's earlier thoughts on quantity – and this rubbish included the bundle of money.

"And 'ose bag is this?" he asked Derek.

Derek was in two minds to say, "Well it's not mine, Dearie," but didn't. Should he say it was Sally's and that it was unwise looking in it without her permission? No... Should he point out he was being a naughty constable and shouldn't be putting his clumsy big fingerprints all over it? No... Should he...?

Oh *shhhh-ugar*... The money.

If that's found, how could they explain it? It might be suspected to be part of the Supermarket stolen cash and Sally would have to explain all her dilemma and stupidity – and they might not believe her anyway. She'd already made this pair out to look foolish, hadn't she?

"*Miss Donaldson*," Alfie shouted and Sally appeared.

"This bag – your's or your mother's?"

"It's mine – *and why are you looking in it?* Why didn't you *ask me* in the first place," she exploded.

Sally is a right little firebrand when she's riled it would seem. But isn't it nice to see a policeman blush, something that Derek wouldn't have believed was possible.

She quickly gathered the bits and pieces together and started pushing them back in.

"What's the bundle?" pursued Alfie.

"I really don't think it's any of your business but if you must know, it's the spare knickers I carry with me in case of emergency. Do you really want to *see* my knickers?" she asked innocently.

Look – another blush. Well done Sal. Derek wanted to cheer her, even though it seemed unlikely that she'd been believed, but Constable Alfie wasn't confident enough to continue with that line of investigation.

"Is it just you and your mother that live 'ere? Does Sweaty reside 'ere too?" he continued, trying not to look directly at Sally.

"It's Derek," Sweaty tried to say.

"My father and mother both stay here but my friend *Derek* is just visiting, thank you," Sally informed the constable.

Derek found it objectionable that Constable Alfie had directed his question at Sally and had expertly managed to get up Derek's nose at the same time, but he did admire the skill.

"And your father, where is 'e?" continued Alfie.

"I've no idea. I've just arrived back myself. He's probably out trying to find my mum," Sally threw back at him, "... the job you should be doing at this moment, should you not?"

It was then it suddenly struck Derek that these policemen weren't aware that Sally had been with her mum at the time of the robbery or that she'd been tied up overnight in the furniture van.

Sally hadn't offered to make them any wiser. She appeared to resent this particular pair of policemen being there, though Derek accepted they were only doing their job.

He had discovered Sal just a few hours ago hadn't he, and he was the only one who *knew* she'd been tied up in the van – so how could the police possibly be aware? And unless the staff at the supermarket had actually seen Sally with her mum yesterday and reported that, again, how would they know?

And there surely must have been some video evidence somewhere – there are always CCTV cameras...

Could be that these two coppers have not been properly updated for the day, or just didn't listen at the briefing when they were told.

Shouldn't Sally tell them? Derek suspected it was just pig-headedness on Sally's part. She had been an eye-witness and was even physically involved. But he'd have to leave it to her to judge the moment herself.

His knowledge was limited to what she'd told him earlier before they came into the house, and naturally as an ambitious newspaper reporter he was very curious to know more. And that bundle of money? She shouldn't have it, should she – her boss's cash? He had a naughty thought – could he persuade her that they should run away together and just spend it? The mood she's in, she might say "Yes".

Policeman number two came back down the stairs.

"Nobody up there," he said. "Better leave some work for the other lads to do. They wouldn't be happy if we solved this ourselves would they Alf? Right then, we know you live here Miss. Where do you live, sonny? We will be contacting you again."

Sonny... *sonny. That was the second time.* Derek saw red – but held his temper. These two are worse than Granny Smith and I'm more inclined to thump them, he thought. But at least they didn't call him Sweaty again. That really would have been pushing it. Derek gave his name.

"How do you spell that?"

"D-e-r-e-k."

"Your surname..."

So, he gave him the gory details plus the address and home telephone number and waited for some sarcastic comment regarding 'Toozlethwaite'.

What a disappointment – they made no comment.

"We'll be obliged for you both to remain in the country, please, and be available to attend at the station if required," and they left.

"I'm worried about Mum. I do hope she's alright, but I haven't had anything to eat or drink since yesterday lunchtime. I must have something to help me think. I'll nip upstairs for a quick shower and change my clothes. Rolling about on the floor of a van doesn't make me feel very feminine, and I guess this could become a long day."

Meanwhile, Derek made himself useful. He discovered the kitchen and started searching cupboards and fridge to find food, and he didn't have to look hard, there was plenty. He'd never had to bother about preparing meals at home, thanks to Granny Smith, but here today he wanted to make his mark. The fun his Gran could have in a kitchen like this – but she'd be exhausted just having to walk the length of it...

The kitchen had all the appliances you could possibly buy or he could think of, except maybe an automatic shoe polisher and trouser press, but they would probably be somewhere else, waiting to be used. And how all these pieces of equipment worked he could only guess. He also wondered if some of them had simply been taken from the packaging and placed there to impress visitors. If they had been – he *was* impressed – *big style*.

He knew nothing of Sally's background or family, but they weren't short of a bob or two, obviously. Perhaps there was a cook used this kitchen, it looked grand enough for that. They maybe even have a maid as well, and while he was at it, he concluded a butler would not be out of place in a house this size.

As he stood there daydreaming again, gazing open-mouthed into the enormous fridge, a sudden practical thought occurred – what about the garage, this big house's integral double garage...? He'd recognised it from the outside but hadn't seen the access from inside the house. Had any of the earlier searches for Sally's mum included looking there? Could she be lying in there, bound and gagged the way Sally had been – scared and alone and unable to shout or even see? He shuddered and imagined it and was grateful it hadn't been one of *his* first-hand experiences. He'd barely coped with yesterday's...

He wasn't aware which door accessed it – and, of course, Sally or the two policemen could have already looked there, though it certainly hadn't been mentioned. Then Derek's brain started working overtime. If the gang had been in the house, had it been one of the family cars they'd taken?

This seemed a really well-off family. Would there be three cars – one for each? And what types – Jaguars, Daimlers, Mercedes, Range Rovers? They would be expensive types, no doubt, and personalised number plates, probably a family set because it would be cheaper to buy in bulk? Maybe they'd even have their own chauffeur? He was curious now. He also had slight pangs of jealousy ...Oh to be well off – but not if it brings a lot of trouble with it. Then again, what use would a car be to him? He couldn't even drive.

Then he thought about Sally's mum. Just where was Mrs Donaldson? He'd read so many stories in the national papers that were about people being found dead – all over the place. He was glad he hadn't had to follow up on any yet. Bodies had been found in dustbins, in rivers, up alleyways, in plastic bags, pushed off cliffs, in cars, in lofts, in trunks, *in garages... Stop...* Or at least slow down... Think positive thoughts – he told himself.

Had they dumped her off somewhere or taken her as a hostage right enough? Would they just release her unharmed – he hoped so, for Sally's sake – and her mum's.

He shouted upstairs.

"Sally, have you checked the garage?"

"No I haven't Derek, it's a good idea, why did we miss that? At the end of the hall – the locked door – key hanging beside it."

It was a big garage and looked bigger because it was empty, that is except for a couple of small lockers, two bicycles leaning against the wall, one a male's in dark blue, and one without a crossbar, in pink, a solitary little plastic floor brush and shovel set, and a dusty calendar which was four years out of date hanging on one wall. Definitely, there were no cars in this space, nor was there any sign of Mrs Donaldson.

Sally had hurried down the stairs and joined him in the empty space. "Pity, they've even taken the cars?" Derek sympathised.

"*No. Don't be silly.* We don't have any cars. We just use our bikes or walk," said Sally. "That's mine and my father's. He uses it a lot but not quite as much as he used to. He uses a taxi now and again. Mum's bike will be..." Her voice broke. Derek thought she would burst into tears but she took two deep breaths and controlled herself.

"Oh..." was all he could think.

There was nothing different in there, according to Sally, just a lot of the usual unused space. A quick change of subject seemed appropriate. "Would you like bacon and egg, or a sandwich, Sally?"

He hoped she'd opt for a sandwich – he could cope with that.

"Oh please, Derek, bacon and egg."

She showed surprise by his success at the cooker, whereas he was amazed – *he* didn't think he could do it. And there he was having a second breakfast in the space of only a few hours.

Gran would probably say "He's a growing lad."

Grandad would say, "G-g-greedy p-p-p-pig."

As he ate his second breakfast this morning, feeling a tad guilty, he learned a little more of the detail of her ordeal. She had felt really bad after meeting him at the park, mainly because of the way she'd messed things up for him, so she'd gone on walkabout before the money exchange was due. She'd been passing the Supermarket and had gone in, as she'd done many times over the years. Access to her mum's office had never been questioned and she was able to toddle in anytime. Most of the staff in Bisko's knew her well, but yesterday, she'd popped in the back entrance because she didn't have a lot of time to spare.

Sally and her mum had been the only ones in the office and were sitting chatting when the raid happened. They had been pushed to the floor. It was a menacing group with their faces covered and they threatened to stand on her mum's fingers, and break them if she didn't open the safe. So, she had to. And guns, they weren't actually displayed but Sally was sure the threat was implied.

The two of them had been tied up and blindfolded.

The blindfolding had been the part that she had found most terrifying. Not being able to move and only hearing what was happening seemed to make it even worse.

Sally was aware that the gang had been surprised to find her there with her mother and they'd argued about what to do with her – leave her or take her? They'd obviously decided beforehand to take her mum as a hostage but it wasn't clear what else they'd planned.

Walking to the van had been frightening, not being able to see, being pushed along through the storage area with very few words being said. She had never before appreciated the sensation of hearing only, without sight. Although she'd been terrified, it didn't stop the thought of how terrible it must be for someone to be blind – her hearing had suddenly become incredibly important, and sensitized.

She'd been pushed and made to walk along the concrete floor, then on to what she'd taken to be a metal ramp, noticing and feeling the different textures on her feet, and a change in the levels, and finally onto a wooden floor. Hearing how her footsteps in the open warehouse changed to an enclosed echo also told her she could only be inside a large van. Sound had never been so apparent and she found it could create clear pictures in her mind. That walk had only taken a few moments – but had been new and horrifying feeling.

Her captor's had tied her ankles and left her more or less totally helpless on the van's floor. Sally only sensed her mum was beside her – they couldn't see each other or talk. She was unsure if she could hear her mum's breathing – her own breath and her own heartbeat seemed so loud.

It had been an uncomfortable journey which lasted some time and it seemed as if they had gone a great distance but they had actually doubled back to the house.

"Could that have been just to confuse us," she asked Derek, "...or do you think they could have been lost?"

Derek was able to contribute about that.

"If it's the driver I saw, and if she wasn't using her specs, I'd say – *definitely lost.*"

Sally thought another car or van had been waiting for them and possibly her mum had been transferred to it. A vehicle had roared off a little later – and suddenly she'd felt very scared and very lonely. Lying there, alone in the hot van, not able to do anything but bang her feet every so often had tired her out and done no good. She had exhausted herself and fallen into a broken sleep. She'd kicked around again when she wakened and that's when Sweaty/Derek/Mr Wonderful came on the scene.

Sally ate greedily, talking excitedly all the way through Derek's make-shift meal. He found all of this fascinating, but after being brought up to date and after drinking three cups of tea, Derek had to ask directions to the loo.

"There's a shower room next to the garage door – you can use that," Sally told him.

He was a smart little cookie, he told himself, as he walked jauntily along the hallway. He was actually getting some things right today. He'd guessed earlier that there were at least two loos in this house and he'd been proved correct. Yes, he was on a roll... (It didn't take much to please Sweaty).

It was a large shower room, but somehow as he'd entered he'd felt a sixth sense kicking in – something was odd. Could it be the effect of the whole space being covered by shiny tiles maybe, or the several mirrors showing his reflection from different angles? He smiled at himself, as you do, in self-admiration and pulled in his tum...

The WC was at the far end of the room. He went to it, took up the standing and firing position, but, just before he lowered his zip, he sensed a presence. He stopped breathing. Thank goodness the zip was still closed. A man feels truly vulnerable with his fly open. In the silence he could just hear the rapid breathing of someone else.

There were obviously only towels in the glass-fronted cupboard he'd passed on his right as he'd entered but the cupboard on the opposite side had a mirror-fronted door. Could someone be hiding in there? Could it be a gang member?

Should he shout to Sally or be a big brave boy on his own. It'd be nice to impress Sal but only if he left the bathroom alive.

He tip-toed over and... and... He opened the door suddenly – but there was nobody there... Just his imagination again...

No, he was correct. There was someone. There was a barely perceptible movement again and his nerves were taut. What was it?

The shower curtain – *it twitched.*

Hell... don't panic... He'd have to do something... Should he just run...? No...

He went cautiously forward...

He got ready to grab the curtain and... PULLED.

"What the..."

The figure moved forward and Derek jumped back – and tripped.

CRACK.

He didn't remember seeing stars when his head hit the tiled floor, as they say in stories. He felt only incredible pain...

"Ouch..."

Darkness was closing in, but so was the female figure that was coming towards him.

She had something in her hand...

She was going to hit him with...

It was a – it was – *a pink loo brush...?*

"Ohhhhhhh..."

15

He was being borne aloft by the two angels, one for his head and the other for his leftovers.

Hmmmm... He felt so light... And... at peace with himself... But why were they wobbling...? The picture faded... but back it came... a little wavy at times. The two angels were still there. One was wiping his brow. It felt so cool... And... he was...

floating......

floating......

floating......

His angels were so... *beautiful,*

just emanating... love, and they had such a gentle touch, and they were caring... just for him, so tenderly...

"Reach out and touch me," they seemed to be saying – but you can't touch angels, he knew, they were like... ghosts, and you passed through them – unless... you were an angel too...

"Reach out..." was repeated, so he reached out, and there was a touch, a feeling like one he'd known – long ago – when he was alive...

So now he knew – he... was an angel too... *Fair ye well... dear Sweaty* – now Derek – is angelic...

This divine shape looked just like his Sally, his dear, dear Sally, his loving Sally, his...

"We were together... for such a short time... The feeling was so... *beautiful...* We had been too, too happy... Why did it have to end so suddenly...?"

And the other angel...

He turned to her, reached out and again he...

"My God..." Her hair came away in his hand and he was suddenly wide awake.

"Who the hell are you?" he blurted out.

"Ehm – I'm Sally's father," the voice said.

"But you are a woman," he said.

"Not really," the voice said again.

"Dad – leave him please. Get changed – *now*." Sally was angry.

Derek was in the master bedroom lying on the water-bed. He hadn't known this type of bed still existed and felt that he was actually floating – an odd sensation. He could only see hazily, because his glasses were missing and his head was throbbing, but standing in front of the wardrobe was a shapely female figure but with a short haircut and she (or maybe he should be referring to 'her' as 'he') was removing the dress.

This exposed the ladies underwear in a striking shade of scarlet, and legs sheathed in black silk stockings with a scarlet suspender belt, and scarlet high heels displaying a pair of very shapely legs to advantage.

"Calm down," he told himself, "It's a *man* remember."

"My father has some funny friends," Sally informed him.

He's just a little strange himself, Derek thought.

"Why aren't you at work anyway," she asked her father, who was laying his other clothes on top of the bed, preparing to change into something a little less daring, it would appear.

Derek's eyes could just about distinguish a very sensible pair of spotty boxer shorts, a lightweight white vest, a pale blue sports shirt, and a conservative looking pair of light brown cotton trousers, all being laid out carefully on top of the bed, by this strangely fascinating figure. This attractive shape then bent over to select and lift a pair of gent's casual brown shoes from the floor of the wardrobe.

Derek couldn't prevent his eyes being drawn to the sensual movements of this red underwear, and he lay there, gazing in admiration – and lust – at the shapely bottom before him... *Stop it – it's another fella...* And he quickly looked away, embarrassed, which made his eyes and his head hurt.

"It's Friday, Sally, Sweetie, and I told you before that I was having today off. Have you not wakened yet? Anyway, did your mum go into work early today? The burglary must have been after she left I suppose. How annoying. Didn't you hear them?"

"I wasn't here. And Dad, Mum has been kidnapped, we think. Why don't you know that? Haven't the police spoken to you? Where have you been?" Sally sounded deeply concerned.

"Why would the police speak to me? We had a special celebration last night, a Very Special Night, if you know what I mean, and a little too much to drink, I guess. I slept on a settee – somewhere, and got a taxi back to find this place in a bit of a mess. I went into the loo and heard noises and thought it could be the burglars returning, so I hid – behind the shower curtain – until this young ruffian..."

"But you must have known it was me. You must have heard me surely," said Sally.

"I did, but there were other voices too and I didn't think you'd like it if I'd appeared in my special clothes," he whimpered.

"When are you going to enquire about Mum? Don't you care?"

"Of course I care but wait a moment. I must take off these shoes." His voice was now a whine. "My feet are *killing* me. Oh yes, that's better. Now you were saying?"

Derek's head had cleared a little though it was throbbing like mad and at least he could see that 'Daddy' had thrown on a bathrobe but somehow he still managed to look effeminate.

Could be the eye liner and the lipstick he supposed...

"Your mother kidnapped? That sounds a bit unlikely to me. Anyway your mum's a tough old bird – she'll manage" he said as he made for the door. "Must get something to drink – I'm parched."

Sally stood glowering at him as he turned and left the room.

Now it transpires that this gentleman (or should it be gentlewoman?) is the manager of the bank in the next town. Derek wondered how well this gent's customers knew of these funny habits. He was aware of many organisations having 'casual clothes' days. Comfortable wear one day a week had become quite common but is it possible that this guy's bank was trying to buck the trend?

'The Bank that liked to say – DRESS'.

He couldn't help smirking at that thought.

"At least you are looking a little cheerier," said Sally.

And as he thought of Sally's dad's 'away from work' habits, wasn't *he* supposed to have started work today? He was lying here, when he should have been there.

His day had begun, so recently, full of hope and 'joie de vivre', but what chance was there now? Here he was in a strange bed and beginning to feel seasick, wearing what felt like someone else's head. He'd have to get up. He had to get to that job.

"Don't move yet." Sally pushed back him down flat and he didn't resist. "Rest some more and I'll make a phone call. I'll tell the boss we'll both be in later and that we have a front page story for the next issue of the paper."

Sally sat on the bed beside him as she dialled. It was nice with her being close like this. He knew he had better not say to Granny Smith that he had been in the same bed as Sally – she might not understand. "You're not too old to have your ear clipped," she would say primly – and then she'd clip his ear, even though he was nearly thirty – especially if she thought he was pulling her leg...

The phone was switched loud enough for him to be able to hear both ends of the conversation but he could see by the expression on her face that Sally hadn't expected some of her boss's comments.

"Hello. Is that Rob Sheldon? Ah, yes, Rob, of course it's you. Sorry I'm not in yet, Rob. I've been delayed a little."

"Not half as bloody sorry as I am... Where in hell's teeth are you? And what have you done with my money?"

"I've a great story for this week's edition, Rob."

"My money... Where is it?"

"It's safe, Rob. I have it here with me..."

"You've what? And why have you still got it? You were supposed to hand it over yesterday, weren't you?"

"Yes, Rob, but something happened that..."

"Are you trying to get me killed?"

"What do you *mean*, Rob?"

"The least that will happen is that my bookie will arrange to have my legs broken if the money's not handed over pronto."

"Your BOOKIE?"

"Yes, my bookie. Who did you think the money was for? If I don't pay up quickly he'll be sending his boys round... And incidentally, there's one of his men sitting here waiting for YOU. You apparently gave him a job yesterday. What bloody job is this you've dreamed up?"

"Oh Rob, I'm sorry, I..."

"Just get that money in here right away – and I mean RIGHT AWAY or you are out of a job, Missy."

"Yes, Rob...I'll..." She looked at Derek. "He's hung up..."

And it had been Derek who'd been worried about his job. Oh dear, the tears were about to start again. No, Derek didn't cry. He'd given up all hope, but poor Sally...

"Can you come with me, Derek – please? Do you feel well enough yet? I could do with some support. We'll get a taxi."

He felt bad just lying there and when he moved he felt terrible, but this was big trouble for Sal and therefore it now was important to him. He was the one who would have to be strong. Of course he would help – even if he felt lousy.

The taxi arrived fairly quickly.

Because it was a short journey, this taxi driver felt he had to tell his passengers his full life story even faster than taxi drivers usually do, and that was in addition to his current take on the political situation.

This didn't help Derek's head.

And to make matters worse, this driver seemed to know Derek's head was throbbing and was deliberately cornering too fast and slamming on his brakes as if he was in an American Cop film... well, he wasn't really doing that – but it sure seemed like it to Derek. They arrived in one piece and Sally paid – Derek couldn't. He was very pleased to leave the taxi.

The vehicle moved off but, just as he pulled into the traffic, and just too late to stop him, Sally realised something rather important was missing from her shoulder – her bag – with the money in it. She'd left it on the seat.

Yesterday, Derek felt he'd coped with a struggle when running away from the guys in the park and their policeman pal, but today – he'd a cracking headache, but he was obliged to chase that taxi – for Sally's sake. So, yesterday would have to be considered only a rehearsal – *and after that taxi he went.*

Thank goodness for traffic lights – the taxi had stopped. Damn, it was off again, and quickly, and Derek found he was having another opportunity to dodge through traffic. He amazingly survived once more.

"I'm not keeping up. He's stopped again. He's picking up a passenger. I might catch him this time. No. He's off again."

He was sure he couldn't keep going.

"Thank goodness it's a straight road – I can still see him. He's slowing down. He's stopped beside two policemen. He's handing them Sally's bag. They're opening it."

He surprisingly found the stamina to keep running but what would he say when he reached them? At least the taxi hadn't gone off again – the policemen were writing out a receipt for the driver.

"Don't move off yet – please..." Derek implored sotto voce.

He couldn't keep up this pace for much longer.

"*Oy,*" he yelled at the top of his voice and they heard him.

At least the taxi driver recognised him as 'the quiet one with the glasses' who'd been with the pretty girl who must have left the bag in his cab.

"Nice girl she was," said the cabbie.

Derek could instinctively tell that the nice police constables didn't think he was very nice. It was the same pair who'd visited Sally's house today. Derek gasped out that he'd run after the taxi to retrieve the handbag – thanks very much...

"Got any identification, Sir?" Constable Alf asked.

"You saw me this morning and spoke to me. You know me."

"I said, got any..."

"Oh, just a minute" and he could only find his library card in his wallet.

"Will this do?" but Derek just knew there would be a reason why it would not do.

"Just gives your name, Sir," Constable Number Two said pityingly.

"Nothing with your name and photograph as well, like a driving licence? You could 'ave stolen this from someone."

"Yes, and I'm into stealing books from the library. Been doing it for years... *I don't drive.*"

"That's a pity, Sir. 'int of sarcasm creeping in there, y'know. We don't like that, do we Samuel?"

"No, we don't Alf," said Samuel.

And now, at last he knew both their names, how lovely – but it's the bag he wanted.

"And 'ow do we know that this bag will finish up with the correct owner? We'd better check if there is some identification inside," Alf said as he started to open it and all Derek could think of was the money. They mustn't find the money or they're going to start asking questions – questions that he didn't want to be asked.

And that's when he went a bit crazy because he grabbed the bag from Alf's hands, leaving Alf just looking startled, and took to his heels once again.

Two breakfasts that morning and his previous days' training sessions stood him in good stead – but his head started pounding again in rhythm with his feet as he retraced his steps back to Sally.

"I shouldn't have done that... I hope Sally can obtain a 'get out of jail' card for me," was all he could think.

If only he'd kept calm, but as it was – he had to keep running. If only the policeman had been *walking* back with him to Sally they might have all lived happily ever after, but they weren't...

If only... if only...

He was into deep breaths – involuntarily.

Finding that the two pursuing policemen, galloping along behind him, were neither as fit nor as fast as he was had given him both a small feeling of consolation – and a small lead.

He'd have to come up very quickly with a convincing explanation for his actions but his feet were pounding faster than his brain, and his feet weren't nearly as painful. He would be paying a hefty price when they caught up but it was all for Sally – she was worth it.

Sally was still at the office entrance.

He threw the bag to her. "Run Sal, *run*. Get the money back to your boss or hidden – quickly – before they get here. I'll stall them."

Sally vanished into the building as two pairs of thundering boots screeched to a halt beside him and two pairs of hands lovingly grabbed hold – *and held on*... Nothing was said by either – they couldn't speak – they just stood, chests heaving and their faces a bright shade of red. He decided not to mention that he'd run faster and claimed the prize.

"Right Sunshine," gasped Alf, "You... are for... the book."

"I'm sorry Officer. I know I was wrong but I had to. It was a matter of life and death for the young lady. She was about to lose her job."

"No young lady here *(gasp)* and no *(gasp)* bag either. I'd say the charge *(gasp, gasp)* would be assault on a police *(gasp)* officer and the theft of the bag with *(gasp)* the help of persons unknown." This charge had been pronounced by Constable Samuel, as his lungs eagerly searched for oxygen.

Derek suggested in a suitably pleading manner that they all go inside, because he was sure that it could all be sorted out to their total satisfaction, and then he proceeded to identify the excellent qualities being displayed by the two gentlemen who were apprehending him. Never before had so many words of a flattering and complimentary nature been uttered towards the police force by someone without the use of a thesaurus, and said with such totally incredible sincerity, but neither policeman believed a word being spouted by this smarmy little shrimp, and decided to give him just a little more rope. They had rushed about sufficiently for the day and hoped that inside there would be a chance of a seat and a cup of coffee. They sorely needed a break...

Derek's memory wasn't functioning. The name of Sally's boss – what was it? Bob? No, it was Rob something? And *he* complained about people not remembering *his* name... He wished he'd listened more carefully earlier, but then he had been poorly, hadn't he? He still was, but he knew he wouldn't be getting any sympathy from his companions in blue. The three trooped into the building, two of them with hearts still pounding furiously, and the third with a head pounding as well and just as furiously.

At least the receptionist knew Sally well and phoned her office. It was the boss who answered and the receptionist didn't smile at his reply. Rob Sheldon was a well known figure in this building too and had always displayed impeccable behaviour towards whoever was on Reception over the years, and she really liked and respected him. Something very serious must have happened to make him explode like that. She gave the visitors an *edited* version.

"Mr Sheldon says to go up. First on the left upstairs."

Sensibly, they should have taken the lift, even for the one level in the state they were, but no, they trudged wearily up. Linked by the common bond of exhaustion, they entered the outer office of The Newingsworth Weekly Gazette.

Mr Rob Sheldon, the Editor, looked red-faced, with arms waving, and displeased. Sally was in his office with him and her cheeks were flushed. Derek could see she'd had a few tears already, but Derek was thankful that at least her boss would have the money by now and all could be easily sorted out... But Sally was still holding the bag. The money was still in her possession. *Give him the money, please, Sally,* he willed. *Get rid of it.*

When he looked round, he found he was the only one who'd

observed the inner office activities. The two coppers were sitting on a desk and laughing and joking with a tall skinny bloke who was seated. They obviously knew each other very well.

"What are you doing 'ere, Spider? Been kicked out of the bookie's 'ave you? Found you out at last, eh? But I didn't think you were into this sort of thing."

"Gone up in the world I 'ave. Got this job yesterday – 'ead'unted I was. Started this morning." Spider informed them.

"So, what do you do then?" asked Constable Samuel.

"Dunno," he said, "Just sit 'ere and look attractive, so far. Can't complain."

"Some punters 'ave all the luck. Good for you, mate," said Constable Alf. And that's when the main office door opened with a crash and two rather hefty gents barged in, rough and tough, written all over them. These guys had a purpose in life and were determined to get the job done, a little sub-contract for 'Saddanbroke's – The Bookmakers You Can Trust'. They had the build of rugby players and wore t-shirts, which would have done a great job of display, if they'd had sponsors, because of the vast available advertising space. Today, both shirts were identical. Black with white letters *'Hell hath no fury like...'* They didn't notice the two policemen and made to go into Rob Sheldon's office.

"*Oy,*" shouted Constable Samuel."Where are you two going?"

"None of your business – a private appointment," was the cocky reply, and they opened Mr Sheldon's office door and walked straight in.

"Right, where's the dosh?" was the demand to Rob Sheldon.

The editor looked ashen and sort of choked – they'd been expected, although not invited.

"I've... not... got it..." he gulped.

What was about to happen to Mr Sheldon if he didn't pay up immediately could be heard loud and clear by Mr Sheldon and the other listeners in the office – and it wasn't pleasant. The two bruisers stepped forward and grabbed the editor to frogmarch him out. The dirty work wouldn't be done in front of interested observers and they preferred the open air.

"*Help,*" squealed the editor.

Sally stepped in front of them.

"I have the money. It's in my bag..." she said softly.

Her bag was pulled roughly from her shoulder and she was pushed aside as this pair went to step from the office with the money – and Sally's bag.

"That bag is our evidence," said Constable Samuel to Constable Alfie, and "*STOP.*" He officiously held up his hand like he was controlling traffic. The two policemen blocked the path of the two bully boys.

"Just one moment, please. You are going nowhere."

Now this statement was apparently considered debatable, but the debate rapidly escalated beyond what was normally considered to be calm and reasonable discussion round a table.

In other words – *it got rough...*

During the ensuing scuffle, police hats were knocked off, an eye was punched and a desk was knocked over. The visitors were ultra protective of their new T-shirts, and having them wasted on the first day of wear hadn't been the plan. They'd also taken a great liking to the handbag and refused to part with it – but that was police evidence and the two constables had to uphold the law, and anyway, it wasn't every day in Newingsworth that they had the chance of a good punch-up.

Sensibly Rob Sheldon had remained in his office. Derek was delighted to see that the editor had put a protective arm around Sally's shoulder. The two of them stood horrified and transfixed as the outer office calm disintegrated before their eyes. Spider looked as if he'd had previous experience of situations like this and had hidden under his desk.

Derek became a minor hero in the eyes of the editor because not only was he calmly moving about lifting items that had been knocked over and replacing toppled chairs as they fell, he'd skilfully caught a laptop, which had been sitting on a desk, before it smashed to the floor. In truth Derek wasn't being a hero – he was in a terrified nervous panic trying to find a way of escaping from this mad space but things kept tripping him up.

The bloke with the bag had managed to break free from Constable Alfie and dived for the door. Although Alfie grabbed an ankle, a quick shimmy and out the door he went. Alfie yelled in agony as he was used as a doormat by the other villain leaping through the door after his mate, but worse still, Constable Samuel chose the same route and left his footprint on Alfie's back too. Alfie, in agony managed to get up and rushed after the others, down the stairs and out onto the street.

And suddenly the office was silent...

16

Constables Simpson and Gilbert were standing rather shamefaced and hatless. These were the two policemen that Derek knew, and had come to love, as Alfie and Samuel respectively. The grilling they'd received from their Sergeant when they'd reported back to the station hadn't been pleasant.

They'd returned only after they'd succeeded in bringing their breathing and heart-rates back to near normal. That had been about half an hour after a less than totally successful chase, thanks to the two individuals who'd galloped off with their police evidence – the large handbag.

The chase out of the newspaper office building had started well enough for the two constables. The two thugs had rushed down the stairs and knocked over the carefully arranged pots containing the everlasting-flower arrangements prepared painstakingly two days ago, by the Receptionist, to brighten up the entrance. She was just about to phone for the police when first, Constable Samuel, closely followed by Constable Alfie, came clattering down and caused an even bigger mess. What was more galling for the Receptionist was that these four clod-hoppers had ensured her *everlasting* flowers *were not.*

Along almost the full length of the High Street the four of them had gone, with the two policemen getting some satisfaction from feeling fitter and doing a lot better than the two they were chasing. Their earlier warm-up with Derek had helped a little and they weren't in the mood to be losers this time.

Still well ahead, the two in front took a sudden right turn down Vincent Lane, but there was uncertainty where this would take them. These guys were from out of town and didn't know their way around here particularly well, but had had plenty practice at vanishing quickly when *The Law* became involved and had left many a copper standing feeling stupid, and not knowing which direction they'd gone.

They arrived on Stevenson Street. Outside 'POUNDSWORTH BARGAIN STORE' they had an inspiration and shot through the swing doors. Surprised shoppers jumped out of their way as they barged along the corridors between shelves. The same thing then happened when the two policemen appeared, but by deliberately knocking over the promotional display of the giant tins of 'Celebration Toffees' their quarry caused a mess, and a noise, and a delay for the two policemen, although the various kids in the store at that moment did a great job of clearing a lot of the stock into their pockets before staff could catch them.

At the far end of the store there was little choice... Either to return into the waiting arms of the law, which they had no intention of doing, or to leave by the doors marked *'Fire Exit only – Do not use except in an emergency'*. They chose the doors they shouldn't use, which triggered the fire alarm. Customers stood holding hands to ears as a surprised and confused manager failed to remember the code number to stop the bell ringing and had to go in search of the piece of paper he'd scribbled it on.

This took them into the back alley. They knocked over the various piles of cardboard stacked ready for collection, just to make it a little more of an adventure for their two pursuers. And then the two thugs went the wrong way altogether and found, to their cost, that it was a dead end. Having cornered them, Samuel and Alf eased off. Samuel moved towards them reaching into his pocket for his notebook and pencil, his essentials – and received the full force of Sally's overloaded handbag swung into his face.

The blow knocked him off balance and he was pushed aside into the arms of Alfie. Alfie was lucky enough to grab the strap and the body of the now Very Important Bag, and he hung on.

But the other two didn't give up. They held on too and started dragging Alfie back along the pavement – until the strap broke. Alfie's knees were pleased to come to a halt as the other two fell backwards, and Samuel jumped at them, but a swift and agonising kick in the groin had Samuel doubled over in agony and, not surprisingly, he collapsed.

At this point, the other two decided enough was enough and didn't take advantage of their adversary's temporary inconvenience. They decided it was time to retreat and to live to fight another day – and surrendered the bag to Alfie. It wasn't their money anyway, only 'a job' and they'd have another chance. They ran back along the lane – and into the busy road, pretty sure this time they wouldn't be followed, maintaining their excellent escape record.

Alfie had the bag, but at what cost? His elbows and knees felt raw and bruised but, he thought graciously, that seemed nothing in comparison to the state of Samuel's bits. Alfie's eyes started to water, in sympathy, with just the thought. Their Sergeant hadn't offered *them* any sympathy. He had criticised them for the state of their uniform and for being improperly dressed and even worse, for having failed to apprehend the criminals – but sergeants weren't sent into the world to be loved, now were they?

He took a lot more interest when the content of the handbag was poured onto the table, particularly when he saw the bundle. When he asked for details about this package, he doubted his constable's answer. "It's... um... err... 'er spare knickers," Alfie was able to say proudly, and with a little smirk. "I asked 'er about them earlier and she told me."

He received a cold hard stare from his senior. "And you saw them?" Alfie coloured a little.

"Well, no... it was 'er... knickers, Sarge..." he squirmed a little.

"You haven't seen the contents of this package?"

"No Sarge."

"Well, shouldn't we see exactly what it contains by checking *properly?*" There was a critical and caustic tone to the Sergeant's question.

"Yes, Sarge..." from Alfie, and opened the package.

And there in front of them was the cash, in large notes, to the value of three thousand pounds. "It's *not* knickers..." said Alfie.

17

She'd slept well, but felt guilty because of that and Sally was the reason. Muriel had fallen into a really deep sleep, probably due to nervous exhaustion, and had a pleasant dream of when she had been young, but she'd stopped worrying about Sally for that brief time and that felt wrong. Muriel cared deeply for her daughter. She would ask them, but she guessed she would only find out if they were willing to tell her, and only of course if they knew...

She was desperate to be told that her off-spring was safe and well. So far, the gang hadn't proved as fierce as those first impressions back in the Supermarket. She thought she'd probably been fiercer than them when she'd been brought into the house at first. Although she'd seen nothing of their faces, she had an idea from the way they moved, that they were fairly young, all four of them, and probably of a similar age to her Sally, maybe even younger. She felt sorry for them to a certain extent and presumed extreme pressures had forced them to carry out a robbery. However that unspoken sympathy towards them hadn't improved her chances of escape, or release, as far as she could tell.

Breakfast had been brought to her by Beakie just after nine o'clock, and she was told to eat in the bedroom. Someone had cooked bacon and eggs, and there were two slices of toast with a little pot of marmalade on the tray. It had been nicely prepared. She doubted that a male would have been thoughtful enough to have added some marmalade but could be wrong.

Beakie wasn't wearing a balaclava this morning but Muriel

still couldn't see her face. One of them must have had the idea during the night to use some card and string and they'd cut out a face mask. Had they been looking over Muriel's shoulder when CBeebies was on last night perhaps? Anyway, choosing woolly balaclavas in the middle of summer – a right bunch of idiots, she concluded, and she felt confident on that thought, but she was also pleased to see they wouldn't be quite so uncomfortable now.

She remembered a case of a robbery and maybe it was a bank, where the thieves had worn plastic Disney character masks. Was it real life or a film, or did she read it in a book? She couldn't quite decide. Her memory used to be better than this. There was a bizarre picture in her mind of the jolly masks contrasting with the guns in the hands of the robbers, and of the terror on the faces of the bank's staff and the customers lying prone on the floor and all recorded by the remote control cameras.

When you are confined to a room the mind wanders. It would be so easy to reach out and pull away that paper mask she thought as Beakie leaned across, and she was tempted. But she was glad she resisted. Having their faces exposed would make her more of a threat to them, more vulnerable for conviction if caught obviously, but tougher on the way they would treat her for their own protection from then on.

But balaclavas in the middle of summer... did you ever?

Muriel was desperate to know what was to happen to her, but more so, where was Sally? Was she ok? Surely Beakie would tell her? She'd ask anyway – but it wasn't Beakie who collected her tray. "My daughter... can you please tell me about my daughter?" she pleaded with this new individual.

"How would I know anything about your daughter? I only know about you." The voice behind this paper mask was a girl's and now in the daylight it showed obviously in the body shape. The clothing was lightweight and loose fitting but a female body was discernible. This girl's hair was cut short and was bright red and showed over the top of the mask. Muriel guessed that she'd be a bit of a tom-boy.

"But my daughter... you took her with me ...in the van or whatever... She's not here is she?"

"Was that your daughter? Oh, we didn't know that..." replied the tom-boy and left the room hurriedly.

This girl was christened 'Tich' in Muriel's head.

Did she lock the door? Muriel went over and gently tried the handle. Yes, she had. Be patient, she told herself.

With no television in this room to distract her, in the silence the voices across the hall could just about be heard, if they weren't careful and if she listened very carefully. Tich had carried the news about Sally back to the others and none had realised the relationship was mother and daughter. Anyway no-one actually knew whether or not she was alright. She'd been abandoned by them when they'd driven off from Muriel's house last evening.

An unanswered question maybe, but if they'd known would it have made any difference? They'd been concentrating so much on having Muriel as a captive they'd almost forgotten the other person they'd taken. This sad fact made the four of them feel guilty and anxious. They were not hardened criminals by any means. They really weren't very good at this robbery lark they realised.

And the discussion began on how they could confirm that Muriel's daughter hadn't come to more harm. Should they phone the police and tell them where the van was and that the girl was inside? It was going to be another hot and sunny day and she could cook in there. No, the police could trace the call probably.

Contacting a neighbour to tell them was another idea. They couldn't do it by phone because they didn't know any numbers to ring. Should they ask Muriel? No, that would be a big psychological advantage for her if she thought they had to ask for her help. They didn't want it to encourage her to become awkward. She'd behaved like a nice little old lady up to now – if you ignored the cursing and swearing. Let it continue like that. Or could one of them go and look? Yes... The conclusion was that one of the boys would go and reconnoitre. He'd have to walk –

they had no transport of their own. That shouldn't be too difficult a task because they weren't far away from Muriel's home.

It was a few weeks back when they were making plans that they had discovered the house they were now occupying had been lying empty since early summer. A chat in the local pub and they'd learned the owner and his family spent almost all of the summer in Italy. The four of them had decided to take a chance and make use of it. They hoped it wouldn't have to be for long. If someone did question their presence, they could claim they were renting it for the summer. And what the owner didn't know wouldn't hurt him...

It was a nice house and they'd planned and agreed to avoid any more damage other than the minimum that they would have to inflict on entry. The back door lock had been the casualty. No need to put another lock on the door though. A slip-bolt would give the effect required to anyone who checked and at least one of them would always be inside the house, except during the robbery. They wouldn't be leaving until it was safe to do so and they didn't expect any visitors. If they kept the hostage tied up or locked in the bedroom, she would be well secured, once they'd placed a few bars on the outside.

And so far the plan had worked a treat. No-one had been near them, other than the Pizza Man, and the hedge was wonderful for screening them from both traffic and from the other houses, and the rare passing pedestrians. No-one seemed to have noticed the house lights being used, or if they did, they'd considered it to be none of their business. It was that kind of neighbourhood. Keep yourself to yourself. When they came and went from the property they tried to avoid being seen by neighbours, but none were very close anyway. Large houses on large tracts of land set well back from the roads were the norm, but after the robbery, why had they gone back to the home of Mrs Muriel Donaldson, the woman they had abducted? Was it to burgle that home? No, it wasn't. It was because they were naive, or just plain dumb and should never have decided to become criminals. They were out of their depth.

The two girls thought that Muriel would appreciate having clean clothes of her own to wear and therefore which fitted her. She would appreciate their thoughtfulness, the girls declared, and be a very well behaved hostage because she would realise that this gang cared. The lads were certain this was a load of cobblers. As it happened, surprisingly, the girls were actually correct...

They'd established Muriel's address relatively easily. They also found out that at work, Muriel was the one always in the supermarket office, and, it had been decreed, she would be the only one they'd take with them. It had been a shock to find Sally there as well when they burst in. They'd presumed wrongly that Sally was a Bisko employee too. Taking her had been done in a blind panic although it seemed the right decision at the time.

After deliberately taking a lengthy drive all round the town, the access to Muriel's house had been achieved with the minimum of fuss. They'd used the keys from the shoulder bag, without realising it belonged to Sally, or they might have questioned why the keys from this other woman's bag fitted the locks in Muriel's door.

When inside, the male members of the gang felt they'd had to create a creditable macho image. It would look odd if they didn't leave some sort of mess behind they argued – the girls insisted that it hadn't to be a *messy* mess. The boys put the foot down when it was time to leave the house – and upset the girls.

"We'll have to tidy up before we go," the girls had said...

Well, can you blame these guys? The boy's were beginning to have regrets – it should've been a boy's only gang, but a bit late to change that...

The departure from Muriel's house was to be by a different vehicle and it was Sally's mobile that was used to call the other two males to bring this other vehicle round. The hostage was to be transferred, and the furniture van abandoned where it stood. They'd planned that no identifying clues would be found and had behaved accordingly in the use of the van, but they still had all crossed their fingers when they left it and they hoped that no-one had slipped up. They also waited with trepidation to see what the getaway vehicle would be like. The girls, in particular, hoped it would be big enough – they didn't fancy sitting on the guys' knees on a hot day like this...

Luckily for the gang, Mrs Masterton, next door, was out at Bingo in the Old Astoria in town and didn't arrive home that night until after they'd gone, or they would not have succeeded so easily.

Mrs Masterton didn't normally miss much of what was happening in the neighbourhood. She was an expert at picking up information with her eyes and ears, absorbing and remembering everything that happened around her, but she was even better at saying very little about her own goings-on. Bingo was her little secret vice and she wouldn't have been pleased if any of her posh neighbours got to know of it. It had been her compulsion for many years. Anyway, she called it 'housey-housey' and she won small sums quite regularly, thank you very much, though she had no need for the winnings.

Her husband, Albert, when he'd passed on, had left her well provided for. He had been a very successful greengrocer owning a string of stores across the country. These were sold for considerable profit when he died, making her a very rich widow. So, although she certainly didn't do it for the money, only ill-health would make her miss her daily bingo sessions.

When she returned that evening, she'd noted that a common furniture removal van, and a not very clean one at that, was sitting outside the Donaldson's. She wondered why, and presumed it had broken down. It wasn't obviously anything to do with the Donaldson's. They weren't moving. Could it have been a delivery of a piece of new furniture? Mrs Donaldson hadn't said, and as her neighbour she would have expected to have been informed, *surely.* No, it couldn't be that, she decided, they only bought from Harrods and that was by very special delivery. Just as long as it's not still there in the morning...

If she'd been around earlier, she certainly wouldn't have missed the roar and the screech of brakes from the borrowed

Range Rover as Bill and Freddy Watt came to a dramatic halt in front of her house. Bill could be a bit of a show-off driver. The Range Rover had been his selection at Bisko's – he liked big cars, no matter who the owner was. And she certainly wouldn't have missed the transfer of Muriel from the furniture van to that Range Rover.

Bill and Freddie Watt were not part of the gang proper. They considered themselves to be associate members, co-opted for this job only, and would deny all knowledge of everything if the fuzz caught them. After taking the car from the Supermarket they'd pulled over for a moment and swapped the number plates to avoid being caught right away and so far had avoided detection. They'd had their jaunt into the countryside, as they'd said truthfully to Derek, to pass time. They weren't into telling lies to a buddy – though, *if Stinky had joined them...?*

The time in the house by the gang had been brief and Muriel was hurriedly transferred into the car. However, large though the vehicle was, after the seven people were seated, with two large bags of Muriel's clothing added, everyone except Muriel had the feeling of claustrophobia. She didn't suffer only because she could see nothing and the journey had been in silence. The others were dropped at the destination house and Bill and Freddy took off again for a last spin. It seemed a good idea to them to leave the stolen vehicle in woods many miles away so it wouldn't be found too soon.

What they hadn't really thought through properly was how to get back home. They finished up having to trudge for nearly two miles, along the edge of the wood, climbing over stiles, and then passed the cow fields stumbling along rutted pathways which the local farmer would not negotiate with anything less than a tractor, before eventually reaching the bus stop – and then found they would have to wait almost three hours for the country service bus. Stout footwear would have been so much more suitable for that walk. Two pairs of their favourite imitation 'Italian Original Design' dress shoes would be going into the dustbin when they returned home.

Who'd be stupid enough to live in the country was a well discussed topic, but they were philosophical about their outing – they didn't see the countryside too often, so anyway, the walk probably did them the world of good. They grudged the cost of a taxi. Then it sank in that they could afford it, when they got their money from Thelma, so they splashed out and the taxi had them home in their own little house in no time. They didn't join the others. They weren't part of the gang. Thelma had only arranged with them to sort out the car – and anyway, they liked their own cosy little beds. To all except one person, the day had been a great success.

What had not been discussed by the gang yet, or rather what hadn't been disclosed to the others by Dozy, was the content of the money sack stolen from the supermarket. When the plan had been discussed in those early days, when this had seemed the perfect answer to all their money problems, a few facts had been misinterpreted.

Point one: Thursday was pay day – yes – but wages for all the staff went directly into a bank account. All Muriel was doing was checking the books and sorting out the payslips to be distributed on Friday.

Point two: At varying times each day all cash, except for the daily float, was collected by the Security Company, and on that day the takings had been removed one hour before the gang arrived.

Incredibly, one hour earlier and they could have taken away a fortune, as it was, and sad but true – the total success of the robbery amounted to a measly *£3000.*

He'd have to tell the others shortly but there was someone he'd have to contact first – *the scary lady – Thelma...*

18

He was either hyperventilating or just doing a very good impression. Today there had been too much happening on his patch. Rob Sheldon was at death's door, his time was up, his life forces were ebbing away, he was fading fast. He would have explained the process, in detail, if he could have stopped wheezing for a moment. All the excitement had been overwhelming.

This was an editor normally who had to force himself to generate some self-enthusiasm to compose a half-page article about a Senior Citizen's one-hundredth birthday bash, or a repeat article about the Primary School roof that was still leaking, or when things became really lively, announcing the winners of the Women's Guild lucky dip, and other such non-news, for a once-a-week edition of the paper.

Sally was being his nursemaid – attempting the good old paper bag technique and seemed to be succeeding. She had already refused Derek's solution of throwing a bucket of cold water over Rob.

All this was happening on top of his failure to capitalise on a story for this week's edition about the Bisko's Superstore robbery, which had occurred just along the road. Rob was still kicking himself on the bad timing of the robbers. Twenty-four hours earlier and he would have had a hot story, but printing once a week still had to meet a strict deadline. A day late was too late – a penalty of being a weekly paper. The consequence was that *The Evening News* carried the story that he would have liked for a change.

The thing that brought him back to the land of the living was finding Sally had inside knowledge of the robbery. He hadn't linked the person who'd been taken hostage with the attractive young lady whom he employed – the one who'd messed up his accounting arrangement with his bookie. Now this was something he *could* use in the next edition – the heart-rending story of a Newingsworth mother and daughter torn apart – even though it would be a week out of date, an exclusive, with his employee as the central character. It was local and it was news, wasn't it, and a great deal more exciting than a leaky school roof.

Eventually, when he had calmed down and was breathing like a real human again, Sally had let him know some details of her involvement, informing him that the police didn't yet know about her part in it.

"Why not?" and this had been an inevitable response.

"They weren't being very nice," was her reason.

"Oh..." and although he wasn't convinced it was a good reason, he did sense a bigger story. "When are you going to tell them? It might help them to find your mother," her boss suggested.

"I'll go and see them this afternoon. I want Mum back – safely. They should have my handbag by now and I want it back too," she replied.

If the police had in fact recovered the bag, Rob Sheldon hoped for his own sake that his two ugly visitors were the ones who'd removed the money first so that his well used, but demanding bookmaker would be happier. That debt had to be removed to clear any future threat. But – if not...

"You'd better start recording all the detail and build up a good story of what's happened so far, Sally," he added and tried to forget the 'if not...' possibility while his mind kicked around some interesting headlines to lead this article.

"Isn't that something that our new reporter can do? He played a part in it too. I couldn't write a story to save myself," said Sally.

"OK then, but *which* new reporter?" asked Rob.

"What do you mean – which reporter? Why, Sweaty, of course"

"It's Derek actually..." He'd been standing silently by Sally's side, not sure where it would all end, and hoping he had not been totally forgotten. For a moment he'd had a horrid suspicion that he may even have been fired – before starting work – and without realising it.

"And what about the other one?" continued Rob.

"What other one? Oh, *that* other one..."

Spider had returned from a stay-out-of-trouble under-desk position and was now seated ready and waiting and trying to look as intelligent as he could. He felt his big moment would come shortly. That's what happened when you'd been 'ead'unted...

He had been christened Alfred Webb – *Spider* had come later at school. He'd liked it and had always been delighted to answer to it, but he wasn't the first in his clan to be dubbed by that moniker. The surname Webb had meant his grandfather, Albert Webb and Alfred's dad, Anthony Webb, had already been carrying the nickname for most of their lives, and like young Alfred, had difficulty remembering their correct first name if they ever had to complete any official forms. In consequence at home, Grandfather had been known as Spider, his son as Spider Junior and Spider Junior's son as Young Spider.

Grandfather died a number of years ago. With then only two remaining, Spider Junior retained his lifelong name, and Young Spider became simply *Spider*. There was a feeling of pride in graduating to the simpler name and he had thoughts of the future and the prospects of having his own little nest of spiders one day. He had been born thirty-five years ago and for most of his life had been as skinny as a rake but again that seemed to be a family thing, the standard male Webb shape.

It had been Spider who'd always answered the phone in the bookmakers, his previous employers, and he had received and taken Sally's message as his personal invitation. He'd become a chosen one – he'd always wanted to be 'ead'unted.

Spider had been very much left to his own devices since he'd arrived at the office, bang on time at 9.00am that morning. When he'd made his way to the office he'd reported to Rob – who'd looked at him blankly. That silence had encouraged Spider to explain in minute detail, firstly the pleasure at receiving Sally's phone call and how good he'd been at his last job, and also that he had been offered his old job back if this one went belly-up, and that his father had worked for the council for over twenty years and never been in trouble. He'd also expanded on the fact that his had been a difficult birth, and that his mother had blamed him for most of his life, that he'd worked at the bookies and was *good with the 'orses*, and oh, yes, he recounted the tale of his family of Spiders.

Rob Sheldon hadn't a clue what Spider was talking about.

He hadn't expected him to be there and when he spoke, it had seemed, to Rob, to be at high speed in a different language... So in an attempt to maintain some of his sanity, Rob asked him if he could make a good cup of tea or coffee, to which Spider claimed he was 'The Best'. Rob had then enjoyed a near perfect cup of tea, and on that basis, after having proved that what he'd said was true, Spider had been told to twiddle his thumbs until Sally arrived. It would all be sorted out then.

Sally therefore was the one who had to inform him that, even though it was accepted that he was the number one tea and coffee maker, his days in the office might be numbered. She was grateful that Spider took it so well when she explained it had been her mistake. He said he'd be happy to do the various jobs around the office that Mr Sheldon and Sally didn't like and, the part that pleased Rob Sheldon, he was willing to do it for very little pay. So, much as it went against Mr Rob Sheldon's principles to spend any more than absolutely essential to run the paper, he agreed, at Sally's request, that Spider be allowed to stay for a trial period.

In future, Derek would normally be the roving reporter, a new post. He'd go out and about, keeping his ear to the ground, selecting and developing stories of topical events, and searching for new subjects which would have general appeal. He was expected to propose new ideas and inject that magic 'something' that would increase sales and keep them there. Sales takings would *have* to rise, Spider would have to be paid as well, remember.

The four of them, together, tidied up the office. Most of the damage had been superficial, thankfully. It had all looked so much more serious during the scuffle. After some bending and stretching and shuffling around, a semblance of normality was established.

Sally had no mobile phone. It was lost forever, she presumed, possibly to the robbery gang, and she felt naked without it. Derek had no phone either. There was an easy solution – claim expenses – and so a new one was purchased by Sally, and at the same time the new reporter, Derek, was given his. It pained Rob to sign this first authorisation chitty for his new team to spend money.

And first things first – Sally rang her dad and gave him her new number with strict instructions to phone her the moment any fresh knowledge arrived about her mum. She didn't want any information being delayed in reaching her. She knew her father could be quite thoughtless at times, even with the dramatic events that had occurred. Sometimes he thought only of himself. Was he drinking heavily? She suspected that he was.

There didn't seem much she could do about her mum, but just sitting around to mope didn't seem to be an option, so she had to try and concentrate on other things, like the office routines. She began by giving Spider some basic training to justify her 'ead'unting him. He was a quick learner. Answering the telephone was a speciality but he had to stop saying automatically "You've reached Saddanbroke's – your favourite bookies – 'ow can I 'elp you?" Sending e-mails and operating the printers proved a doddle to him, and there was no doubt he could cope with analysing a lot of internet information, monitoring other newspapers and any breaking news. Learning by trial and error on his computer at home had been a great help. And he was proving to be a nice bloke.

Derek was given the laptop he had saved from destruction earlier and was getting to grips with the intricacies of its programmes. The new mobile also took a bit of fiddling to understand and at one point he almost disgusted himself by having to resort to reading the 'instructions for use' – but he resisted and managed.

Rob Sheldon was thinking over how valuable Sally had become to him. It was weighing on his conscience that he'd been annoyed at her earlier, even though he told himself it had been totally justified. Not only had she been his nursemaid for a short time today, when he'd had a panic attack, she was the one who remembered all the family occasions that he inevitably forgot. She guided him on the most suitable presents for his wife, and in many cases, what to give as a peace offering, and she always had the supply of indigestion tablets for the pressured days.

In fact it was probably thanks to her that his marriage was still in one piece. So, he had to forgive her for messing things up this time, though the threat from his bookie hadn't gone and he'd have to come up with a solution soon, even if temporary. He tried not to think of his lack of knowledge of the whereabouts of his £3000, but it would be nice to have it back...

The phone call he'd received from the local police had surprised him, but was not unusual. They wanted the media to play down the Bisko's Robbery story. Something to do with giving the kidnappers zero publicity, they said. Ah well, he thought, nothing will be printing for another week anyway. Restrictions would probably be lifted by then, he surmised.

Putting aside this morning's odd teething problems, The Newingsworth Weekly Gazette had a new team and Rob had a good feeling about that. Pastures new were beckoning and this team was raring to go. Those thoughts settled him into a pleasant frame of mind and he was almost at the point of starting to do some fruitful work when the outer office door opened.

In came Elizabeth, his dear wife – and his two darling sons. So much for work...

19

Plain Clothes, as a department, felt chasing such a trivial amount to be embarrassing and demeaning. Only three thousand pounds taken in a supermarket robbery – it was pitiful...

These criminals had let the side down and ought to be ashamed and, in fact, this department felt that *failing* so successfully should remove any rights to them even being called criminals. Since the robbery, there had been some tough talking about the circumstances by all the team at the Station and strong feelings had been displayed. Unusually, opinions had *not* been divided, although to be honest, this team could find arguments about any subject you could choose, being influenced by the draught from the office fan as much as the way the wind was blowing, whether they felt strongly or not.

They liked to think of themselves as Devils Advocates, looking at a subject objectively and fairly, but in fact when it came to a discussion they simply formed a den of Devils. It could make a dull routine and a long day seem livelier, but on this occasion there was unison. The collective opinion was that maintaining standards was important and that *being* a professional criminal should be something that a professional criminal should be proud to be. And as with any profession, a poor public image rubbed off on all who could be involved and Plain Clothes may be the opposition but they were definitely involved. This gang had let their side down. Tut, tut, tut...

Each man in this department (currently it was only males and, in the minds of these males, only males could tackle the job) liked to think that it was an intelligent, cunning, and ambitious type of person who made up a *good* criminal. That was the type they liked to chase and catch. Sometimes they were quite pleased if a top quality criminal escaped justice, but that was rare because it was a slight on them at the same time. They were, however, big enough to admire *real* skill when they saw it.

The culmination of their effort was experienced when they strode cockily out of a court after a successful prosecution of *their* case. The 'poncy' prosecuting team, of course, would normally claim the credit, but it had been Plain Clothes, *they* knew themselves, the success had been thanks to them doing the hard graft ...and of course they, as detectives, were a notch above the criminal class, two notches in many cases. They did winning work, even if others took the credit. They saw themselves to be 'The Good Guys' in the eyes of the public, and that was important to them – though not always true.

A high standard of competition between detectives and criminals was expected and appreciated by them – a stiff challenge – it was all part of the game and they relished these severe tests of their superior intellect. In their heads, failure was acceptable only if they could claim it had been 'very tricky'. If it had been seen beforehand as *an open and shut case,* failing to solve it then meant being *recognised* as a personal failure and was most humiliating.

So, for this ridiculously low-value theft, which had *definitely* been deemed too easy, didn't common sense say it should be left to the Uniforms? Why not let them take the blame for a failure? No-one volunteered to take on this one. General agreement was there once again. On the other hand, this gang had taken a hostage – that was much more serious and came back into Plain Clothes territory. It was equivalent to kidnapping, even though no ransom note had yet been received. Hmmm..? No demand for ransom, but only as far as they knew. Experience told them that often, and foolishly, the ransom note, when received, was kept secret by the recipient who then would make a right codswallop of the whole thing by handing over cash, therefore removing any chance of the glory that every man in this department craved.

Ordinary criminals dealt in goods and didn't harm people – much... Nasty villains tried to bargain using *people* to barter for money. Therefore it was the detective's task in life to track down these nasty villains – but in this case, *they hadn't a clue where to start*, which should have been another reason to leave it to the Uniforms.

There was one young Detective Constable, Andy Woodstock by name, *aka* Andy Pandy, who foolishly went so far as to *bet* his fellow detectives that this gang was so stupid that they would send the hostage back with the money – and a 'Sorry Note'. Not surprisingly his colleagues smilingly jumped at his kind offer, confident the outcome would not be to Andy's liking... and a bet's a bet, and he had offered...

Moments later, Andy regretted having done this, but he couldn't lose face – so the bet was on. How could his colleagues, these superior beings, have the gall to criticise this gang's skill? The reality was that the robbers had just vanished, leaving few clues. This had come as a fact they refused to accept. Gloves had been worn as you'd expect, but the raid was cleverly timed and done during the supermarket back-shop staff tea break – swiftly and quietly. The tea-break, like many tea-breaks, tended to extend beyond the official timing and this had contributed to the success of the robbers. On top of that, the fact that a robbery had taken place and hadn't even been *recognised* by the store staff until about half an hour after the robbers left the premises, had been pretty incredible. Yes, that part had been slick. The gang were given a good deal of credit by these lawmen, for the planning.

In truth it was pure chance that the timing had been so fortunate – *and the gang hadn't realised that at least they'd got that bit right...*

As for the CCTV system being out of action – the whole system – the Store Manager was given a real pasting for that failure, and he had received the same lack of appreciation from his Bisko Regional boss and his boss's boss, very shortly after. Bisko's wanted this played very low key because they reckoned that it didn't show the company in a very good light. No CCTV – at all – the thieves had walked in and out, and nobody noticed. All the crooks in Britain would be along to Bisko's shortly if the word got out. The top man in Bisko's had contacts in Whitehall and when the telephone rang at the Newingsworth Police Station everyone leapt to attention as the message was transmitted down the line, *"No publicity – and that's an order."*

Had the engineer been part of the gang as well? This had to be a consideration. Investigation found he'd worked for this trusted security company for many years and every month earned more than was stolen, so we'll ignore him, they concluded.

Outside the Supermarket, nothing had been out of the ordinary. No one had noticed anything – nothing untoward seen or heard, other than a furniture van being driven dangerously.

This had been recorded by the Uniforms, Constable Simpson in particular. He'd been involved at that time with the theft of a Range Rover in the car park, and with the severe damage caused to a Mini Cooper by an overfilled trolley. It also had been driven dangerously – and it had faulty brakes. An individual called 'Stinky' had escaped from the scene and could have been involved. Constable Simpson had also logged that he'd had to spend some time in breaking up a fight which began between the owner of the stolen Range Rover and the owner of the Mini Cooper with the side bashed in.

What other clues did they have? The theft of the four x four could have been a cunning diversion was one thought. That vehicle hadn't been found yet. And anyway, they were clutching at straws. Had the runaway trolley been part of it too?

The whole team wasn't needed for this simple exercise. Eventually from Friday lunchtime, Andy Woodstock would be the only detective assigned to continue the investigation. His boss had added his money to Andy's bet of bravado. He certainly wasn't as stupidly optimistic as Andy, and on top of that, he thought this young dick had too much to say – this wasn't the first time Mr Bigmouth had sounded off – and it would be an easy tenner. So, Andy Woodstock was given his instructions and, other than Andy, the case was abandoned and the individuals who'd had so much to say about the subject earlier in the day, lost interest.

Andy decided to make this *his* big opportunity.

For starters, he didn't have a great deal of sympathy for the owner of the four x four, the Range Rover, a gas guzzler – it polluted the air. He disliked four x fours – he couldn't afford one. He was also a little niggled that two of the Uniforms had been at the hostage's home before him. He liked to be first to review a scene of crime and gain the credits – and anyway what did they know about solving crime? This required *detection* and he was the specialist...

He'd visited the victim's home but hadn't learned a lot there. The interview with the husband had been weird. It was as if Donaldson, the husband, had been suffering a severe hangover, and had probably enjoyed himself excessively with the vodka the night before. When he'd asked about this guy's sister, he'd just been given a blank look.

"Your neighbour, Masterton, next door, the old nosey parker, said she regularly sees your sister visiting – an amazing family likeness. Said she was your spitting image. Does she live here?"

"She saw my sister? I haven't... She hasn't been... *OH*... No – no, no," was all he'd succeeded in eliciting – very frigging helpful. To be followed up, shortly... Another observation he'd noted down to question later – had this guy been wearing make-up? Andy didn't like men who wore make-up.

He had always disliked the taking of drugs and though there was nothing to suggest drugs were involved in this house, where there was one obvious problem there would probably be others, hidden. Consumption of alcohol during the day was a big no-no of his, and in his eyes, almost as bad as drugs.

Andy's salary was paid monthly into the Co-operative Bank Slatterfoot Branch and there was always *less* in his account than he expected. This guy was the bank manager and Andy suspected that he'd be creaming off the profits of *his* savings account, and many others. It came naturally to people like him, didn't it? The fact that Mr Woodstock regularly spent more than he earned, had little to do with it. He just didn't trust bank managers and, whether he had good reason to or not, he would not permit these sorts of facts to influence his logic. If this man was guilty of anything, Andy Pandy was going to get him.

He sat there at his desk and thought – alone.

Some of the hostage's clothes had been stolen and a few bits and pieces had been knocked over. And the daughter's bedroom... that room had been the worst in the house. It had *really* been trashed. What a mess. He didn't like messy rooms – he'd had to share with his little brother when he was young and his little brother had been at the opposite end of the scale from him in the tidiness league. The world had been held to account for that ever since.

Had this been a separate house burglary or was it connected to the superstore robbery? He was undecided on that.

Could it be all to do with the daughter? Had the gang been looking for something special in that room? Had they found it? Jewellery? Drugs? Secret papers? Blackmail? What could it be? Was she 'on the game' or perhaps involved in the White Slave Trade? Everything had to be checked. Then suddenly it occurred to him, why had it been presumed to be *a gang?* Could it have been a set-up?

There were no witnesses, little evidence other than the Manager's report of the money involved. Add to that a missing wife who could have gone off with her lover, a wife who had a husband who didn't seem to care a damn. Was it an inside job? These very often were. Could there be a close relationship between this Mrs Donaldson and the Store Manager? Had they been fiddling the books? Had they just been pinching food big style? Were they *lovers?* Now be sensible, they weren't youngsters were they? *Had* to be the food then... As for the house... locks hadn't been forced. A ladder had been used at the rear of the house but, he'd been told, this had been the way in for the daughter, her boyfriend, and two policemen who'd also managed to add their fingerprints to all the others that were around.

There was the furniture removal van parked outside, it had been there since Thursday evening. Yes, there was some rope lying on the floor and some broad adhesive tape, but neither was unusual in moving furniture...

Although, hadn't a furniture van figured at the Supermarket? No, it was unlikely to be the same one. That sort of thing only happens in fiction. That would be too easy and again this could all be innocent speculation... Further investigation had not revealed anyone locally who was moving home, nor were there any furniture men walking about looking for a lost van, as far as he knew. The van belonged to a company about fifty miles away and hadn't been reported as stolen but that could be carelessness on the part of the owners. He'd phone them later.

Andy Woodstock had also found out something else and was made to promise it would remain a secret with him – Mrs Masterton, next door to the Donaldson's, the nosey one, went out every afternoon and was a *bingo* fanatic. Unfortunately, she'd been out that afternoon and seen nothing and was of no help. There was always one in an area who saw and knew everything about the neighbours and this old busybody would normally have been 'it'. Her and her stupid Bingo.

The neighbours next door on the other side of the Donaldson's were on holiday in Malta. Pity, he would have enjoyed a chat with them. He could have told them Mrs Masterton's secret. He didn't like neighbours who had secret vices, who *should* have been able to help.

Neither did he like people who went abroad for holidays, leaving their house unattended for any burglars that fancied easy pickings. Either that or they came back home and complained to the Police that their house was full of squatters – as if the Police were to blame. It made life hectic for people liked him. However, it wasn't all negatives with Andy – he did like ice cream.

It didn't make sense to his logical mind that any self-respecting burglar would want to enter a house and steal a bundle of clothes that could easily be bought cheaply in an Oxfam Shop, and leave the house taking nothing of value, but that's what it looked like. Nothing other than clothes appeared to have been removed from the Donaldson's and only the wife's. That was odd.

The Donaldson's house was big and he liked it. If he could have afforded it, he could imagine himself ensconced there, with a girlfriend in every room. A fanciful thought he realised because the likelihood would be more that his recently estranged wife would want to return to him, and probably insist on bringing all her large, idle, sodding family with her to fill the rooms. That thought made the house instantly less appealing.

He looked at the notebook again. He'd recorded the Donaldson father saying that his daughter had been home earlier in the day but hadn't been in last night, and neither had he.

Donaldson seemed shy about his own whereabouts, saying he'd been at his club overnight. He was apparently a respected bank manager but could he be into drugs or fraud or something underneath the facade? In fact, Andy Pandy wondered, was he too innocent? Andy hadn't pushed him for more details on his 'Club' – he disliked men who did *clubs*... He might come back to him later on that.

And where had the daughter been the previous night? She definitely had something to do with this robbery – he'd convinced himself. No evidence, but that had never restricted his actions before – he'd find it. The pressure would have to be put on her and Andy Woodstock would be the little boy who would apply it – with pleasure. So far his day had been all questions – four pages – very few answers...

Today, the daughter would be at work, her father said, and had told Andy where. That would be his next call.

20

Friday afternoon and Sally and Derek were in the park again – together – holding hands. Sounds nice but the hands they were holding were not each others.

The experience was being somewhat spoiled by each having to hold tightly onto one of the two little darlings who, since they'd left the office, had been trying to break free – Thomas Sheldon and Raymond Sheldon – aged four and three respectively.

Poor Derek was now suddenly involved in circumstances that were totally beyond his control and he very much appreciated the presence and the motherly disciplines of Sally. She was automatically making the decisions and directing the actions of all three males. Derek was happily complying, and glad to have left the office. He was also very glad to have an office to leave, and the good thing being, he was expected to return again. He was working once more – *yahoo* – but he was not used to having two lively youngsters zooming off in different directions the moment their hands were released and he realised what 'living on the edge' was all about.

He reminded himself it was a park. There were no vehicles moving about which could endanger them, and he should be able to run as fast as them if they broke free – but only if they would oblige him and both run in the same direction. And there were lots of mothers around with their own bundles of trouble who would help if needed.

And Sally was with him.

Yes, they were safe ...but there were flowerbeds everywhere

with what looked like prize blooms waiting to be destroyed, and there was the model boating pond slap bang in the middle of the park and, although it wasn't deep and today it wouldn't be cold, if anyone had to fish them from it, it would have to be him. He was pretty sure he was going to get wet. They were doing this as a favour for Rob Sheldon. He was the boss, now to both of them, and both were grateful to be working for him, one thankful for a new start, and one even more thankful for letting her continue.

Rob had been grateful to Sally, knowing that she had almost always been willing to tackle anything including child-minding, for a limited period and she'd commandeered Derek into helping.

Mrs Elizabeth Sheldon had phoned to remind her *dear* husband earlier in the day that she would be meeting him for their joint visit to the solicitor. Rob had already been given a reminder at breakfast, before he'd left the house, but his wife was well aware how poor his memory retentive powers were, especially for family matters. When she rang, he'd agreed to arrange someone to look after the boys for the duration, but he was a busy man – and, oh dear, he'd forgotten.

Sally hadn't been there to remind him and, of course, she would have been the one to make some temporary child-care arrangement for him. She was good at that sort of thing and, when Rob thought of it, at most things.

So, at short notice, the temporary minders had become Sally and Derek, and the park had been an obvious safe place to spend a few hours. There was only one motorised non-council works vehicle permitted to enter the park, which, once in position, had to remain stationery until the end of the day. During this very warm spell of weather it would have been sadly missed by everyone who entered through these gates. Now and again, if the queue diminished, the happy little jingle sounded which put everyone in the mood once again. As the four of them were passing, 'Oranges and lemons' rang out for the regulated eight second blast...

"I want an ice cream," demanded the four-year-old.

"I want an ithe cream too," demanded the three-year-old.

"Have you forgotten the little word?" asked Derek.

"*Now,*" stated the four year old.

"*Now,*" repeated the other.

So, Derek joined the queue at the brightly-coloured van and the little darlings were given what they'd asked for – and it dribbled down the front of their shirts.

Now wasn't that a surprise...

"Swings," demanded the four-year-old.

"Swingths," repeated the three-year-old.

At least that area was surrounded by an iron fence and Derek relaxed ever so slightly until Raymond, the three-year-old, fell off. Derek experienced fear because he'd 'helped' him swing. The three-year-old *bounced*. Derek noted the 'Can't Hurt Yourself' surface and was thankful for it, but that didn't stop the yell.

"Boo-hoo-hoo-hooooo."

"You pushed him too hard," said the four-year-old "...and I'm going to tell my Mummy. I saw you push Raymond off the swing and that's *naughty*."

"He puthed me. Boo-hoo-hoo."

So, they were given another ice cream, and this time Sally and Derek were ready when it melted, but it still dribbled onto the shirts.

When Master Thomas Sheldon decided to gallop off into the middle of the dahlia bed, it took both Sally and Derek by surprise.

"Come out of there," the child was told.

"Why?" was the reply.

"Just come out – *this minute,*" demanded Derek.

And the three-year-old ran in to join his brother.

"Come out of there, the pair of you, this instant or... or... *Come out...*" yelled Derek.

"Derek, you'll frighten them. Don't shout at them. They don't understand," offered Sally. And some other people may also have difficulty understanding, thought Derek, the people who care for the flower beds. And sure enough the noise they were making initially just caused a few heads to turn, and then, as the shouting continued, a few others began to take even more interest.

Now, Charlie and Arthur were the two main men when it came to the flowerbeds. Derek should have guessed that, now, shouldn't he?

"Come – out – here – or – there – will – be – trouble." screamed a panicking Derek at the two little angels, who were just staring insolently back at him.

"Whatcha doin' wiff my flowers?" sobbed a distraught Arthur, as he ran towards them. "My luvverly flowers...Why d'ye let 'em?" he directed at Sally.

"We're very sorry," said Sal. "They just sort of... just did it, but they are only young children. Derek will get them out."

And Arthur noticed Derek this time and his finger pointed threateningly at him.

"It's you init? Our ladder... pinchin... yea, it's *you*."

Luckily for Derek he had Sally with him and before it became physical this time, she stepped in, and he stepped back, away from the flowerbed, and from Arthur.

"Look, we are *very* sorry and I'm sure you're mistaking my friend for someone else. They are only little children. Don't you like little children?" she gently asked Arthur.

"Yuss," he replied meekly.

"Well, you must know what they can be like, don't you. I bet you were a little rascal yourself, now weren't you?"

"Yuss," said a subdued Arthur.

"And I'll bet you did naughty things, as well, things you knew that were wrong. Did you then?"

"Yuss," Arthur replied, looking guiltily at his feet.

Is she going to tickle him under his chin as well, wondered an enthralled Derek? *No, she didn't.*

Charlie had run up and joined them now. He took in the sight of the mangled mess – the dearly loved dahlias. He was about to explode, but stopped when he realised that Arthur had everything under control. He didn't need to get involved. His mate would give them a right bollocking ...but, he stood amazed

– then mesmerised, and watched intently, as his mate, Arthur, was gently, but firmly, twisted around Sally's little finger.

"And anyway, Derek is the new reporter with the Newingsworth Weekly Gazette and was looking for someone like you for information about the lovely flower displays in the park. They are really nice this year, Derek was just saying. Are you the one he should ask?"

"Yuss – an', an', an' Charlie's me mate," he'd gone sort of coy.

Derek was expecting Charlie to curtsy when Sally turned and smiled at him but, in fact, he just nodded shyly.

"So, if you could just help us get these little vagabonds out of there, you can get on with the job of making them lovely again and Derek will be back on Monday to do the interview and take your pictures for the paper. Now, is that agreed?"

"Yuss," said a proud Arthur, who was going to be a celebrity.

"Lovely," said Sally with a smile that made Arthur's face light up with a big grin. "We'll leave you both to do your excellent work, and see you on Monday, byeee..."

And off the four of them went, waving back to Arthur and Charlie, who were still grinning, and waving to Sally.

Derek's mouth had hung open for almost all of Sally's speech.

She was wonderful. He was in love...

He even felt grateful for the children's help...

21

Hands were held securely as the four ascended the stairs, and were not going to be released until Mummy Sheldon took over.

Both Sally and Derek by now were looking forward to being relieved of this excessive responsibility and both had decided that if ever they were partnered there would never, ever, be any children involved. A wild animal as a pet would be an alternative if anyone became broody in the future – much simpler...

The solicitor's visit was over and Mummy Sheldon had returned and was waiting to welcome her boys into her arms. They ran to her.

"Well, did you have fun?" she asked them.

"Yes, Mummy," said Thomas.

"Yeth Mummy," said Raymond.

"And did you behave yourselves?"

No-one answered that.

Further questions were to come and answers were required, after Mrs Sheldon and her offspring left, because the two constables had returned and they too were waiting to see both Derek and Sally. There was another person with them but he wasn't wearing a uniform. He introduced himself. He was a detective constable. Andy Woodstock was this one's name and he wanted to discuss the Bisko's Supermarket robbery.

Rob Sheldon offered the use of his own office for the interview to give some privacy. He sat outside. The sound-proofing wasn't very efficient so Rob was able to hear every word that was said. Convenient as it wouldn't have to be repeated afterwards.

Andy Woodstock explained that it was a coincidence that the two police constables were here at the same time as him, but it might save some effort if all five were involved together, at least to begin with.

The names and addresses of Derek and Sally were confirmed as correct. "Your 'andbag, Miss?" asked Constable Alfie holding up the damaged goods.

"I'm not sure. The strap's broken on that one... What's happened to it, constable?" asked a frowning Sally.

"I'm not at liberty to divulge that, madam. Part of an on-going enquiry," he replied.

"Surely you wouldn't be returning it in that damaged state then, officer? If you were, don't you think there could be a compensation claim coming from the owner?" said Sally, still frowning.

"I'm *not* returning it – yet," said Alfie.

"There's a little matter of the contents," said Constable Samuel.

"I've never been very tidy, I know. Always meaning to clear out some of the rubbish," apologised Sally.

"Your knickers," said Alfie, "they're not knickers..."

"Oh?" said Sally.

"There was three thousand pounds in the package."

"Now there's a surprise," said Sally.

"Oh," thought Derek.

"Oh, no... no... no..." thought Rob listening outside. He went slightly pale and felt faint. *He* needed this money, his *bookie* was demanding it, but *they* had it...

"You all right Guv?" asked Spider, who'd blended beautifully into the office. "I'll get you a glass of water"

Oh dear what do I do now, wondered Sally? She didn't think she should say that it was Rob's money without him having accepted that she could, particularly after her failing to hand it to the correct people yesterday, but she couldn't think of a plausible reason why she would have it otherwise, so she decided to try a diversion.

"I've been meaning to tell and it's been on my conscience and now is as good a time as any," she began. All ears cocked up and she became a very important person. "Did you know I was there – when it happened?" she continued. "The robbery, I mean. *I – was – there.*" Hooray, at last, a lead and a confession at the same time, without having to put on any pressure, thought Detective Andy. "And I was in the van. And so was Derek. He helped me," she explained, very clearly and simply, she thought.

This case has been cracked already, thought Andy. That's the two of them pin-pointed, as I predicted. He could foresee promotion coming from this...

"I thought you were too sweet to be wholesome, this morning," said Samuel. "So it was the pair of you did it, was it?"

"I think you could be misunderstanding what Sally is telling you," a nervous Derek interrupted. Sally had been saying the words beautifully but telling a helluva story...

"Oh yes, 'ere we go. Trying to back out of the confession already," said Alfie.

"Were you at the Supermarket, last evening?" Detective Andy asked Sally.

"Yes," admitted Sally.

"Were you at the Supermarket, last evening?" Detective Andy directed at Derek.

"No... err... yes...err.. no," spluttered Derek.

"I think we can take that as a 'yes' from both of you. Were you in the house of Mrs Muriel Donaldson this morning?" asked Andy.

"Yes," both Sally and Derek replied.

"And made the mess?"

"Oh, that was me and me alone, Officer," admitted Sally, "...but I was in a bit of a hurry to get out."

"I think you are totally misunderstanding what is being said, your honour," said Derek, forgetting that the case hadn't yet reached court – he was already visualising himself standing in the dock.

"I was in the furniture van last night," explained Sally.

"I think we've heard enough, thank you," said Detective Constable Andy Woodstock, becoming officious, "...and we'll continue this more formally down at the station. Take them away, Constables."

22

Steve sat there, head in hands, regretting every single thing about this whole affair. This was the gang member that Muriel had dubbed Dozy. He was the leader and sincerely wished he wasn't. Why had he ever thought that they could pull it off? He should never have been persuaded by the scary lady.

No money worth speaking of had come out of it so far, and the worst part, the part he was dreading, had still to be tackled – by him... If only he'd been born rich...

Going into that pub that particular night was the start of a chain of errors he'd made. If only he hadn't stepped over that threshold he might never have met her and he would be a lot happier than he was now... Sitting there he blamed strong drink to have contributed to him slipping into this stupid mess. He made himself a promise that if he survived this catastrophe intact he would never touch another drop of alcohol – but deep down he knew that would be very unlikely.

There was no turning back unfortunately.

He'd been on his own that night. Maddie, his partner, had been visiting her parents up north or she would have been with him. The music had been the attraction. He'd heard that local band before and liked them, the atmosphere in the pub was always good, and there was no entrance fee, he had been on his own, so what could have been more natural than to go. The place was busy when he arrived and he'd thought himself lucky to find an empty seat, beside a young couple, and an older woman who was on her own, as he found out later. The young couple went when the music ended and he'd found himself chatting to this woman, and bought her a drink. She was well made up and looked good, initially – that night: long dark hair and teasing eyes. It hadn't been anything sexual – a few drinks and some provocative banter, yes, but she had been much too old for him and anyway he had his Maddie – she was the one and only one for him.

However interesting and absorbing the conversation with that woman in the pub had been, there was no getting away from the fact when he thought back – she had been strange...

Call me *Thelma*, is what she'd instructed.

It had been obvious that he had little cash, and after a few drinks, and a little encouragement from this woman, he'd started to spill out his life story... He hadn't hidden the fact that he had a steady girl who wanted a family, but slowly it emerged that he was in debt, debts that he had no likelihood of paying off. It had started as a joke. Then why not rob a bank? She'd had all the answers on how it could be done and not be caught. It seemed all fanciful that night but then she'd said to think about it and come back next week – and he had...

"I'll set up a target for you and prepare a plan," she'd offered on a much later occasion, and even then he'd thought of it still as a fantasy, "...but I'll have a third of the profits. And if you take a hostage you can demand a ransom and make even more money. You just have to do what you are told," Thelma had said.

It had seemed so easy, but the suggestion of taking a hostage was definitely not to his liking, but that was just talking big, he concluded, and would never actually happen... and then came the meeting, many weeks later, after hours of more and more detailed conversations, when it became much more serious.

"Just do as I say – *or else*..." Thelma had changed the mood.

He hadn't liked it when she'd started to threaten the safety of his girlfriend. He'd never been the violent type himself and this shocked him. Thelma had money and contacts, he was told. She wouldn't be involved in the rough stuff. She had people who'd be paid to do that for her and it would never be possible to be traced back. There was a sinister edge to everything she said to him from then on and he began to dislike her intensely and, for the first time in his life, felt fearful of a female. She'd said to call her Thelma but in Steve's mind she'd become the 'scary lady', and he'd believed every menacing word she'd said.

Although she was not young, she still looked good. The glamour must have been from a bottle, he reminisced, and she could hold her drink far better than him. He didn't want to continue his dealings with her but he was too chicken to pull out. His pal, Michael had been up for it from the beginning. Michael had always been a bit more cocky and confident in his abilities than Steve himself had ever been, and the plan had continued to move forward.

When told, their girlfriends had initially laughed it off as a joke and had been sure it would never happen, but over the weeks they eventually saw the plan as likely to be a success and greedily thought of all the money that could be on the horizon. They actually became eager to take part.

Only one of them could drive and that was Jane, she was Michael's partner. Steve had never had the cash to learn to drive nor had there been any likelihood of him owning a car. Jane would have to be the driver of the getaway vehicle. Steve had always felt uncomfortable sitting beside a woman driver, even though his own mother had been a bus driver, or should that be *because...?*

Thelma had a source for a vehicle that wouldn't be easily traceable. She'd also decided that another car would be used as well for a swap over to reduce the chance of them being caught, and she'd arrange a driver for that one. Then, as the deadline was reached, Thelma was the one who came up with the target. It wasn't a bank – it was a *supermarket*. And there had to be a hostage. "You'll take the cashier," he was instructed – she'd be the only one they'd have to bother about.

So, they'd done the job today, as instructed and it had appeared at the time to have been 'mission accomplished' – until he'd inspected the money bag. He'd steeled himself and phoned Thelma. It had to be done... He'd used Sally's phone, and why not he thought.

Thelma had exploded when he told her how little they'd escaped with, just as he thought she would. She blamed him totally for not following the instructions correctly. He wanted to argue back but felt too vulnerable, but he thought that he'd followed her instructions implicitly and somewhere she'd got it wrong, but the job had to go forward. Thelma reminded him the next stage was to send the message about the ransom. He'd never felt so nervous in all his life.

"What if they refuse to pay?" he'd asked her.

"Then you'll just have to dispose of her," was the cold reply.

Dozy was disgusted at the callous way Thelma threw away that instruction, but he didn't dare argue. He was deeply disturbed by the thought of actually harming another human being. Muriel didn't seem a bad person and certainly didn't deserve that fate. In fact she seemed a very nice woman, but he also realised that if ransom money was not forth-coming he would have an even bigger problem to deal with.

He composed the message but he was reluctant to send it. He would do that tomorrow – when he felt stronger willed. He sincerely hoped that the woman they had locked in the bedroom had a caring husband, and more importantly – *that he was loaded.*

23

"Dear Auntie T," she'd begun, and then had to stop and think long and hard. How do you write a letter of conciliation to an aunt that you've never met and know very little about? And where was she living now anyway?

The young Sally had felt this compulsion such a long time ago. A wrong had occurred, as far as her innocent ears could gather from conversations over the years that she shouldn't have been able to hear, conversations between her mummy and daddy. As an adult she now recalled, this split had happened nearly thirty years before, just about the time she was born. Sally remembered herself as the little girl who had grown sufficiently to feel that she was the only one in the family who cared enough to *do* something about it. All those years ago she had decided that something *must* be done, but what could a little girl do?

"Dear Auntie T, you don't know me and I don't know you..."

This second attempt did not seem to move her along any faster, so a deep breath and she did it once again, using another piece of paper because her earlier try wasn't very neat, certainly not as neat as she wanted it to be for a special letter.

"Dear Auntie T, you do not know me, and I do not know you... and I do not know where you live either so I am not sure that this letter will ever reach you..." She was warming up now. She just had to keep it going... *"...but I am going to write it anyway and even if it never gets sent, at least I will feel I have done my best. I am now ten years old and living with Mummy and Daddy and I just know that you would be my most favourite Aunt if we ever meet. I don't have any other Aunts.*

I've only just found out that I have an Aunt last night. Mummy and Daddy were arguing and making a loud noise and I could hear them without having to listen at the door as I usually do. Mummy said it was your fault, Alexander Donaldson. She only says Alexander Donaldson when she is angry. When she likes him she calls him Dear Heart. Daddy said it was nothing of the kind, it was her own damn fault, and she shouldn't have been so headstrong. He said he didn't ask for the money but would have been bloody silly not to take it. Mummy said there was no need to swear and Daddy said he'd bloody swear if he wanted to. I don't know who was right. Mummy said it was sad that we never see his sister and Daddy said he didn't have a problem and couldn't care less. If Daddy has a sister then that must be my aunt mustn't it? I think they said your name is Thelma. You are my Aunt Thelma. I like that. I think that Thelma is a nice name and so you must be a nice lady. Why doesn't my Daddy want to speak to you? Did he argue with you the same way that he argues with my mummy – all the time? He always thinks he's right, Mummy says. I would like to see you and we could go for picnics and go to the cinema or the zoo. I would get money from Daddy if you haven't got a lot. Daddy says the last he heard of you, you were desperate for cash, so if I got money from Daddy, I could pay. Mummy says you have probably mellowed over the years but I'm not sure what 'mellowed' means, is it good? Please come and visit me. I would like that. We have a lot of bedrooms and if you wanted, you could come and stay with us. Daddy would have to talk to you again then, wouldn't he? Mummy would be happy to have someone who did not argue with her all the time. Well that's all I think I can say to an Aunt that I've never met but I hope that I can meet you soon. Lots of love and kisses from Sally."

Sally could remember writing the letter, but also remembered that it never was sent.

24

He was going to have to pass on the bad news. At least he had a mobile. Get the number right first. Success, it's ringing... It's still ringing... And it's still ringing...

"H-h-hello..."

Oh no, it's Grandad... "Grandad, I'm going to..."

"Just a m-m-minute," said Grandad, "I'll have to t-t-t-turn d-d-d-down the radio," and he put the phone down on the hall table.

Now that I'm working, thought Derek, we will have to invest in a portable hand-phone for the hall – one that could be carried about the house, but Grandad would not be allowed to take it into the toilet when he's doing his crosswords. Having money to do that and all future plans could be affected by him continuing working, of course.

"H-h-h-h-hello ag-g-g-gain..." Grandad was back.

"Hi Grandad, can you hear me all right now?"

"D-D-D-Derek, is that you?"

"Yes, Grandad I was just..."

"Wait a m-m-m-minute. I'll g-g-g-go and g-g-g-get your g-g-gran..." The phone was placed back on the hall table. Derek could hear the loud music continuing in the back-ground and his grandad shouting to his gran.

"Hello... Hello... Hector – who did you say it is?" his gran shouted over the radio-noise which was still fairly loud.

"It's D-D-D-Derek," shouted back Grandad – eventually...

Did his gran actually swear at Grandad? Had he heard correctly? Surely not... The music suddenly stopped. Yes, she probably had.

"Hello, Gran, I'm not..."

"Just a minute, Derek, the potatoes are boiling over. It's nearly teatime, you know. You picked a bad time to call. Hold on, I'll have to turn down the gas a little... Right then, now... what is it? Why aren't you here? The tea will be on the table shortly. Are you going to be late or something?"

"Yes, Gran. That's why I'm phoning. I'm at the Police Station..."

"Will I keep your tea warm for you then? Why are you at the Police Station? Are you chasing up a story?"

"Well..."

"Is it about your grandad?"

"No Gran..."

"Well, what is it then? Spit it out. You're taking an awful long time to tell me this. The potatoes will be getting burned, you know..."

"Gran. I might be getting arrested..."

"Derek, don't joke with me when I'm trying to get the tea ready. Hector... Turn off the gas under the potatoes, please. No, Hector...the other one...the potatoes... So, you'll be a little late then. I'll keep it warm. Ok, see you soon. Bye"

"...Bye Gran," said Derek.

At least he'd tried, but she'd thought the call was about Grandad, hadn't she? Had he been involved with the police too? He'd find out about that later. Right now, he was concerned for Sally. She'd been the one that the Detective Constable had decided to question first. She wasn't being arrested, he told her, but he'd a lot of unanswered questions about her circumstances so he couldn't guarantee that the interview would remain informal. He had been wearing a confident smile.

Friday early evening and the atmosphere in the Police Station was subdued, but in only a few hours, there would probably be a lot of bodies being bounced, supported, restrained, and mopped up, if it was to be a normal Friday – pandemonium.

Derek hoped he wouldn't still be there then, but if he was,

and could force himself to maintain a positive outlook, there may be some stories to be picked up. What he would do with them then could be doubtful – if he was locked up...

Dear me, and there he was being negative again.

Sally, meanwhile, was feeling fidgety.

She'd explained to Andy Pandy, or whatever he was called, that she had been in the Supermarket at the time of the robbery, and he'd believed that. She'd then told him how seriously depressed she'd felt last night, but hadn't given him any detail of why. He'd wanted to know why, but she'd told him it was none of his business – and he hadn't liked that...

"Well... to get some comfort from my mum," was the reason she'd gone into the office, she told him grudgingly, "...you know what I mean," she'd said then.

He hadn't empathised with her, as she felt he should have – and she didn't like that, so slow progress was being made. He'd accused her of being part of the gang and that she'd gone ahead, to lull her mother into a false sense of security, so the gang could take her by surprise. "My mother?" she reacted in amazement. "I love my mother and would never do anything to hurt her. How dare you. Don't you love your mother?" She was undecided if the silence that followed meant that HE was the one to ask the questions or – maybe that he just didn't love HIS mother.

"But you were in the van, you said," he persisted.

"I was tied up..." She almost added, "You Dimwit," but then she remembered she hadn't told him that before.

"But you weren't when the Constables discovered you breaking into your mother's house."

"Sweaty found me – I mean Derek. He untied me..."

He looked her straight in the eyes and continued to stare. He'd seen this staring technique done years ago in a Clint Eastwood movie and it had worked for Clint.

"And we weren't breaking in..." her voice just faded away. She was getting fed up and exasperated with these questions and he kept giving her strange disconcerting looks. At one point he seemed to go cross-eyed...

"I believe you are BOTH part of this gang... you and Toozlethwaite – and your mother? Is she part of the plan too?"

Now this is getting silly, thought Sally. At least he hadn't questioned her about the money.

"Now about the money..."

Oh dear... What could she say now? "What money?" she asked innocently.

"A package of money was found in your handbag today by two law officers when they were apprehending two villains." As he said it, he put a more heroic and successful sounding spin on that event that had little to do with the reality – the two villains had escaped. He didn't really look down on his Uniform brethren. Plain Clothes and Uniforms have to support each other in times like these and the public have to be kept in check – or in the dark even, but the Uniforms never could get it right, in his mind.

"How do you know it was my handbag?" she continued innocently.

"Because..." and he remembered that the handbag, after it had been snatched from her in the office earlier, had never been confirmed formally as hers.

Damn, he said inwardly... "Just a moment please," and he left the room to collect the bag from the Front Desk Sergeant. He stomped back into the interview, bag in hand, slapped it down on the table and leaned over her, nose to nose.

"Is this your handbag?" he barked.

She could see the hairs in his nose and that wasn't a pleasant sight. She looked away hurriedly. He told himself to be patient. He could tell he was wearing her down, the strain was showing. He was good at this. "It looks like mine... Ah yes, I recognise the rubbish. But you said there was money. I don't see any."

"It's... it's... it is separate evidence." She was succeeding in really getting up his nose.

"Could the men who stole my bag maybe have added the money? As compensation for the inconvenience they were about to put me through?" and again the innocence.

He ignored that – with difficulty but pressed on. "And no doubt you'll be able to tell me why it matches exactly the amount stolen from the Supermarket yesterday afternoon." He was back in control and felt like the kill was near. This was the part he liked best.

"What? Three thousand pounds? Is that all they got? And they took my mother too – all for three thousand pounds. I...I... I don't believe you." It was her turn to splutter it out and then she started laughing, normally at first, but then it became hysterical.

And he felt she was laughing at him. How humiliating...

Sally was taking deep breaths and getting control of herself – and of Andy Pandy. There now...she was calm again.

"Three thousand pounds... Oh dear me. At least Derek will be delighted about this." Sally started to giggle again. "No-one else knows of this. Oh thank you. This is fresh news and it could be Derek's first scoop." She was laughing again, very happily.

This was wrong, Andy Woodstock said to himself – not going to plan – he'd lost control of the interview. The sum stolen was to be deliberately kept from the public. It had been a tactic decided by his boss, an instruction from on high. He'd blown it – so he decided to give up for the moment.

"I'd appreciate it if everything we've discussed between these four walls is kept strictly confidential," he stated – hopefully.

"Oh..." was her only smiled response.

He didn't hold out much hope.

Derek was pleased when the two of them came out of the Interview Room. Sally was happy, Detective Constable Andy was not. He was surprised and delighted to be told they could go – for the moment – but to remain available. Andy Pandy couldn't face any more today.

Outside, the pair of them hugged.

He asked her if she'd like to go home with him to meet his gran and grandad. Sally said yes.

It was a warm and pleasant evening and, being Friday, there was a relaxed atmosphere all over town. The working week was over. Bring on the weekend. They'd known each other for only a short time but a lifetime seemed to have been crammed into these few days – a lifetime of togetherness. They laughed and joked and were comfortable as they wandered along hand in hand, and arm in arm, and sometimes just a little bit closer still. Sally hoped his grandparents would like and accept her. Derek was sure they would.

He told her of his gran's fussiness and her 'crossword' thesis. He explained her doorstep farewell routine, and her non-stop housework. When he spoke of his grandad and the daily newspaper round, it brought a smile to Sally's face. She laughed when he explained about Grandad becoming the reluctant subject of Gran's thesis – her 'almost-human test-dummy' as she put it – and of course there was the squeaky bike he'd had for many years – and his stutter. She readily accepted that Derek had loved growing up with them both.

They just arrived at the gate when Sally's new mobile rang out. At least it was easy to find in her pocket – no large handbag to have to dig into, but...

It was bad news and Sally started crying.

25

Dozy had informed the other three how unprofitable last night's activities had been. Their reactions had been just as bad as Thelma's, although they didn't blame *him* – well not totally. Each of them felt more that they'd been stupid and duped into becoming involved at all, with him and the robbery, even though beforehand they had been eager. This may not have been fair to Dozy, but isn't it the way people tend to react when it's all gone wrong?

They, however, remained loyal to each other. They were all in it, like it or not, and *had* to stick together. Of course, that conclusion was reached only after voices had been raised and tempers lost and the rights and wrongs had been spewed right, left, and centre, but they all agreed that the way ahead, if they were going to become rich, would be a successful payout from the hostage's spouse.

They read the phone message that Dozy had prepared on the mobile. Now it had to be transmitted. With difficulty, all four trembling fingers were placed together on the send button – the four fingers pressed simultaneously – and the text went.

They knew it would be received instantly on the mobile of Mr Alexander Donaldson. What they didn't know was how he would react.

"DO NOT CONTACT THE POLICE RE THIS MESSAGE OR YOUR WIFE WILL GET IT. OBTAIN URGENTLY £100,000 FOR HER SAFE RELEASE OR ELSE. YOU WILL SOON BE TOLD WHERE TO TAKE THE MONEY"

Muriel had been listening and heard only a small portion of

their arguments and discussion when it had been mundane and calm, but she'd heard almost everything when the voices were raised. She'd begun to experience a dread of the 'scary lady' they had talked about. The one who was out of sight but definitely in charge – THELMA. And that name seemed familiar...

No. It couldn't be...

Beakie and Tich had come into her room together. Muriel presumed it could be as moral support for each other, rather than physical. The task they had come together to do was the removal of her shoes and her glasses, they informed her. Initially she pleaded with them not to take them, at which they apologised but insisted. Then she bravely said she wasn't letting them have them – they'd have to take them from her – which they *did*...

Suddenly she was helpless and in tears of rage. Being short-sighted she felt rather lost, even though she was only in the confines of the bedroom. The specs were part of her.

They were obviously afraid she would attempt to escape. Little chance of that now, she had to admit. She'd never find her way out of the house, even if they released her.

Reading without glasses she could do, but that was a very small consolation. A load of magazines and an assortment of soft-backed novels had been supplied to her. She'd no radio or television in the room. The day felt very long. Reading was not a favourite pastime and she'd glanced at some of the magazines as a time-filler, and then slept fitfully for a little while.

When she forced herself to pick up a book and attempted to read, she'd found it to be a surprisingly enjoyable experience. She hadn't spent time like this, doing nothing, for years – though here she had little choice and reading didn't remove her disquiet about the future.

The television, that she had been dumped in front of when they'd arrived, was rarely off. Mainly it was tuned to one of the music channels and the music wasn't too bad. She was used to hearing music playing in Bisko's each working day. It helped the sales she had been told, so unintentionally she'd absorbed the words of a large repertoire of songs and she would sing along when at work. Here she listened only. Singing didn't seem appropriate.

She also knew that the gang kept up to date with the news but frustratingly at a very low volume to prevent her hearing.

Beakie and Tich came in regularly to check on her and carefully locked the door behind them each time – she'd checked – *every* time. If they came in together, little talking took place, but individually they proved chatty.

A vacuum cleaner, having been left in the room that morning, gave Muriel something to do other than read and sleep. It took up very little of her day, but because the house had not been occupied and cleaned recently, she had fun sucking up the cobwebs, and the little spiders that were foolish enough to become visible to her and her trusty vacuum.

Even with her short sight, she got 'em. She enjoyed the opportunity to do something, but there was a limit to the fun she could have with that.

In no time at all, not a spider remained in the room. It became web free, and dust and fluff free.

On the outside of the window, if she pressed her nose hard against the glass surface, she could vaguely see masses of spiders and webs, but she could not reach them.

They remained free.

If only she could be free, she thought wistfully.

Neither of the males ever entered her room but one of them had been out to reconnoitre. She had been told that he'd confirmed her daughter was no longer in the van, so therefore must be safe. She didn't know how they'd found out but she was willing to believe the news to be true, mainly because she wanted it to be.

Though she'd tried very hard to hear, she'd failed to pick up the detail of the text message they'd talked about, but she gathered it was about her and was some sort of demand. It would be money no doubt, "...and do you think he'll pay?" was the one comment to reach her.

Of course he will, she told herself, but really she was thinking, *he'd better...*

However there wouldn't be much she could do about it if he did not. That was a very unpleasant thought, but as long as Sally is safe.

26

The text message had been from Sally's father. He'd been at 'his club' when he'd received the ransom text about his wife and had passed it immediately on to Sally – a problem shared? More like a problem off-loaded... Whatever the motive, it was bad news.

Standing at Derek's gate, Sally had burst into tears. It was a shock to receive the ransom demand and she wanted to return to her own home. She'd be poor company for anyone she insisted. Derek successfully convinced her that going home to mope would only make her feel worse. Being with others was a much better idea.

And Derek had been correct, she reluctantly admitted later. She felt bad about meeting Derek's grandparents in these circumstances, and she couldn't stop worrying about her mother's predicament, but being with them turned out to be a pleasant experience. Derek was overjoyed not just because she liked his guardians a lot, but because they liked *her* even more. And it helped Sally that evening being with people who were not involved – but who cared.

When her father had called, he'd told her that there was no quick way he could get together the money that was being demanded. What shocked Sally, however, was the callous way he'd said that he was against ever paying a ransom for kidnap victims – it just encouraged other rogues to do it as well...

"*Bloody hell,*" Sally screamed down the phone at him. "*It's your wife you are talking about – not just anybody.*"

He then replied calmly he'd have to see what he could arrange – but it *was* a Friday.

"But you are a banker. Surely you have contacts and can pull strings."

She was disgusted by his attitude.

"I'll see what I can do. I'll be at my club. You have my number if you want to contact me. I won't be home tonight."

And that was her loving father... He'd changed over the years...

Derek's gran suggested that Sally stayed over. Going back to an empty house in these circumstances couldn't possibly be a good idea. Sally had said it was very kind, but no. That's when Granny Smith got stroppy and *insisted* Sally stayed, and went to air the spare bed. So, Sally was staying. Although she felt she'd been bullied into it, she had been pleased to give in – happy that someone else was caring for her and who, at least for a short time, had almost taken the place of her mother.

"It's the weekend anyway. And you must be tired after all this nonsense." Yes indeed, Granny knew best. Just don't argue.

Sally was aware the house belonged to Granny and Grandad Smith but in her head it had became Toozlethwaites'. She was getting used to that name – and liking it.

So, she made herself comfortable in Grandad's favourite chair at Grandad's insistence, as Gran took control.

"Let me get a glass. A drop of whisky with a little hot water, take it to bed with you. A hot toddy's is what you need young lady," was Gran's decision.

"Wrong..." said Grandad, "You've g-g-g-got the p-p-p-proportions all wrong. It has to b-b-be a l-l-lot of whisky. F-f-f-f-f-f-f-f-forget the water." The other three in the room were relieved to hear the word eventually come out. Each had been expecting something much worse...

"Thanks but I'll be fine. It's nice that I can stay. Thank you. Thank you very much," said Sal.

And there were tears again. Earlier for Grandad it hadn't been so much tears of sadness – it had been more of annoyance and frustration.

Grandad's bike had been pinched – *again*.

He'd been doing his normal routine. The paper round took several hours and he'd almost completed it. His delivery route wasn't far from home but the newsagent's was in the opposite direction. Most days he would have several bagfuls to deliver that he couldn't take in one go, and it saved him time and energy, going by bike over the longer distance, but the bike was more of a nuisance when he was doing the house deliveries because he'd have to return to where he'd left it each time and move it to another spot along the route. In truth, it could be more trouble than it was worth, all the lifting and laying, and hard to pedal because it needed oil, but as Derek would say about old dogs... they go barking mad – sorry – are unwilling to learn new tricks. Indeed, both could definitely apply to Grandad, thought Derek.

He'd left it parked at the normal place, and wandered off along the lane. Rarely did he meet anyone. Generally the houses were large, and the occupants, who tended to be retired gentlefolk who were content to sit and read and ruminate about world affairs all day, bought the broadsheets, the heavier expensive newspapers with enormous supplements. Well, they always seemed enormous to Grandad. No tabloids here – no sirree.

Some households even had the 'special' men's magazines delivered. Retired Forces personnel he reckoned. Grandad had to be careful they didn't become folded the wrong way in his crowded bag. It was bad enough where they put the staples sometimes in these magazines without folds as well. He always made sure they were in perfect condition when he delivered them by checking every single photo when he stopped for a rest. Technically, they were second-hand when delivered. He didn't dare buy them himself – Gran would have kicked him out the house if he'd tried to skip in with something like that. Some of the photos were shocking – but that's why he had a peek.

He wasn't hurrying. He had almost completed the final stage for the day, and the bike had lain a while at that one spot, and it was a lovely sunny morning. There was no need to rush. His working day was nearly over. He was starting to relax – until he returned...

There was no bike and nobody to be seen – the place was deserted – hence the visit to the Police Station.

The Desk Sergeant had been amused, firstly by the fact that Grandad was still doing a paper round and secondly, by his stutter. He had difficulty hiding his smile, but wisely did. It made a pleasant change from the knifings, the muggers, under-age drinkers, and the sex workers. His other work was up to date anyway.

He had been glad that it was still a quiet morning – he couldn't have spent the time with Grandad and his slow rate of explanation if he'd been busy. He was very patient and unusually sympathetic towards this older victim as he laboriously went through the details.

"And how would you describe the bike, Sir?" the Sergeant asked him. He'd recorded this old fellow's name and address, contact telephone number, where it had happened, but it had taken nearly four times longer than it would normally.

"R-r-r-red with chipped p-p-p-paint and a squeak."

"Is there no numeric identification?" the sergeant had asked. "It's usually somewhere on the frame..." he continued, "or maybe the manufacturer of the bicycle – the people who made the bike?"

"Eh?" Grandad blinked. "No."

The Sergeant didn't hold out much hope.

"Oh, and a saddle that would c-c-c-cut your b-b-b-bum in half..." Grandad suddenly remembered.

The Sergeant went through the motions anyway. It was Granny Smith who took the brunt of his anger when he arrived back home – on foot. She just smiled... Sometimes she just had to be like a sponge and absorb it. She'd found over the years that it helped him get it out of his system and calm down again.

Before he'd come in to the house he'd checked where he normally left his bike, beside the back door – in case he'd got it all wrong and hadn't taken it with him. This time, the good fairies hadn't brought it back.

27

Monday morning, and Sally had stayed all weekend at Toozlethwaites'. She had slept well in the comfortable bed and woke this morning with the sun streaming in the window, and the noise of a blackbird sounding off about a prowling cat in the neighbourhood.

She'd had no more word about her mum, but she was not confident about her father keeping her up to date. He'd remained all weekend at 'his club' and his whereabouts had been the only information he'd passed on to her, after the ransom text. She was worried about his drinking and hoped he'd be fit enough to go back to the bank this morning. She could see him starting to be criticised at work if he wasn't careful, especially him being the manager.

She was desperate to know if he had been successful gathering the money – she didn't have much confidence in him anymore. The temptation to ring his mobile and start shouting at him again was strong, but she resisted.

It was another warm and, so far, sunny day, but the weather might be changing, some wispy clouds were starting to appear.

Both Derek and Sally were up sharp. It was a working day and it seemed only sensible to them both to be maintaining some normality, but Derek hadn't foreseen the ablutions problem looming. He now found getting access to the bathroom doubly difficult against the competition of both Grandad and Sally. He had to be very patient but ready to make a dash the moment the door opened and someone came out, and this had been the case all weekend. Grandad behaved like a gentleman for a change and always insisted Sally take priority, but zealously made sure he was in before Derek.

When they arrived at the office Spider was already at his desk and eager to get started. He had been studying hard over the rest days, keeping up to date by carefully analysing the racing pages and current racing results. He'd also been contacting racing friends, resulting in some hot tips for Rob Sheldon. The question would be whether Mr Sheldon would trust the skills of this 'ead'unted bloke from the bookie's.

Today was the first outing for Derek, the roving reporter. He would be working in the field today – or rather in the Newingsworth Public Park. He had to follow up on Sally's promise to Arthur and Charlie and make them 'stars'. He was at a loss as to how he could do it...

It was morning break time. Arthur and Charlie had been going hard at it for several hours and considered their break was much deserved, anyway it was their entitlement. They'd been looking forward to this since they started that morning. Mondays were the same for everyone it seemed, even those who loved their job – Mondays did spoil the weekend.

Arthur had reminded Charlie about Sally's promise but Charlie was sceptical. "Betcha 'e won't appear..." was Charlie's reaction.

So, when Derek did appear, Arthur was a little more pleased to see him than Charlie. It was only a quid, but he'd won.

Arthur offered Derek a mug of tea and put the kettle back on, while Charlie listened to Derek's spiel, but he had a suspicious look that said, "You look like trouble. Where 'ave I seen you before?" Derek found this a little unsettling but the mood changed when he managed to spill part of the mug of tea over his trousers. These trousers... they certainly weren't good ones now, so it didn't really matter, but Charlie and Arthur both found it funny. The three of them began to get on better when Derek joined in the laughter too, though he felt like crying. At one time, which *seemed* long ago, these had been his favourite trousers...

Finally down to business – with notebook at the ready,

Derek gritted his teeth and started to use his real writing skills again – the bit about reporting he didn't like. Shorthand would have been quicker and easier he had told himself for years, but had done nothing about learning – so – onward... The usual cold hard facts of their working life with the council parks department were duly recorded for starters. He progressed onto where they'd learned their craft, and followed by a listing of all the types of flowers they used for the displays. The quality and type of fertilisers had to be an important topic obviously. Natural animal materials being preferred always and could be best judged by the smell.

"Ye gotta smell it – *an' smell nuffink...*" was Charlie's simple explanation for fertilisers.

"An' best t' be cowshi' – cowshi' always – unless it's 'orseshi' of course," added Arthur.

The tea break extended and gradually they were chatting happily together. Both Charlie and Arthur had relaxed totally. Neither had a good word to say about 'Elf and Safety' and the silly safety rules that had to be complied with. Way over the top, was their opinion, common sense was all you needed. They'd even had to attend a course on how to climb ladders, a waste of Council Tax money and their time.

"But there was a bloke last week, 'e 'adn't a clue, 'e lifted our big ladder all 'imself. Could've done 'imself a mischief..." said Arthur.

"Served 'im right an' all though – an' 'im tryin' t' pinch it." added Charlie.

And they all laughed at the stupidity of this bloke, although Derek's was more of a nervous giggle... his cheeks flushed. He was very pleased that their combined short term visual memories were perhaps suspect – and changed the subject.

Vandalism – they became heated about that. The "yoofs oo cum overafence," when the park is closed and bring cans of beer – they were worse than the kids, by far.

The big palsy-walsy breakthrough came when Derek opened up about himself and it came out how his nickname had become

Sweaty. That caused big grins. They liked that a lot and, from then on, they used it at every chance.

Arthur turned out to be a closet classical music lover. This had begun with the three tenors and the World Cup song. He'd then stumbled onto Tchaikovsky and Wagner and found them to be particularly stirring. His actual words were, "Boaf shi' ho' man – shi' ho' – *def-in-ately* man. 'Ese buggers is grrreat." Derek thought Arthur's turn-of-phrase could be a bit strong for the family readers. He'd have to remember to make an editorial adjustment.

Arthur also gave full marks to Charlotte Church's voice but Derek suspected in that case it may not have just been the music which got Arthur excited. Derek was feeling quite proud of his interviewing skills. He'd discovered that Charlie, Arthur's very good mate, hadn't even been aware of Arthur's musical passions.

When it came to heroes, it was Charlie who started spouting. Unsurprisingly, Alan Titchmarsh was on the list, but then again so was Lady Gaga, Madonna, The Sugababes, and the girl from page three of the Sun that day. Derek would obviously have to think a bit more about the slant he'd give to that part of the article.

Both Arthur and Charlie modestly admitted to having run three charity marathons over the last five years, achieving moderate times. They'd run the distance one year wearing Nun's outfits, the following year it was as Gorillas, which Derek thought very appropriate, and the last was in very large pink tutus. They asked Derek if he'd any ideas on what they could wear next spring for their fourth attempt. That could become a readers competition, Derek thought.

Arthur asked Derek if he was runner and did he fancy the marathon?

Derek had a smug feeling – was *he* a runner? *He sure was.* Wasn't he the guy who'd outrun this pair and their policeman pal only last Thursday? Had they caught him? No. Was he fit? Sure was... Could he run a marathon? *Of course* – no problem. Then the little voice in his head pointed out to him that, last Thursday, he'd beaten them by running about two hundred metres – a marathon was twenty-six miles.

"Me...? ...Definitely *not.*"

The three of them happily rambled on until lunch-break by which time Derek had picked up more than enough of interest to make an article attractive and good to read. He'd wisely taken the office camera with him. So, the grand finale was some photos – close-ups of the two 'stars' and artistic shots of their handiwork.

This had been a fun visit to the park and what a difference to his recent jaunts. By the time he left them, all three had become bosom buddies. It was lucky that there was no alcohol involved or the whole business could have become maudlin.

He arrived back in the office, sober but in high spirits, to find a tearful Sally being comforted by Rob Sheldon and Spider. The cause – at long last there had been a call from her father. Another text message had been received, more or less repeating the previous one but this time giving a deadline of Thursday for payment. In bold capital letters it had emphasised, "OR ELSE"

Bad enough for Sally, but it was again her father's apparent lack of concern that was getting to her. Yes, he admitted he had enough money to pay them but no, his principles didn't allow him, and anyway, the value of his stocks would be ridiculously low if he sold now. He preferred to wait and see what the 'OR ELSE' actually meant. He didn't believe they'd go through with any violence. Sally was truly shocked but no matter what pleading she did for immediate action, he was adamant – he was doing nothing.

And all this had happened during Derek's absence, but Spider and Rob Sheldon had been around to support her physically and mentally. They were fully up to date on the dilemma, and emotionally involved too. The day progressed in fits and starts, outburst of rage from Sally, followed by tears. The other three were desperate to help but there was little they seemed able to do. Eventually they found that keeping their heads low worked best...

It took a little of the shine from Derek's success but, by the end of the day, he'd progressed well with the 'It's Your Parking Place' article, glorifying the roles of these two council employees, and Rob was delighted that obviously he's made an excellent choice by interviewing and choosing this young man – even though, in reality, the choice had been Sally's. On the day of the interview she had heard everything that had been said in Rob's office as she sat in the silence alone, on the other side of the flimsy wall. She'd believed every word of Derek's 'flannel' obviously and had been swayed by it. Rob had been lukewarm. Sally had been decisive, but that didn't spoil Rob's feeling of triumph.

He was also delighted with *his* other find – Spider.

Rob had listened carefully to Spider's tips for the day and acted on them. He'd taken chances and gambled a large sum (which he didn't actually have) with gambler's confidence. The nail-biting wait proved worthwhile as the afternoon progressed and by the end he had incredibly brought his debt down by almost one thousand pounds.

Spider would be a permanent feature he decided.

When the working day was over, Derek and Sally left together. She had agreed to stay on at his place. She knew that she needed company to see this through and Toozlethwaite's did it for her.

Life had also to continue with a little normality, and that was to include a visit to the supermarket by the two of them on the way home. It was 'Bisko's Red Hair Day'. All over the store there were people wearing red wigs. All Bisko's staff had them on, but so had many women customers, lots of children, and a few males as well with big grins, feeling very foolish ...and it was all for charity.

This had been a new venture this year and sponsored by a large hair products organisation who'd supplied cheap wigs to sell for the cause – made of a material which no doubt would be blowing all over town in a few days and clogging up drains on wet days, thought Derek. Cynically negative thoughts again, following on a very depressing afternoon because of Sally's troubles, so not too surprising. The pair of them made a donation to the charity as good citizens but declined the wigs, although Derek was tempted to take one for Grandad.

Sally was immediately recognised by the staff and sympathy was showered on her followed by question after question about her mother. Everyone was surprised how low-key the whole incident had been treated by the newspapers and local radio and television programmes. Many suggested it must be part of a complicated plan to catch the people who'd done it, and whispered that they'd heard that... Sally was reluctant to listen to the gossip and moved on at that point, but then would meet another sympathiser and there would be another stop.

It seemed hours before they joined the queue at the checkout carrying the very few items that were all Granny Smith had asked for. Normally it would have been a five-minute gallop around the store for Derek.

The red wigs fascinated Derek. Almost everyone wearing one gave a strange effect to his eyes, making every face look the same, but in a silly or grotesque way, he thought, although that girl, just a few places ahead of them in the other queue, she looked nice. Ah, the difference – her hair wasn't a wig. It was real and she had a nice short haircut that suited her. He could see she was buying a lot of books.

He hated standing in queues but tonight he was standing much longer than normal because the checkout girl was another who recognised Sally. There followed yet one more chat, somewhat shorter than the many previous long discussions, because it was a busy spot and becoming rather congested. Eventually they paid and arrived in the fresh air again.

Derek was wary as they walked in the bustling car park. He knew what it was like to be attacked by a runaway trolley, and it was still a fresh memory. In his heightened awareness, he noticed the girl who'd passed, the red-haired one he'd already noticed while queuing. She was wearing glasses now and they suited her as well. She was cycling but she seemed familiar, other than in the queue, of course. Her bike didn't half need oiling, he thought. It had a bad squeak just like Grandad's.

They walked on – and then *it hit him*.

The van – the furniture van – *she had been the driver*.

Too late – she was gone...

28

In the short time of her confinement, Muriel had become a voracious reader. Being limited to the bedroom space meant her day comprised of doing some rudimentary exercises to avoid totally stiffening up, and attempting crosswords and Sudoku puzzles. Attempted only because few of the crosswords and puzzles were completed correctly and she tended to abandon them part-way through. These pastimes had never been included in her skills. She tended to become rapidly frustrated by her lack of ability to solve them and stopped trying. Her reading, though, had been varied and enjoyable – while there was a stock of unread books available. Already, very few remained unread.

She had found the relationships with both of her female captors, Beakie and Tich, to have become reasonably amicable in the short time. It had almost become normal, talking to someone wearing a paper mask over their face, and not to even notice.

In this case, it had been Tich who'd been with her. She'd said about reading material running short and how she was enjoying it, influenced very much by little else to do of course, but satisfying none the less. A conversation developed about the books that each had read over the years. Whereas for Muriel reading had been occasional and tended to have been limited to continuing what she'd enjoyed previously, Tich had a vast knowledge of varying authors and titles, and that had impressed the older woman.

It was an amicable chat. Both women could have been sitting relaxing and having a cappuccino in the local cafe, but one was a hostage and one was the jailer. The conversation was not generalised as normal conversations could be, and some topics were deliberately avoided, but it was still enjoyable for both, none the less.

Tich promised that she'd get Muriel some good books.

The two males had decided to take it in turns to leave the premises cautiously to obtain daily supplies, fresh milk and rolls and newspapers, at a local shop.

They found that the Friday evening and Saturday morning newspapers had carried a report of the robbery but with scant detail, referring simply to an 'incident' that had occurred at Bisko's and with no mention of their hostage, or what had been stolen. This puzzled them. They were also concerned that Muriel's husband would make the ransom public which would put considerably more pressure on them and their freedom. To 'watch that space' was the decision.

They had, however, acquired a bike – ancient and a little squeaky unfortunately – but a bike nonetheless. It had very clearly been abandoned and with that squeak it was obvious why, but they were pleased to have it. They had no other transport, although they weren't really planning on going anywhere – yet...

Dozy had found it, abandoned, lying against the hedge. There was nobody about and it looked a bit sad just dumped there, chipped and uncared for, probably had been pinched by kids and abandoned. Kids nowadays... dear me... He only did what he felt any caring ratepayer should do – he removed some rubbish from the street and he felt self-righteous doing it.

Dozy, Mick and Beakie had all been for a wander around individually with no incidents, making a point of doing nothing to attract attention. There was rarely anyone to be seen about these roads. Either their neighbours just didn't go out, or else they only used cars, the gang concluded, but all their wandering had been done on foot. No-one had actually used the bike until Tich, the only one who hadn't ventured out, decided she'd go farther afield than the others. Using the 'new bike', she made the Supermarket her planned destination.

She wanted to go back to the scene of the crime. Would it feel any different as an anonymous customer? The thought of doing it fascinated her and gave her a buzz. Would she feel guiltier?

It had been a beautiful spell of weather for many days and it was a lovely feeling pedalling along with a slight breeze cooling her head. Until two weeks ago she'd had long flowing blonde hair. A sudden urge to do something wild and adventurous resulted in having her lovely locks shorn, and the remainder coloured red. She may have been driven by the thought of her impending criminal involvement – no matter, she'd regretted the action immediately after, but, as the days had gone by she'd come to like it, and now she preferred it this way. Wearing her glasses with the long hair had been less attractive than with the short. She looked good, and she knew it, even though it was immodest to think that way.

Today she had set herself a task.

She wanted to give Muriel the best choice of reading she could find. She liked Muriel and felt very sorry for her predicament, and the part she'd played in it. Her target was to please her if she could. Wearing the paper mask all the time, when she went in and out of the bedroom, seemed silly, but essential she was told by the others. Deep down, she knew that Muriel would know her immediately, if they ever met again in different circumstances, without ever having seen her face.

This supermarket had a large stock of books. There was little competition nowadays from specialist bookshops. Superstores like this had taken over the market and the world – well – almost.

There was no rush she told herself as she parked the bike, took some deep breaths, and prepared to enter the store, but walking in and finding masses of red headed people suddenly all around her made her heart flutter like mad. What's going on, she thought in a panic. It's surreal. This is most unsettling – I'm going crazy.

She came back to reality when the voice beside her made a comment. "I don't suppose you'll want to buy one. Yours is really nice." It was the young sales assistant at the special charity counter.

Tich gave the money over anyway, for charity but no, don't bother with the wig...

The store looked different from the view she'd had on her last visit. What had she seen then? Not a lot...

For a start she shouldn't have gone along with Steve's suggestion not to wear her glasses on the job. She would be less recognisable, he said. He may be her boy-friend's pal, and was acting-leader on the job, self-crowned because no-one else wanted it, but she thought he had lousy judgement in many things.

She hadn't felt comfortable driving like that and had been lucky to get away with not hitting anyone or anything. She'd seen an out-of-focus car-park, a blurred loading bay and after a very short wait in the van, the bustling out-of-focus car-park again, on a wing and a prayer and almost blinded by the sunlight. Afterwards, she had been relieved to remove the hot balaclava and to replace her glasses at the traffic lights. That's where she'd clearly seen a fellow spectacle-wearer on a bike at the traffic lights giving her such a glaring look that she suspected he might have been one of her near misses.

What a lot of books they had – excellent... Now choose – hardbacks or paperbacks? Let's go with paperbacks, easier and lighter to carry. I'm on the bike, she reminded herself.

She lifted and replaced many. Slowly the collection grew. She wanted to be sure that the choice she made would be the correct balance to satisfy and maintain Muriel's new love of the written word. The stack she'd selected was reviewed once more and a couple of changes decided on, and then she was happy. Mission accomplished, and she smiled to herself.

There were raised eyebrows at the checkout when she lifted the ten books from her basket to pay – the books she'd carefully and lovingly selected. "Where do these young people get the money to squander on all these books...? That's what I'd like to know," the grumpy-looking old fellow who was behind her in the queue said in a stage whisper to his equally grumpy-looking wife, "...and how does she get the time to do all that reading – she should get a job – they're bone-lazy nowadays." He took a breath, "...And if she had to live on the pension like us, she wouldn't be wasting money like that... books... *Huh*. We have to make do with Sky Television..."

"That's a great book" commented the red-wigged checkout girl lifting the fourth one. "I couldn't put it down until I finished it and I read it in a day. I like *your* wig. You suit it more than most people. Did you buy it here?"

Tich loaded her plastic bag and paid cash, which would have come from these tills in the first place. As she went by the cigarette kiosk, she had a sudden thought – to buy another four weeks' worth of lottery tickets. Habit is a wondrous thing and she had the feeling that she'd be tempting fate if she didn't continue after... how many years was it? It must be five or six.

She said angelically to herself, *I'll* buy them for the group – but she was using stolen money anyway. So, the usual numbers were marked on the card, she couldn't possibly change them or forget them – mustn't tempt fate. Anyway, the same old routine – if it's a very good night they'll be getting a tenner – and be happy at that.

Back on the bike again for a leisurely ride home – she corrected that thought. How could it be a leisurely ride with that saddle? – It felt as if it could cut your bum in half...

29

Tich didn't cycle straight back to the others. She was curious about the apparent police inactivity and decided brazenly to go by Muriel's home.

She knew exactly where she was going in this town. She'd studied the maps for long enough beforehand, and it had been she who worked out the convoluted route carefully to confuse the innocent hostage and hopefully the police if there was a chase, and all her hard work had paid off after the robbery. She'd memorised the area so well, she'd navigated the way with ease – once she had put her specs on again.

The furniture van was gone from outside the house and the street was deserted. She considered this road to be overly tidy. She saw it a bit like her mother's house used to be when she would be told off every time she left any of her stuff lying around. She and her mother had always been at odds about that. The house she and Michael shared wasn't like that by any means. They'd never had any more than limited cash and were just delighted to have a roof over their heads – but tidy? *No...*

Not a soul to be seen, she thought. No – I tell a lie. There's a sweet little old lady going into that house, next door to Muriel's. I'll bet that's the first time she's been outside in months.

How wrong Tich was...

Mrs Masterton was returning home early from a visit to the bingo hall and today she was a happy bunny. There was a beaming grin on her face that Tich couldn't see. Although she was regularly lucky, winning small amounts, it wasn't every visit that gave her a profit of five hundred pounds. She couldn't wait to get inside and open the bottle of sherry in her bag, and have a personal celebration – or two. And then she'd make her tea. Bingo was one vice – *maybe* sherry was another, but you wouldn't get her to admit to that one.

Next door in Muriel's house, there was no sign of life. Tich had seen a cat during her brief visit and hoped someone was looking after it. She remembered it being frightened by their presence but she also had a mental picture of it scurrying out via a cat flap. Anyway, cats can look after themselves, not like men, and she smiled to herself and pedalled on – squeaking.

Muriel was pleased to see her return with additional reading material, but ten books?

"This isn't a good sign," she said to Tich, "...am I expected to be here for a long time?"

"I hope you are," was the reply.

That seemed a bit odd to Muriel. Is that because she likes my company or is it indicating something else? She didn't want to think of what something else might be ...but looking on the bright side, she had all these books, and she started into one right away. In no time, she was deeply engrossed and any unpleasant thoughts for her future had gone.

Good book or not, it was not easy to stay awake, when all she was doing all day was lying around... reading...

... And she dozed off.

When she wakened it was pitch black. She'd slept all evening, but she sighed, she knew she would not sleep during the night, but she had the new books. She switched on her light.

They were making a lot of noise next door. That could have been what wakened her, she realised. It was happy sounds she recognised. It was far more pleasant than the feeling of impending gloom that had descended on the house during the early afternoon, but no-one had told her then what the problem was, and frustratingly she couldn't hear what they were saying. They had deliberately turned up the music again.

There was a knock and her door was unlocked. It was Beakie bringing some supper. There was a glass of wine on the tray as well. Unusual, but Muriel didn't refuse it.

Beakie sounded a trifle 'happy' as she talked this time – the effect of more than just one glass, Muriel assumed. She said a few pleasantries and left Muriel alone but as she closed the door, there was not the usual click of the key being turned. At least Muriel didn't hear it. Could she have been mistaken? Could the effect of the wine have made Beakie careless? That was Muriel's sincere hope...

She listened until the door across the hall had closed, waiting excitedly, then rose quietly and moved towards the door on tiptoe, even though she had no shoes and didn't make a sound anyway.

She gently turned the handle – and pulled very cautiously...
The door opened...
She closed it again and went back and lay on the bed again, her heart pounding.

What should her next move be?

She decided not to act immediately, although if someone returned to check the door, her chance to escape could be lost. She would wait until they'd all gone to sleep and then find a way out. The book which had been so absorbing a moment ago couldn't quite capture her mind now as it had. Too many thoughts were tumbling around. She hadn't seen any of the rest of the house. She had a feeling it was substantial but she had no way of knowing. How would she find a way out? Where were the doors? ...particularly the outside ones, and how carefully do they lock them all? She had no idea. Could it be similar to her home? Too much to expect, she supposed? Where did they all sleep – upstairs or downstairs? Were they sharing rooms?

She presumed there would be more than one access in and out of the house – a big house would normally have a front and back door. Which should she aim for? Would it matter – she didn't know where they were anyway? She had no footwear, and no glasses, but she did have a determination to leave this house, no matter what.

The small clock sat at her bedside – ticking. She lay and she watched the second hand sweep around the dial, oh so very, very slooooooow-ly... The story she had begun earlier, and had found so engrossing, had completely lost its attraction. It was once again just a paperback sitting on the little table. Her mind was on other things tonight. *Escape.*

The noise across the hall diminished gradually as the night progressed. She heard one, "goodnight," being said, and then another moments later, and doors being closed, then at long last – silence... She had to have patience... *She* wasn't sleepy...

One o'clock and now not a sound in the house – her time to move...

She opened the door gently, hoping it wouldn't creak – it was an old house. It didn't. Then – out into the hall.

Now which way?

Her instinct said the front door was on her left but it was pitch black in the hall. She stood still hoping her eyes would become used to the darkness. She closed them tight and opened them again – with little improvement.

She worked out that she been brought, blindfolded of course, straight across the hall to the bedroom from the living room, so that eliminated the door opposite. Her eyes became a little more accustomed to the darkness but, being without her glasses, it didn't help a lot. She'd have to be careful that she didn't knock over any ornaments or chairs that she guessed could be decorating the place. She turned left and felt her way forward.

Ah, a door on the same wall as her bedroom. Could be another bedroom maybe? Don't open it in case it's occupied, but it could be only a cupboard... Aim for the front door. *Oops* – a chair, yes. Keep going – slowly – a hall table – correction, a corner table. She'd reached what she presumed was the front wall of the house. *Yes...* She felt a glass panelled door – could be into a porch. If only she could switch on a light it would be easier.

The inside door opened and it was a porch entrance, a coir doormat jagged her feet, but disappointment for her – the front door, it was locked. She felt around for a key – people tended to hang them at the side or put them on the ledge above – no success, all she encountered was a handful of dust.

So, back into the hall she went. Slowly and carefully back along the same route, passing the two doors, there was a third on the same wall. She was about to try that when a door opened upstairs and she was suddenly blinded by the light from one of the rooms. It was panic as she shrank back against the wall and tried to imagine herself being the size of a mouse. The door closed. It was dark again. She heard the padding of bare feet across the floor. Another door was opened and there was more light for a moment – and dark again. The sound of a flushing loo, then two brief moments of light were repeated – and then darkness.

It seemed even darker than it had been until her eyes adjusted again but she'd picked out some detail of the hall.

She'd seen that she was standing not far from the wall at the far end of the hallway and almost directly opposite the front porch – and there was another door. Her guess, and hope, was that this might be into a kitchen or pantry at the back of the house, a bit like her house, and she was right. The door opened, and through she went – then lost her balance and fell forward down the two steps to a lower level. She hadn't expected that... One of the new swear words she'd used a couple of days ago was repeated as the pain shot up her leg, but at least this time it was only mouthed silently, *and it did help*. When she had confirmed that no serious damage had been done, she reached back up and closed the door gently behind her. If she could find the switch perhaps she could have some light. She stopped herself. If there was a window in this room the light shining outside might be noticed upstairs, particularly if everywhere is pitch black. She gave herself a pat on the back for smart thinking and moved forward.

"Damn." She couldn't stop herself speaking out this time, as she banged her knee against something solid – a heavy kitchen chair?

She froze – and listened – no sounds...

Her hands reached out and she moved forward again this

time feeling her way along the edge of a long table. Part way along, her hand brushed against an object lying there. It moved. She felt carefully. It was a mobile phone.

That goes with me she decided and put it in her pocket, and carried on.

There was a slight glimmer of light and she could see vaguely it could be another door. Or is it a cupboard? No... Again she was lucky. She was into another porch and at the back door. Her feet hit something lying on the floor next to the door, and she stumbled. It was a wellington boot – and there was the other. Could be handy...? Another bristly coir door mat...

She tried the door. It didn't move. Disappointment... It had been too much to hope for... The door handle and lock seemed loose... And then her hands felt a slip bolt. Move it slowly...so... quietly... and turn the door handle ever so gently...

AND THE DOOR WAS OPEN...

Stop, she told herself. Let your heart catch up. She stepped outside. It was pouring down rain in bucketfuls – but she didn't care. *She was out.*

"Ouch," she cried out, but softly, as she left the doorstep and placed her foot on the loose gravel path.

"Ouch," again as she took the weight of her body on both feet.

"Rain and pain – could be a job for boots..." and she reached back in the doorway and brought out the wellingtons from the dark. It was difficult for her to judge whether they were two or three sizes too big, but loose-fitting or not, that was her only choice, so she went along the path towards the house front wearing them, flapping around her legs. They were miles too big. With each step they were threatening to drop off her feet.

It was hard to control her eagerness to leave. There was now a little more light reaching her from a lamp-post on the other side of the high hedge, but it continued to be awkward to move quickly.

And then she noticed the bike.

It was sitting upright against the house wall and was just crying out to her to jump on.

She grabbed it, but as soon as she started to roll it along the path, the noise began.

Squeak – squeak – squeak – so she hoisted it on her shoulder.

She smiled to herself in the pouring rain, as she remembered that only a week ago, after she'd had a lovely luxury bubble bath, followed by a little nightcap, she had gone to bed and slept soundly, thinking that nothing out of the ordinary ever happened in *her* life.

The over-sized wellingtons and the slippery grass didn't help her balance and she almost fell over.

Deep breaths, and again, moving forward, calmly.

Walking on the grass at the side of the path made less noise than the crunch of the gravel and she reached the front gate silently.

It seemed wise to walk some distance along the road away from the house before cycling because of the squeak, and she did. Then out on to the road she went, eagerly, and being an experienced cyclist and on a man's bike, she thought nothing of swinging her leg over the saddle and free-wheeling away – she almost lost a wellington with that manoeuvre.

"What the...?" she said aloud as her bottom contacted the razor sharp saddle. "They will probably be glad I took this away with me," she thought as she gritted her teeth and pedalled.

To her, the squeaking sounded very loud in the silence of the night although the rain probably deadened it somewhat. The wellingtons slipped and flapped, but on she went. She wondered how far from home she was, but her main concern was to be as far away from her prison as quickly as possible. The surroundings were vaguely familiar to her, blurred – and then suddenly recognisable...

She was only a few miles away from her home – she'd expected to be in the next town or farther – and she was cycling the wrong way, but she kept going. Returning and passing the house would be chancing fate.

She was on a long circuitous route, with a painful saddle,

wellingtons flapping about, and in the pouring rain, but she was happy, free, and going home to her loved ones.

If she'd looked back as she'd gone out the gate, and had been wearing her glasses, she might just have noticed the four pairs of eyes that had been watching her secret departure...

30

This was another 'Toozlethwaite' household tradition – a second Gran/Derek tradition. *"Happy Birthday to you... Happy Birthday to you..."*

There was the 'good-bye kisses' routine, and there was the 'birthday waken-you-up-and-get-you-out-of-bed' routine. The latter annual event had arrived again, today.

Granny Smith, who could sing no better than Derek, in fact, considerably worse, had been at his bedside every birthday morning for as long as he could remember to warble him awake. Today, it was something that he didn't really want to hear – especially now he was getting old. He was *thirty*. It seemed no time since he was a boy but this last week he felt he'd grown old rapidly. In truth, he'd matured only in some ways, and that was thanks to meeting Sally.

Downstairs there were two presents on the breakfast table – a large parcel, and an envelope.

Sally was upset and embarrassed when she came down because she hadn't known. She was annoyed that Derek hadn't told her that today was special for him, but he said she'd enough on her plate, and anyway, a hug from her would be better than a present. And hugging was still the state of play when Grandad appeared.

"You're p-p-p-putting me r-r-right off my b-b-breakfast," he growled but he didn't really mean it. He ignored them and pulled in his chair and waited expectantly for another morning of bacon and eggs. Having a visitor had created this unexpected bonus for him. No doubt, when Sally left, he'd be back to fetching the cornflakes himself. He was in for another day of walking, having no bike, so nothing would stop him enjoying this large breakfast to see him through his work – certainly not their hugging and a kissing. At one time the youthful Hector and his dear wife had been like that, hugging and kissing at any excuse – but that was a long time ago. There was less effort needed for a quick peck nowadays.

Derek opened the big parcel – from Granny Smith, a hand-knitted pullover. Pity the sleeves were too long but she'd done it secretly and used Grandad as the model and he was obviously a monkey by comparison to Derek. It will be altered right away, said Gran. Derek was a little relieved that he wouldn't have to feel guilty about not wearing it today – it was a lovely summer's day outside again. He broke sweat just thinking of it.

"Thanks Gran."

The envelope was from Grandad. It was a year's subscription for a men's magazine – one of the 'special' men's magazines.

"It c-c-c-can be changed – you c-c-c-could have the P-p-people's F-f-friend or the B-b-b-beano. Something t-t-t-tamer if you want," he offered. The glare from his wife forced him to continue the little speech, "...ehm... I'll take it b-b-back and get an ordinary b-b-b-book t-t-token and you c-c-can m-m-make your own s-s-s-selection." He smiled weakly at his wife but she continued to glare back.

To make up for no present, Sally offered to take Derek back to her home that night and make him a special meal as a birthday treat. And it would give her a chance to tidy and clean the house in the hope of her mum returning soon.

Granny was a bit disappointed but hid it with a smile. She'd really enjoyed Sally's presence in the house. Wouldn't it be nice having her as a *grand-daughter-in-law*? What a mouthful, she thought. If it did work out for the pair of them, she'd simplify that title – it would be nicer to welcome a simple *Sally* into the family – yes that's what she'd say. She was a nice girl, had a nice name, and she hoped she'd be able to welcome her soon.

Interestingly, Sally was now part of the house farewell

routine.

'Gran kisses' for both as she and Derek left together.

Back at the Newingsworth Weekly Gazette, this had been a good week for Rob Sheldon. For him, gambling had become fun again. Spider and Rob were now more like pals than boss and employee and not only was Rob's debt reducing, horse racing and the joys of betting were to become weekly features of the newspaper. This would be a novelty for this weekly paper and Rob was confident it would bring in new readership.

It had, in a very short time, become a comfortable working team and when Rob was told by Sally it was Derek's birthday, the four of them went together for a celebratory few drinks, at Rob's expense, after work. When they came to leave the bar, the weather had changed. Rain had started and was more than just a shower.

Sally and Derek didn't have very far to go but a taxi was called and they went home dry. Derek reminded Sally, as she left the taxi outside her home, to ensure this time that she'd taken all her belongings with her. He didn't feel like running behind a taxi with three pints of beer wallowing around inside.

Mrs Masterton was home and her curtain shook slightly as the taxi stopped next door. She watched as Sally and Derek alighted and walked to the door. Derek had his arm around Sally's shoulder and to Mrs Masterton's keen eye they were looking at each other in a sort of airy-fairy way. Then they stopped at the entrance and kissed.

"Hmmm, Sally..." she thought, but not at all disapprovingly, "It's a while since you were last naughty..." and she sat down to continue watching the Sky Horror Movie of the Month.

Sally's father had not been home.

Inside, various bits and pieces were still all around, as they'd been left, so the first task was tidying up a little, for which Derek volunteered. Sally's bedroom remained the mess that Sally seemed to like, so he didn't offer to do anything with that. Nor was he stupid enough to comment or criticise. He didn't want to upset her in any way.

Derek did a good job, even in his slightly inebriated condition and brought the downstairs rooms back to a reasonable state. He even found that he could operate a vacuum cleaner – he hadn't realised he had that skill.

"Why have a *gran* and Hoover yourself?" he'd learned from his grandad and it had been their working motto, up till now.

Meanwhile Sally had gone into the bottomless freezer and started to rustle up what turned out to be a lovely ad hoc birthday dinner. He was hoping that after dinner there might be some treats to come, but it was a vain hope.

Sally became quite morose.

It could have been a few too many vodkas of course, but she suddenly started to sob and pour out her worries about her mum. It was now five days that her mum had been missing. Sally began to fantasise that maybe something worse than just being held hostage had happened. Derek's shirt front became a wet soggy mess as he attempted vainly to comfort her.

They were alone, and likely to remain alone all night, but any special birthday treat that may have been promised, and that he had been looking forward to, became less and less likely with every sob... So the outcome was, Sally went off tearfully to attempt some sleep in her messy bedroom, and Derek stretched out downstairs under a blanket on the large settee in the living room and they both slept – with alcohol perhaps contributing a soporific effect.

Derek normally would have relied on late night television. He was used to waking up in an armchair with a flickering bluish light around him, and toddling to his bed in the middle of the night. Tonight was different. He'd carefully removed his trousers and his shirt and folded them neatly, thanks to Granny training, and promptly dropped off.

His awakening was abrupt.

"Where am I?" the initial question, quickly followed by, what the heck was all that noise.

It was the doorbell. Someone was persistent.

"It will be the police," he decided, "...because it *always is* in the middle of the night, isn't it?"

He threw back the blanket and stood shakily. It was dark in the room. Luckily the hall light had been left burning or he would probably have stood up, and then just gone round in circles.

Sally hadn't appeared downstairs and must be sleeping through this racket. The doorbell sounded again – and again... Didn't they realise he was on his way? The noise was painful.

He bumped into the standard lamp and switched it on with difficulty, then went and opened the outside door. It was still raining heavily. Standing there was a bedraggled figure.

"*Oh, my goodness...*" the female voice said.

Derek should have put on his glasses. Who was it? He should also have switched on the outside light. He stood with the hall light behind him, a shadowy figure. At least he was wearing his underpants.

"... Sorry, I've come to the wrong house, I... Wait a minute this *is* my house. *Who are you?*" she demanded. "And what are you doing in my house? I am Muriel Donaldson and I live here."

"It's Sally's Mum? *Wow...*" and Derek totally involuntarily stepped out into the rain, wrapped his arms around her and gave her a big bear hug.

Muriel Donaldson suddenly thought she'd walked straight into a trap. This was another of the gang and she started to struggle and pull herself from his grip – but just before she screamed for help she saw what looked like *her Sally* appear in the hallway – Muriel had no glasses on either, remember.

"*Mum,*" was the yell and the three of them stood in the pouring rain hugging, and crying, and laughing, all at the same time.

An unusual way to meet her future son-in-law she thought afterwards, as Sally blurted out, "Mum, this is Sweaty."

The oversized wellingtons and the bike had done a good job, but they could now be left at the doorstep.

The next stage for each of the wet but happy trio was a warm bath and shower.

Derek was last, and on his own – which for him was another

disappointment. So he sat in soggy underpants and finished off the wine while he waited.

Mrs Masterton was pleased to observe all the next-door doorstep goings-on from her upstairs window – she really didn't mind being disturbed like this, she was a very light sleeper anyway – and she would hate to miss anything. She happily went back to bed. Muriel was such a nice neighbour – she must have been on holiday...

Oh, and this dear little old lady *really* liked that young fellow in the y-fronts – *and she was still capable of a naughty dream or two...*

31

Andy Woodstock was not a happy chap. He'd had a dressing-down from his boss – his second in only a few days.

The first had been for disclosing the value of the small sum of stolen money to someone who'd been earmarked, by Andy himself, as a suspect. How amateurish can you get, he had been asked? Especially as it had conflicted with his superior's instructions.

The recent criticism had been for having made little, if any, progress in his assigned case – 'a piece of cake' as his boss had described it. That senior officer knew very well it was proving to be difficult to solve, but junior officers have to be driven and, in the case of Mr Andy Pandy Woodstock, driven hard. Having few clues and awkward interviews was totally *his* problem. *"Get on with it,"* he'd been instructed and, *"...of course you are not getting any help."* The others had important cases to solve, *"and we mustn't forget the bet..."* he was reminded.

His boss was convinced that Bisko's had been an inside job. The woman in the office must have known and wasn't really a hostage, in his opinion. "Prove me wrong," he'd told Andy Pandy, something Andy would dearly love to do, but how?

The money found in the handbag, three thousand pounds, he had now concluded, was coincidental. According to the Store Manager it would have been mainly small denomination notes destined to be used for the tills that would have been taken. The package found in the suspect's handbag had been *large value* paper money. He hadn't discovered its source but he accepted it could be legit.

He'd interviewed Ms Sally Donaldson, or perhaps she had interviewed him – he was unsure on that... It would have been overly cocky for her to be part of the gang and then carry the stolen money about in her handbag, surely – especially if she was related to the woman who was *supposed* to be a hostage.

And the guy she had been with – he'd been the one who had apparently been causing trouble in the Newingsworth Public Park and then in Bisko's Supermarket Car Park, as his investigation had discovered. "Sweaty..." *Yughhh* – what a nickname to have... Could he be part of the gang too?

The stolen Range Rover had been found earlier today in the woods outside Slatterfoot. It was undamaged. Fingerprints had been found and some identified, the owner and his family had been eliminated. He'd been able to identify Muriel Donaldson's, although not conclusively, by comparison with those from her house, but the others couldn't be found on file. It was likely that this mob were 'first-timers' – hence the low quality standards achieved in this robbery. If it had been seen as a more serious case, he could have arranged for DNA checks as well.

He'd thought at least of charging this Sweaty character in association with the damage to the Mini Cooper – wilful damage, but a witness said he'd only jumped out of the way – pity the trolley had missed him. It was the idiot who owned the Range Rover who'd been pushing the trolley and was totally to blame.

It would be nice to have Sweaty for something – he didn't like suspects to escape 'Scot Free' – even if they were innocent, and especially one called *Sweaty*. That must be a crime in itself. He could imagine having him in court. *'Is your name Sweaty Toozlethwaite?'* He'd probably answer, *'Yes, but would you please call me Derek...'* The sap...

These thoughts tumbled around in the young detective's head, which had become a bit like a cement mixer and in his case the cement was hardening fast. Going over the details had prevented him getting any decent sleep tonight so far.

He knew that he could be really grumpy on the many occasions he'd been wakened from a really deep sleep, so, it was maybe just as well that he was only dozing when his mobile rang...

"Sally Donaldson speaking – I was..." he caught but he was too slow. The message had already started to record on his answer service as he'd grabbed the device.

He waited a moment and then heard the remainder of the message.

"... phoning to tell you the good news – my mother has arrived home. You might be interested. Hic. Bye-ee... Derek please stop – that tickles... Sweaty, I said... now... don't do... hmmmm"

32

It had been Derek who said that the police should be informed right away, even though it was the middle of the night.

"No rush," Muriel had replied, "We can do it later. Let's have something to eat and drink. I feel I need to relax before they start to grill me – I know that's what they'll do."

No-one argued with her. She was the one who'd had the ordeal although outwardly she seemed remarkably robust after what she'd been through.

So they opened a bottle of wine.

Sally made sandwiches while Muriel got to know Derek a little more, in the drier conditions, and he was proving to be a likeable young man. In fact, if she'd been twenty years younger – oh dear, the wine was going straight to her head, wasn't it...

Deep down Muriel didn't want Tich or Beakie to be caught – she liked them and even after her enforced confinement would prefer them to be away before the police arrived to arrest them, because inevitably that's what had to happen once she'd made the phone call. She'd escaped over three hours ago. A lot can happen in a short time. She wasn't to know that they'd helped her escape. Or that they were rich.

Dozy, Beakie, Mick, and Tich, all had smiles on their faces as they'd watched her tiptoe off the premises, in fact, Beakie would have liked to have carried the bike for her. It's not every day that you have *three million two hundred thousand pounds* to divide between four. Tich had been watching the Wednesday lottery draw, late because of some live reporting of another major political scandal. She had, as usual, noted the numbers automatically in a sleepy manner, but then she'd recognised one, then two, up to six numbers, and then the bonus ball. These were the very ones they had been using for their little syndicate for years.

No, she'd told herself, impossible – and she'd checked.

Yes, she'd told herself – and she'd double-checked... and then she'd told the others – and together they'd checked yet again and *still* had difficulty believing it could be possible.

When they collected the cheque, they would each have eight-hundred-thousand pounds – *unbelievable.* If only they could have foreseen the future they wouldn't have had to break the law. They'd only done it for the money. It was small wonder that Muriel was given a glass of wine. The four gang members felt absolutely marvellous, but guilty for what they'd participated in, and utter dislike for Thelma – all fuelled by a bottle of wine each.

So, they'd sat and re-planned their lives.

They couldn't bring themselves to tell Muriel that they were releasing her just because they didn't need her any more. They decided they could let her escape. That would be a better story for her to tell others later – how *she'd* done it...

They had packed up the few items each had with them in readiness for when Muriel was out of sight – knowing almost certainly she would leave on the bike, which would be placed so she couldn't miss it – and then they could depart – rapidly.

Muriel would *have* to inform the police, they knew that. How long after she left before the police appeared was anybody's guess, so they would have to move out fast. They had to make full use of the short time they had – or they wouldn't be collecting their lottery winnings quite as they would like – freely.

Beakie and Tich let their female instincts take over, and annoyed Dozy and Mick, by insisting that it wouldn't be nice for the owner of this house to return to a mess. So the place would have to be clean and tidy before they left. Reluctantly the males went along with it (or they'd never hear the end of it, they decided) and while Muriel was still in her room they set about clearing up any disruption they'd caused. The only thing they couldn't sort was the entry damage to the rear door lock.

So, the plan was, the moment Muriel went out of the gate, they'd go too. They'd walk well away from this house and phone for taxis from different spots. Individually they'd make their own way back to their two homes by different routes to make it less obvious where they'd been. An important point was the splitting of the remaining cash from the Supermarket job. Well, they felt they'd earned it and they couldn't very well hand it back. It was an awful lot of banknotes each had to take – but they were forcing themselves to cope – and then they had a rethink.

It was a good job that Muriel hadn't reversed her cycle route and passed the house, or she would have seen four separate shadowy figures scurrying along the road in the rain – delighted to have no masks on.

It wasn't until later when he went to phone for his taxi that Dozy realised he didn't have Sally's mobile. He'd left it on the kitchen table and he was sure it wasn't there when they'd left. Everything had been clean and tidy...

33

Thelma was a twisted individual, full of jealousy and self-pity. It was not surprising that when Steve had first met her in the pub he'd thought of her as a 'Scary Lady'. Steve had described her as good-looking all right, but in an odd way and it was difficult to say why that was.

Now, she was sitting in the flat, lonely for an adoring husband and jealous of any woman who had been successful in finding one. She had given up hope of finding the right person – a man she could really love, and who would remain faithful. In fact the self-pity had gone much farther to more like hating men.

Holding the mirror steady wasn't easy. As she applied the lipstick, her hands were trembling, a reaction she'd been having lately more and more but it stopped with the alcohol. She'd received the text messages sent by Steve and was deeply unhappy. What a ridiculous sum they'd stolen. She'd screamed down the phone at him – with enough venom to make him waken up his ideas. That outburst had not released successfully the pressures building in her head so she'd lain in the darkened room brooding, and created greater pain.

It was her fault. She had been too eager to make it happen and too spiteful to be patient. She was full of self-criticism for having selected him in the first place to lead and partly organise the raid. He'd proved totally incompetent. Bad judgement on her part – that mistake will happen only once, she determined. She should have read the signs earlier on. He was weak and soft, and had proved much too pliable, little backbone. Never once had he stood up to her or questioned her judgement. Being really tough with him would be the obvious action if the big plan was to succeed.

He'd ruined the effect she'd wanted from the Supermarket robbery. The text telling her how little they'd taken had sent her into an enormous ranting and raving fit. How *dare* he fail in that stupid manner. No publicity from it at all – probably because the Police and the Press had been embarrassed by the gang's incompetence – *she* certainly was. She had given him precise instructions and he hadn't *followed* them precisely.

He will suffer shortly... and as for taking both the woman *and* a girl with them ...that had not been the instruction she'd given – *he had been told.* His timing and his reactions had been totally wrong.

She became more annoyed each time she thought about it... And the ransom text... it should have been more brutal – to force a quicker reaction. No money had appeared yet, even though the deadline had arrived.

The cut-off finger should be next. That will put pressure on the husband. No doubt it would scare that wimp Steve, witless, having to do something tough, she decided.

Yes, we're at that point now.

I'll text him tomorrow and tell him what to say and give him precise timing – and I'll warn him that if he fails this time...

In the mirror, although she could see a few more lines on this face, to her it was a nice face, a kind face, a gentle face... she was becoming upset over nothing, she told herself.

The pressure in her head could not be seen but she felt the pain worsen – and reached for the bottle.

Then she thought, *Am I perhaps over-dramatising this whole thing?*

34

This was real relaxation. Muriel put her feet up on her own settee, yes, her *own* settee, and lay back, slightly tipsy, partially from the joy of being safe and partly from the excellent wine she was consuming freely.

As for Derek Toozlethwaite, what a mouthful for a name, she'd found him to be a very nice young man – so easy to talk to and he had a way with words. He was the choice of her daughter who obviously had impeccable taste, so like her mother. 'It's amazing how strong drink can sharpen up a person's logic' was the thought that went hazily through her mind... and she must remember his name... She had been corrected by Sally twice, and by the young man once, firmly but politely, so she wanted sincerely to get it right.

Now what was it again? Was she *supposed* to call him *Sweaty?*

As the happy three sat sprawled out, she'd recounted all she could about the ordeal, and that included a slightly tipsy and hazily remembered synopsis of each book that she'd read while she had been captive. Sally and Derek learned that there was a female controlling the gang from a distance who sounded really nasty. Sometimes Muriel had heard the gang refer to her as Thelma and other times as the 'scary lady'. That woman had never been at the hostage house, as far as Muriel knew.

That woman – *Thelma?* No... A blast from the past? Not her *sister*-in-law... Couldn't possibly be... Why hadn't she thought of that before? No, she wouldn't... Thirty years almost and she'd nearly forgotten all about her existence. She could be dead for all she knew. Quite a coincidence though – it was an unusual name. *Could be this wine...*

"Top up my glass, please, Sweaty, would you?"

Sally told her mother of the ransom demand and how much it had been. This amount was news to Muriel and she thought of the terrible strain it must have had on her husband. *One hundred thousand pounds...* Was she worth that much? The high value gave her a tiny frisson of pleasure.

She should phone and tell the police all this information too, but that could wait just a little while longer – some more wine anyone?

One thing she suddenly realised, she hadn't yet seen her husband. She blamed the drink for her failing to ask about him earlier. "Where's your father, Sally? He's surely not sleeping upstairs is he? Just like him to miss all the excitement as usual," and she laughed ironically, but Sally didn't know where he was.

"He disappears off to his club, I think. He hasn't been living here since you went missing. I don't think he could face the place without you being here with him."

She said that to keep her mum happy and deep inside she knew that was not the case at all. Her dad's behaviour recently seemed to have become more disturbing and erratic in her view.

"Shouldn't we phone his club and let him know. He must have been anxious about me, and particularly if he's been raising money for a ransom. And such a lot too. He never likes spending, does he?"

That's when Muriel remembered the mobile phone she'd slipped into her pocket. She had to search through the pile of soggy clothes that had been thrown on the floor of the laundry room but eventually she found it. It could have finished up in the washing machine, she realised. She took it back into the living room and sat down again. When she said where it had come from, Derek immediately thought of fingerprints, those of the gang's as well as Muriel's now.

"Mum, that's the same as my phone." ...Muriel handed it to her daughter. "It *is* my phone," Sally declared after looking and recognising numbers on the directory list, "...but a few numbers have been added, and it's filthy." She reached over and cleaned it with Derek's shirt tail, which happened to be convenient, as Derek's fuddled brain tried to formulate the words *"Don't"* and *"Fingerprints"* and failed.

She looked in more detail at the contents and also saw the calls that had been made. "The cheeky sods have been using my phone. Let's see who they called."

She dialled one of the numbers.

"Sam'sa Pizza Palace, whatta you wanna we supplya you tonighta?" sang out an Italian voice.

"Sorry wrong number," and she hung up.

She then found the ransom text. That was chilling – she said nothing of that to her mother. Derek of course was well aware of the content of that.

"Phone your father. There's sure to be a porter or someone at least to give him a message," said Mum.

Sally dialled her dad's mobile.

It rang for a long time and she let it continue.

"Hello... What is it?"

He had obviously been wakened from a deep sleep.

"Hello, who's that? Do you know what time it is?" he demanded.

"It's Sally. I've news about Mum..."

"What? You can't have... Oh... Couldn't it have waited until morning? Did you have to wake me at this time?"

This was the husband who was anxious, was it? Sally's face burned in anger but she controlled her voice.

"Mum's right beside me and would like to talk to you. I'll pass the phone to her"

"What?" And his tone changed entirely. *"Muriel... How are you darling? What a trauma for you. Thank goodness you are back home. The police have been absolutely dreadful. I'll be having a word with the Chief Constable next time he's here at the club."*

Some more idle loving chat ensued, with the finale that he

would be back from his club in the morning – after he'd re-arranged the not-now-required finances.

Muriel ended the call and took another sip from her glass.

"I'd better phone the police – while I'm sober – *hic*," said Sally's mother. "...Better still, Sally, be a dear and let them know I'm back, presuming they care."

So, Sally filled her glass once more to ease the tension her father had caused, took a long drink, and rang.

It was the number that detective Andy Pandy had given her. He wanted any information she could remember, or found out, to be passed directly to him, at any time of the day or night. The phrase had sort of spilled out of his mouth automatically but he hadn't meant it and he'd hoped that the insincerity had been appreciated. He definitely had not said, *Make sure it's about four o'clock in the morning when I'm sound asleep,* but because Sally looked on him as a cheeky sod, she didn't care if it *was* a bother to him.

She'd also had a few drinks too many. So, she rang the detective, left the message, and poured some more wine.

Andy Woodstock was now wide awake, telling himself as he always did in these circumstances that he was in the wrong job. Beachcombing in Australia had always appealed to him – no money and no frigging mobile phones and no police work, and he was sure he'd grow to like sand...

He felt obliged to wear a clean shirt. Being a born-again bachelor, changing his shirt was not always a priority. A wife to wash and iron his shirts for him was one of the few benefits, from his previous short marriage, that he missed. When he'd used all his clean shirts, it meant having to carry out another task he disliked, taking his dirty clothes to the launderette.

He occasionally had a twinge of conscience that his life was becoming filled by incidents and things he disliked – he even disliked having that feeling, but he was also mentally creating a list of all the things he liked. So far it had included only Ice Cream – but now, wide awake, washed and dressed, he could add 'success'. He liked, and craved, success, and in his bones he felt this phone message was about to lead him in the right direction – *at last*. He'd show his boss how good he was.

His middle of the night enthusiasm waned somewhat when he stepped outside and found it was pouring. Living in a flat in town meant leaving the car where you could find a space that wasn't restricted parking. The space he'd found last night had not been on his doorstep – and he disliked that.

He reached his destination, the Cloverton Estate, feeling his wet clothes clinging to him, and it still rained, but in this neighbourhood he was spoiled for parking spaces. He stopped right outside the house – he'd add that to the list – it was something else he liked.

He noticed the street lights here were fairly old fashioned and gave poor light on a wet night like this. Probably something the local residents had fought for – made this avenue special. This place had always given him the impression of being a district of elderly but rich people who were resistant to change but also who probably still had influence in the town, and knew how to get their own way.

In this dim light he found the stolen bike lying flat on the ground in front of the doorsteps – by tripping over it. He also noted that a pair of wellingtons was sitting on the doorstep and filling up with rainwater.

He rang the doorbell.

Being a very observant detective, he also noticed Mrs Masterton's curtain twitch, so he gave her a wave. She waved back... And back to her cosy bed she went yet again. She was glad she didn't have to rise early or she wouldn't have been able to keep up with events.

It was Derek who opened the door.

"Can I help you?" he asked politely, as he held on to the door to keep himself steady.

"Detective Constable Andy Woodstock."

"Was the mistress of the house expecting you?" Derek continued.

"Come off it – you must remember me." Having to deal with

drunken idiots – yet another item for his 'dislike list' – but he bit his tongue. Keep calm, he told himself.

"Have you a card or some means of identification?" continued the slightly slurred voice. "We get all sorts here you know?"

So in the pouring rain Detective Andy Woodstock fished into his pocket to identify himself. He produced the plastic-coated identification card, the only thing that was not soaked through. He was eventually permitted entry. Maybe he should have stayed in bed. *But heavens...* What had happened in the living room? There were two bodies – one on the floor and one on the settee. Both female, one young the other not so young, he noted. Both would have been pretty when alive. No blood to be seen. What had this drunken idiot done to them?

"Oh, it's Andy Pandy... hello again..." said the younger body with one eye open. "Glad you could make the party... d'you want some wine?" and she closed the eye again.

He may be about to have success but he could sense he was going to have to work hard for it. He was a detective – he could read the signs...

35

The interview with Muriel Donaldson had been a total waste of time. It would have to begin all over again when she'd sobered up. However, this had all been done by him in his own time he told himself – his free time – *his sleeping time.* His conscience was clear. He wasn't paid to work twenty-four hours a day.

Rather than feel he'd got out of bed and arrived here to be soaked in the pouring rain for nothing, this detective had succumbed to a drink of wine – and then another, and another.

That is why Derek, who was sleeping on the settee, woke up and was surprised to find he was cuddling Detective Constable Andy Pandy Woodstock. He would rather it had been Sally, or even his favourite teddy bear, rather than this berk. He gave a shudder and jumped up quickly.

The detective snored on.

Derek's head was pounding as badly as it had been last week when he'd had the visitation from the angels, but this time it had been self-inflicted and no accident. The medicine cabinet gave him choices but none which would provide the instantaneous effect that he required.

What day was it?

"It is..." his brain was still asleep – try again... "It is...THURSDAY." See it can be done if you try hard enough...

Thursday... He should have been at the office over an hour ago – and Sally too. Was she still sleeping? What would their boss say? Especially after all last week's capers...

Andy Woodstock, the ambitious detective constable, snorted, and turned over, and continued to snore away.

A phone call was required to apologise to Rob Sheldon. Where had he put his mobile? Derek felt in his trouser pocket – he couldn't find it. What had he done with his jacket? He'd had a jacket last night, hadn't he? He didn't feel up to a house-search for the missing garment. Ah – Sally's old pink phone was lying on the coffee table where she'd left it. He told himself that she wouldn't mind if he apologised for the pair of them, and he dialled the editor's mobile.

There were a lot of funny noises at the other end when that phone was answered by young Master Raymond Sheldon, the three-year-old. Derek went into his special 'speaking to a three-year-old' voice automatically and asked little Raymond for his daddy – and then felt foolish in case the others had heard him. No-one else was awake. Little Raymond insisted on telling Derek a story but it was not in words that Derek's brain could successfully interpret so he said, "Ah... that's nice..." at the end of it and again asked the little fellow to hand the phone to his Daddy.

Derek held on.

At the other end of the phone, Daddy Sheldon had been abruptly wakened by a mobile phone dropping from a tiny hand onto his head. Derek grinned sadly as he heard the 'clunk' and visualised his boss's face.

"Ouch. What the...? Bloody hell."

Derek heard that very clearly.

Derek heard the little voice say, *"Solly Daddy..."*

Daddy Sheldon was feeling just as poorly as Derek, and maybe worse. This distinctly unwell feeling had been due to Rob and Spider having continued at the bar after Derek and Sally had gone. They both had agreed that they should eat, but not just yet. A few drinks later and it had still been much too early to eat. A few drinks later still and it had now become too late to eat and even if they had so desired, Rob and Spider could not have succeeded in finding a restaurant willing to serve two very drunken bums. When they'd left to go their separate ways home, they'd agreed it had been a great night.

Rob had been in serious trouble when he arrived home, unable to put the key in the keyhole. Waking up his wife to open the door for him had been bad. Having failed to phone earlier and say he was going to be late was worse. Having forgotten the planned visit to the theatre didn't improve matters either.

He'd slept on the couch – alone – fully dressed.

So, as far as the office was concerned, Rob had declared it to be a national holiday.

Spider had already been sitting at his office desk for over an hour twiddling his thumbs. He was obviously made of sterner stuff. As he was the only one present, by mid-morning he'd promoted himself to senior executive for each phone call he answered.

Derek was wide awake now and decided he'd play the hero and make some breakfast. He'd been here before, remember, and knew his way around this kitchen. There was a change of mind when he opened the fridge and the thought of actually cooking greasy food hit him. A cup of strong coffee became the alternative end result.

He took his hot drink back into the other room and sank into an easy chair. He swung it round to face the window to avoid having to gaze at the open-mouthed detective. A clock somewhere in the house began chiming. Derek noticed through his bleary eyes that the curtains were still closed and the room light was still on. These were heavy drapes, with a cord-pull arrangement with which he had to cope to get them open. It was now bright daylight outside and the rain had stopped. He sat down again and gazed vacantly out at the beautiful blue sky, and began to doze off.

Sally's phone rang.

The noise disturbed the slumbering detective constable, but only enough to cause him to turn over.

Derek lifted the pink phone and pressed the receive button.

"This is Thelma. Steve, answer the phone, blast you." the female voice screeched.

Derek didn't say anything – he was too surprised.

"Look, I don't know what the hell you think you're doing but you've messed up very badly and you are going to have to pay. Why didn't you tell me she'd escaped? Call me back – immediately."

And the line went dead.

Derek's mouth just hung open. Thelma? *Thelma...* That's the... *Oh, oh.* Should he tell Sally? Yes, for certain...

He looked at the lists on the phone and found several calls had been received from, and some sent to, this very person over the last few days. This looked like a main line of communication to and from the 'scary lady'.

Should he phone her back? No, he'd tell Sally first. She'd be mad if she wasn't involved in this, and he didn't like it when she was like that. He went quietly upstairs. Muriel was still asleep in her own bedroom in her own lovely comfortable bed and was making the most of it. He tip-toed passed her door...

He knocked gently on Sally's door. No answer. He opened it and went in carefully. Not being careful could lead to a twisted ankle by stepping on, or getting tangled, in the 'Sally debris'. He shook her gently and in the gloom she looked at him lovingly.

"Waken up, Sweetheart," he whispered.

"Who is it?" she asked.

"Oh..." was all he said, but thought, *who the heck was she expecting?*

"*Ha...* Got you. Only kidding. Morning Sweaty. How are you today?" she asked in an infuriatingly cheerful manner.

"Good morning Sal. Sal, I've just had a call from Thelma."

"*Thelma...* What? Why would she call you?" Sally sat up – now very awake.

"She didn't... She was calling the gang, I think, on your old phone. I didn't talk and she thought she was on an answer service. I was going to call her back but I thought you'd want to be involved."

Sally nodded, and made a face that indicated, *if you'd dared without me...*

Derek found the number and dialled.

Just as he did, they heard the front door opening and closing.

"That will be my dad at long last. I hope Mum still thinks he's wonderful this morning"

Derek pushed the call button. He heard the ringing at the other end. The female voice started to speak threateningly from the word go. *"What the hell are you up to, you fool? You let her escape. You are stupid idiots. And do you realise what that will mean now? The police... Get out of the house the lot of you – and vanish. And, I'm warning you – not a word about me, or YOU ARE DEAD."*

"Sally can you hear this?" Derek whispered and turned, but Sally was outside the door and had gone down the stairs, following the sound of the falsetto voice that was coming from the hall. Derek followed her.

She was standing looking at her father – he looked like a bank manager with a phone in his hand – *but he'd been speaking in a falsetto voice.*

And she'd heard every single word first hand.

He, or she, was *THELMA*. Her father, the respected bank manager, and secret female impersonator in his spare time – *he was Thelma.*

He stood with a frightened look in his eyes, frozen in the glare of his daughter.

"Please don't tell your mother..." he whimpered, in what was nearer his normal voice, but his screeching had been heard by someone else. Muriel had come downstairs behind Sally and was standing with eyes wide open in disbelief.

At long last Andy Woodstock surfaced. Overhearing the noises, and sharp as a button, he immediately went into officious mode as he stepped into the hall.

"Do not move anyone..." he commanded, although at that point everyone was standing stock still, in shock.

"I am a Police Officer and I am charging you with..."

"You'll never take me alive," the voice screamed out as Thelma again. *I have a gun."* and the hand flashed to the inside pocket.

Both young males immediately reacted. As Andy Pandy leapt towards Thelma, Derek swung around to shield Sally and her mother and two macho males crashed into each other.

Sally and Muriel screamed.

Thelma panicked and turned around, opened the outside door and leapt outside – and tripped over the water-filled wellingtons, falling headlong down the stairs and landing on the bike with a pain-filled cry...

Then there was silence...

Sally and Muriel started to sob and clung to each other, afraid to look.

Andy Pandy moved forward cautiously towards the prone figure and stopped at the top step in case there really had been a gun.

Derek stood looking on with his mouth hanging open in serious shock. Not only was Sally's dad possibly lying dead in front of them – his grandad's bike had come back to haunt him and the wheel was spinning around – squeaking...

Meanwhile, next door, dear old Mrs Masterton had gone to bed and fallen asleep soundly for the first time in the thirty-seven years since dear Albert, her husband, had passed away. She'd missed all the excitement caused by the visit of *Mr Donaldson's 'sister'*...?

36

That had been a bit unexpected and painful, thought Alexander Donaldson. I walked round that ruddy bike *and* the wellingtons when I went in, why did I have to fall over the *bloody* things on the way out?

He was thankful that he'd missed the pedal and it hadn't pierced his chest, however, that didn't prevent him feeling very painful everywhere, and winded. There was one lesson he'd learned this morning – don't treat a rusty bike like a bouncy castle. And don't get caught with your trousers down, by your wife, your daughter, a policeman, and that Toozle... something or other, unless you have a good explanation ready. But at least the rain had stopped.

He was thinking fast because the two males were standing at the top of the steps, peering down at him. This was viewed through half-closed eyes as he lay there on top of the bike. He wanted them to think he was out cold. He closed his eyes, and lay still.

Something had happened with the plan. Muriel shouldn't have been home yet. He hadn't given the release signal to that bunch of amateurs. Now it looked as if he was rumbled but he couldn't admit the whole truth to his wife and daughter just yet, not while that detective, and that Toozle... Woozle... whatever his name was, were there with them. He'd have to think of an explanation on the hoof.

They were coming down the stairs, two of them, and were moving exceedingly cautiously. Of course, they thought he had a gun, didn't they?

He continued to play dead – or at least unconscious...

Andy Pandy moved one direction and Derek the other, both expecting the prone figure to leap up and make a run for it. Derek could imagine the fright he'd get if he did, especially if he shouted *"BOO"* at the same time. Their last encounter had been only days ago. He could still clearly remember the moment he had been attacked by this person – and poor Derek had just gone in for a pee...

"He's out cold," said the detective, "Check his pockets."

"No, you're the nearest. You check them," responded Derek.

Andy reached down and carefully turned over the prone figure.

"I hope he hasn't made my grandad's bike any worse than it was, or else he'll be footing the bill for an insurance claim," said Derek.

Andy Pandy had confirmed there was no gun on the body, then realised he was thinking of this guy as a stiff – he was only unconscious, wasn't he? He felt for a pulse. Yea, he was alive. Where was the weapon? Had it been thrown deliberately, or even accidently, into the shrubs? At least it wasn't visible and was therefore out of reach of this maniac. He'd look for it later. The detective was reaching into his own pocket for his mobile to call for an ambulance, when the figure jerked.

Derek and Andy both jumped back.

A groan came next.

Alexander moved himself with difficulty into a sitting position, flinching – and without having to act that part. The other two stood ready to pounce.

"What happened?" he asked in a weak voice, "Where am I? Ohhhh..." and Alexander *did* act, this time, holding his brow as if his head hurt, although that was the only bit of him that wasn't actually painful. This action he thought would gain the greatest sympathy.

Alexander then added, "*Who* am I...?" and wobbled a bit as he sat there.

Muriel and Sally were now standing at the top of the steps,

holding on to each other, obviously and genuinely shocked.

"Daddy," and *"Alexander,"* came from the females, as they scurried down the steps to help him.

"Don't just stand there, you two. Get him inside – onto the settee," Sally instructed and the two males leapt into action, grabbing an arm and a leg each, ignoring the 'Ouch' noises coming from the bank manager as he was bumped up the stairs, and thrown on the settee.

Inside, Andy Pandy was told to put on the kettle and make a cup of tea, and Derek was sent to get a blanket to keep her father warm.

Alexander was really appreciating both his daughter's concern, and how luxurious the settee felt, as he lay there, particularly after the discomfort of the bicycle, but he hadn't quite reasoned out the way to go yet. Should he be suffering memory loss, and find out the detective's next move? He could gradually return to normal – once he'd rationalised a plan himself? Some of the truth might be acceptable just now, but he'd have to supply it in small doses, and hope he wasn't arrested in the meantime...

"Sit up, Dad, and drink this," and Sally supported him and held the cup of hot sweet tea to his lips. It had been a long time since Alexander Donaldson had felt so close to his daughter, and a rare occurrence to receive sympathy from her. His wife was holding his hand and stroking it gently. He could get to like this...

"Right... now let's find out what's been going on here then," said the officious young detective taking control of the room and its occupants.

Derek felt he should have his own notebook in his hand with a pencil poised ready, because he sensed there was about to be an interesting story coming, but he couldn't think where either piece of his essential journalist's equipment might be.

"Where am I?" asked Alexander in a dazed looking manner, then thought he'd chance it a little more by asking Muriel, "... and *who* are *you*?"

"Oh, my poor darling... I'm your wife, Muriel. Relax now, you are in safe hands and you are at home..."

"Has the money been sent to the charity yet, dear wife?" asked the weak voice...

"What money? Alexander, darling," she replied in a gentle soothing voice.

"Am I... *Alexander Darling?* Is that my name? Is that *really* my name? It's a lovely name," and he sounded so pitiful...

"Dad – *what* money?"

"And you must be my daughter... I didn't know I had a daughter... That's nice..."

Alexander didn't think he would get away with this for much longer. He could sense that the two men were looking somewhat sceptical about his memory failure, but he had to keep going.

"Enough of this nonsense," said Detective Constable Woodstock, "I'm arresting you on the suspicion of your involvement in the kidnapping of Muriel Donaldson, and for being the mastermind of the robbery at the Bisko Supermarket."

"Don't be silly now, young man," said Muriel, "Can't you see my husband is unwell. Anything that he may have said earlier was only one big joke. Any fool could see that, and now he can't remember anything about it and must be exhausted, and in pain. So, off you go now. We'll look after him and phone you when you can speak to him. He's not going anywhere and, anyway, you look as if you could do with a good sleep and a good wash yourself. No arguments please... *Off you go.*"

He regretted it afterwards, but a humbled Detective Constable, feeling very sorry for himself, had been ushered out of the door, and had then driven home before it struck him how stupid he'd been... and then he couldn't find a damn parking place...

Once the cup of tea had been drunk and the detective had left the premises, Alexander Donaldson sat up.

"I think I'll go up and have a warm bath and a lie down, so if you'll excuse me," and he stood.

"Of course, darling, that would be best..." replied Muriel, who was tidying the room a little and clearing away the wine glasses and empty bottles.

Sally had plugged in the vacuum cleaner and was working her way around the room and just smiled at her father as he passed and went into the hall.

Derek sat in the chair and watched all this, lifting his legs dutifully when Sally reached his floor area with the vacuum, but wondering how a man who knew absolutely nothing about himself, not even his own name, was able to stand up and walk straight to the bathroom and never even had to question where his bedroom was... Could be the healing power of the sweet tea, he supposed...

He sat watching Sally. She moved beautifully and she certainly knew how to handle that vacuum. She looked over at him. He smiled back, dreamily...

"Couldn't you do something useful Derek?" snapped him out of his reverie, "... like collecting the post. The mailman's just been, I think," said his beloved. He had, and some letters had been left, and the usual pile of junk mail and catalogues, which were almost sure to be destined for the bin. Derek stood with the bundle in his hand in a reflective mood... Why isn't there a bin at the entrance to each house, or better still at the exit from the Post Office, where the postman could place junk mail and catalogues, rather than through all the letterboxes? Oh, then he'd have nothing to deliver, that's why...

Derek separated personal mail and junk. Four letters this morning, one for Mrs Muriel Donaldson, two for Mr A Donaldson, and one for the Occupier. Seven pieces of junk, which included −four for ladies underwear, one for essential kitchen appliances, one for the bargains at Bisko's this coming week, and a card to inform Mr Donaldson that he'd won the Chinese National Lottery and to claim the prize he would be required to send his bank details to the undernoted address in Slovenia. Derek presumed the card to be junk.

He took the mail through into the kitchen and handed the bundle to Muriel. She glanced at the catalogues without opening them and threw them into the bin at the other end of the kitchen.

To be correct, she threw them towards the bin – Derek had to pick them up, and put them in.

She laid down the letters for her husband but opened the one for herself. She began to read it as Derek went back to the front room.

Sally was seated and looking at a magazine. Derek sat down beside her and put his arm round her waist. He squeezed, and leaned forward as she turned her head. A little kiss seemed appropriate at that moment and lips were about to touch gently – when the scream came from the kitchen...

"Sally... Sweaty.... Come quickly..."

Muriel was standing holding the letter, with a shocked look on her face. She held up the handwritten piece of paper for Sally and Derek to see, and pointed to the signature of the sender...

37

It was most unlike Derek to feel confused – but he'd thought that they'd established it earlier, wasn't Thelma the gentleman who had just gone upstairs? Suddenly he had a vivid flashback to that first moment they'd met – in a bedroom in this very house – on a water bed – the scarlet underwear on a very curvaceous body... and the black silk stockings... and... Was *gentleman* the correct terminology?

He shook his head vigorously and the image went – that's better...

This letter, now being held by Sally and Derek, had been posted in London. It didn't seem to have any threat attached to it, in fact, it was a letter which seemed to want to make amends, but to make amends for what? Derek certainly did not know...

Muriel thought she did, but there were many other things happening today which didn't make sense to her. Should she stop and try to explain them to the two youngsters? No chance... It could be that her errant husband was the one who would help – she hadn't been taken in by his hammy acting. She'd been a supportive wife but she'd been acting that out as well, and would continue to do so – for his sake – for the moment. What Alexander had to say could influence her future thoughts of course, and *now* might be the time to ask pertinent questions... *Alexander Darling* – indeed...

"Alexander..."

"I was just about to run a bath, Sweetie Pie," came the voice from upstairs, "Can't it wait?"

"No, *Alexander Donaldson*, it would be nice if you came

down – *just now...*" shouted the voice from the kitchen, and meant it.

"Maybe I should leave?" suggested a slightly less than comfortable Derek.

"No, Sweaty, if you are going to be part of the family, you might as well be involved with the gory bits too," replied Muriel, who now appeared to be warming up and spoiling for a fight. "And he'd better have a good story," she muttered under her breath.

It was a shame-faced bank manager in a bath robe, who appeared, but a man who seemed to have miraculously regained all his mental abilities.

There would now be a family discussion in the front room.

Alexander was told to sit with his back to the door, while Muriel chose the seat facing him with her back to the window at the other end of the large room. The other two were sort of in no-man's land. Sally sat beside Derek and held his hand. He thought it was a nice gesture – and then had another thought – was it to prevent him escaping?

Muriel was holding the letter she had received. She handed it to Alexander.

"Read," was her clear instruction to her husband.

Derek considered it would be wise in the future to remain on the friendly side of this lady who would possibly become his mother-in-law. It was also obvious to him, that the detective constable, who'd departed earlier, could learn a thing or two about interrogation techniques from Sally's mum.

Alexander read, pausing occasionally to glance at the expression on his wife's face.

"Hmmmm," he said, as his eyes eventually reached the signature, "Interesting..."

"Yes," said Muriel, "isn't it. It's from your sister, your twin sister, Thelma, the sister that's hated you for years, the same name as the one who was telling the gang what to do? Yes, *very interesting...*"

"If, ehm... I could just explain..."

"And you've invited her to come here – to visit?" pushed Muriel.

"Yes, it was meant as another surprise..."

"A surprise...?"

For Sally and Derek this was similar to a tennis match, their attention jumping from one end of the room to the other, but the warm-up was over – the game was about to start.

"Yes, to be a bit like the other part... When you'd come home."

"What other part? *I am home.*"

"Look, this is not the way it was supposed to end... It's true. My sister has had nothing to do with the robbery and the kidnapping. That was my stupid idea. I've been Thelma, the one in the background, giving the gang instructions. *I was Mister Big.*"

Derek saw an obvious flaw in that statement right away, and interjected, "Shouldn't that be *Miss* Big?" and then felt self-conscious when three pairs of eyes glowered at him at the same time.

"The main reason was to bring something fresh, a different type of excitement, into the life of my dear wife. And did it?" he asked Muriel.

She hesitated, and then admitted reluctantly, and quietly "Yes..."

"I was obviously losing you and I didn't want that to happen, so I planned something different, but my plan went askew apparently," he continued quietly. Muriel had changed from being the interrogating officer, and had become a willing listener. "I only did it because I love you and wouldn't have dreamed of doing anything which could have been too unpleasant for you." Alexander stopped speaking, and just looked at his wife.

She had removed her glasses, wiped the tears from her eyes, and put her glasses back on.

Now, this was a really bad sign. Sally recognised it from previous occasions. Something was now about to happen.

Emotions were being tampered with, and that was dangerous... The tears of rage would precede a mad charge across the room by Muriel, with the heavy glass vase in her hand being used to give this smarmy git a good smack. That was the pattern of events predicted in the thoughts of both Derek and Sally. Sally's grip had tightened, painfully, on Derek's hand.

And were they disappointed? Yes?

No... they were relieved.

Muriel rose... and Alexander rose... and they moved... towards each other... slowly... looking into each other's eyes – *and they hugged...*

What? No violins...?

Kind of embarrassing, for Sally and Derek, when these two older people started moving in slow motion as if they were part of a washing powder advert...

Alexander had to get it all off his chest after that.

For a start, there was no club, and he was not a club member. He just had a little flat he'd rented for a few months where he could change his clothes without Mrs Masterton next door constantly observing and getting the wrong ideas, and maybe passing these ideas on to his business customers. He'd joined the Slatterfoot Players, the amateur dramatic group, and was going to attempt to play a female role, but he'd never done that before. The group sadly were desperate for some help, and he thought that if he could fool the public dressed as a female, before the stage performance, he could create a good enough story for the press to become interested, and give The Players some much needed *positive* publicity.

Derek began to perk up at this. He was journalist, this could be leading to a story for him, but he wisely didn't interrupt his future father-in-law's discourse, this time.

Being a manager of the local bank and aware of the business activities of Bisko's, he'd been disgusted at how little they'd helped charities, and the local districts which kept them in business. His contacts had even informed him of how miserly they were about to be with the proceeds of the recent *Red Hair*

Charity Day. So, a few months ago, he'd decided to do something. He'd created a female character for himself and called her Thelma, his sister's name, and tried her out in the local pubs in town, while staying at the flat. He'd used the flat so that Muriel, and Sally, wouldn't become too ashamed or embarrassed by him. The 'gang thing' had started, by chance one night, and had just grown from then on, and taken him by surprise with its success.

The money from the robbery had been destined for a charity. It should have been more, but the plan had been flawed. However the money had probably been taken by the gang members, who'd vanished. As a good citizen, Mr Alexander Donaldson said, he now intended to use, "some of *my own* money," as a donation, then he rapidly corrected that to, "some of *our* own money and with *your* agreement," before an argument started. It was only £3000 and they could afford it anyway.

As someone who would have to go down on bended knee to the bank to borrow *any* money, if he had been wanting to do that, Derek just sat in awe of Alexander's statement.

The cunning bit in Alexander's plan would be that it would be donated on behalf of Bisko's. That would confuse that company, and hopefully embarrass them at the same time towards better habits. It hurt Derek's brain to think of money being played with in this way, but Sally's dad was obviously loaded.

And then Alexander talked of the letter from his twin sister. A month ago, she'd written to him and he'd responded favourably, and now Thelma's latest letter made the future look brighter. Wouldn't it be nice if, at least, they could all meet together? It had been nearly thirty years since he'd seen his twin, and Sally had never even met her. It must be worth a try, to have a good family relationship with her, rather than a silly distant feud ...but that was for the future.

The detective was going to return soon and *Mr/Miss* Big didn't have a plan. How could he avoid going to jail? Help...

Now was Derek's opportunity. It was his turn for centre stage and a chance to impress his future father-in-law. A spark of an idea had come to Derek, and it could work provided Aunt Thelma hadn't a criminal record.... He had their attention.

A simple idea – supply a red herring – use Aunt Thelma's letter...

The real Thelma was innocent, her letter was innocent, but Andy Pandy didn't know that. Let him go on a wild goose chase...

First create a script. What questions would be asked, and what answers required?

Derek was beginning to enjoy this. He could feel creative juices flowing. What they were doing was a bit unusual, but it had been that sort of week, hadn't it?

38

Andy Woodstock had done as was suggested and had some sleep. On awakening, he'd remembered the other suggestion of Mrs Donaldson's, about the shower, so that was done, with extra deodorant, and even a fresh clean shirt. That family had the knack of making him feel uncomfortable and incredibly incompetent. All the way home last night he'd been asking himself if maybe he was in the wrong job?

They hadn't phoned to invite him to return, but return he was now doing. His duty called, whether he was incompetent or not.

Should he park the car on their driveway? No, he wasn't brave enough for that.

The weapon would be evidence. That would force that cocky bank manager onto the back foot right away. Where did he throw it? There was no sign of it in the shrubs on the Donaldson's driveway. It would be more than likely have gone over the wall and into the garden next door. Yes, let's look there. Not a sausage though. *Ouch.* That was surely a sharp shrub, he murmured to himself.

That's alliteration, he thought – I wonder how many times I could say it, and how quickly, and how crisply? That intelligent little thought suddenly made him feel so much brighter – and he tried... *Surely a sharp shrub, surely a sharp shrub, surely a...*

As he was saying it for the fourteenth time, he was startled by the voice behind him, which asked, "Could we 'elp you?"

Mrs Masterton had been perturbed by the presence of a stranger in her garden, skulking about in her shrubbery. "Please,

Sergeant, I'm a defenceless little old lady who lives on her own. Could you send someone round right away, please, please, please..." She'd made the request and there they were, Constables Simpson and Gilbert, again. They had big smiles on their faces. It was almost as if they were his friends.

"Uniforms are always there to defend the public from villains like Plain Clothes Officers," said PC Gilbert with a smirk.

"Shouldn't you 'ave asked permission of the 'ouse 'older?" asked PC Simpson.

Having ascertained it was one of their own that had caused the upset, the two upholders of peace and justice reported to Mrs Masterton, and then were delighted to be invited inside to have tea and cake with the defenceless little old lady while DC Woodstock slunk off over the wall again and rang the Donaldson's doorbell, dreading the next confrontation. He was surprised by the reception.

"Hello, Officer, it's nice to see you again," said a smiling Mrs Donaldson. "Come in"

She led him into the front room, invited him to be seated, and offered him a cup of coffee, and although he suspected it might be drugged and he could be smuggled out of the country under a cloak of darkness, he said, "Yes, please".

He was alone in the room. He glanced around. It had all been tidied up since his last visit, and unlikely anything in there could be used as evidence, he supposed. Then he noticed the letter. It was sitting partly out of the envelope. He could see the bottom part of the page, the part that showed – *the signature*. He looked closer. That signature read *'THELMA'*... They'd received another threat through the post this time. Take a note of the address... Play it casual, big boy, he said to himself, we could be going somewhere now – and fast...

The coffee appeared and so did the three members of the family and Toozlethwaite... What was *he* doing still here?

"You won't mind Derek being here as well, would you Officer? He's practically one of the family now," Muriel smiled.

Derek wriggled uncomfortably as he sat down. Had he

actually proposed last night? He did have a little too much to drink. What a thing to forget, if he had – so he'd better not say...

The little black notebook and pencil was removed from Andy Pandy's pocket. He opened it and silently read the last entry, and then he read it out, in a monotone, as if each word was of vital importance.

"Yes then... *'In the early hours of the morning you were screaming in a falsetto voice into a mobile phone at, what I suspect, was a gang of thugs and robbers, and then you threatened my good-self with the use of an offensive weapon, namely a gun.'* What do you have to say to that then, Mr Bank Man... Mr Donaldson?"

"Well," said Mr Donaldson, in a rich baritone voice, "You should appreciate I had been having some throat problems, an infection which had affected my voice. I'm all right now, but thank you for your concern."

Derek smiled inside. Thank goodness they'd prepared. Scripting something like this in advance could be affected by the questions asked, of course, but his future father-in-law was a smart talker and would juggle the answers as required...

"I am one of the Slatterfoot Players and have been rehearsing a special role for many weeks. I am afraid that I was startled by you all this morning and, after that threatening phone call from the kidnap gang, I over dramatised the whole affair. I have been under a great deal of pressure because of worry about my dear wife. And there was no gun, unless of course, you found one?"

Well done, future *DAD*, thought Derek...

But DC Woodstock was not accepting any of this rubbish...

"I put it to you that you were the leader of that gang, and you were giving them instructions. Either that, or a right good *bollocking* – excuse my French," he said to the ladies, "... for not following instructions. Do you deny that?" he looked aggressively at Sally's father.

"Of course I do. They were putting enormous pressure on me – about the ransom. Don't be a silly fellow now, how could I possibly be telling them what I wanted them to do? They had my wife and were demanding money from me... Anyway, this Thelma character must have been a really rough diamond," responded Alexander.

What was it about this family? DC Woodstock's investigation wasn't moving forward. He was still smarting from the interview he'd had a few days ago with the daughter. He'd lost then too. *Control yourself, Andy, those are defeatist thoughts...*

"The telephone, your daughter's telephone, the one the gang was using, how do you explain the fact that after your wife stole it from the gang, it had calls on it to you?" he demanded.

"You are not going to tell me a daughter wouldn't phone her father, are you? And who were the gang demanding the ransom from? *It was me...* And which phone were they using? It was my daughter's phone, as you have just told us," was the retort from Alexander.

There was an awkward silence. The other heads in the room were waiting for him to say something, and poor old Andy was starting to flounder. Which way next? He would have to keep applying the pressure to the suspect to make him break, although he felt *he* was closer to breaking point than this ruddy bank manager. Aha, thought of something... the phone... fingerprints...

"The mobile that the gang was using, the one that Mrs Donaldson brought back with her, I'll require to have it to check the fingerprints on it. The gang members will certainly be on Police Files," he stated with renewed confidence.

Derek shook his head solemnly, "No good..." he added.

Andy Pandy's spirit dropped once more.

"Why? Why not? *What's wrong?*" he asked, trying not to sob. He really didn't want to know.

"I *cleaned* it properly when Mum gave me it back," explained Sally. "It's a perfectly good phone and it's mine, and I wanted to continue to use it – but not in the dirty state it was in. It was filthy after being touched and breathed on by that gang of villains. I didn't think *you* would want it."

Oh damn, he thought, she's bugging me again.

So, he switched his attention to Muriel for a description of the gang and where she had been held captive, but that took him nowhere as well. Muriel was quick to point out that she was short sighted and they'd taken her glasses from her, and she was now using her spare pair.

"They look *so old fashioned* don't you think, Officer?" she added.

And seeing where she'd been kept had been impossible. When she'd arrived, she'd been blindfolded. She'd escaped in the dark and it had been pouring rain as well. Short sight was such a pain – but not as bad as some diseases she could think of, and she was thankful for that, she said. And as for the gang, she'd never seen any of them without their faces being masked. All she could offer was that there had been four, two males and two females, but they'd really been very nice to her...

Was it worth the effort, Andy Woodstock asked himself? They've closed ranks anyway. This is what happens when you are dealing with a family of crooks. Ah, but the letter... Yes, the letter...

The detective reached over, and lifted it.

"And what's this?" and he held it, pointing accusingly. This was evidence and he could start moving forward again. They'd failed to hide this from him. Bloody hell, he felt sharper now... "It's from Thelma, isn't it?"

"Yes, but she's my sister. She was just arranging to visit us," said Alexander.

"So you say, but I think I'll be visiting her first," said Detective Constable Andy Pandy Woodstock in his most officious manner. He could smell promotion again.

39

So, it's all's well that ends well – is it?

No, it is more likely to be *winners* and *losers*...

Aunt Thelma had been somewhat shocked when DC Woodstock knocked at her door and accused her of being the leader of a gang that had robbed a Supermarket. She'd been a bit of a bitch in her time, and she would be the first to acknowledge that, but she had done nothing which could have broken any laws – well, nothing that she could think of.

Nevertheless, she treated Andy Pandy kindly under the circumstances, pointing out that in her job she was more of a *manager* than a leader. Perhaps it should be the Company's Senior Director he should be talking to – *he* could be a bit of a rascal... Anyway, *she* ran a *team* not a gang. A *team* is a much more *pleasant* term, she'd suggested. When she'd asked him, "Don't you agree?" The detective had grimaced.

Having travelled over ninety miles to interview her, this young man reckoned he'd simply managed to prove that *she was tarred with the same brush as the rest of that cursed Donaldson family.*

At this point he had a difficult decision to take – a choice of having a mental breakdown, or requesting an immediate transfer to Uniforms. He chose the latter – while he was still almost of sound mind. To hell with this investigation and that bloody bet – he'd do something he used to like...

And Uniforms was a wise decision. Afterwards, Andy Woodstock wouldn't think of himself as a loser – he still had a job. He'd settle for just being an out-of-pocket ex-detective.

A definite loser was the poor old Newingsworth BISKO Manager, the final straw for him being Alexander's charity contribution on his behalf.

The story only came to light when Muriel returned to work and found she had a new manager. The previous occupant had been called to Bisko Headquarters and summarily dismissed. His list of offences had been lengthy. He'd failed to maintain company CCTV equipment and lost £3000 to a robbery as a consequence, while at the same time putting a Bisko employee's life at risk and he'd failed to display a sign disclaiming responsibility for accidents occurring on the Company Car Park, thereby absorbing responsibility for the claim by a member of the public for major repairs to a new Mini-Cooper – having been struck with force by a Bisko's trolley. Even more serious in the company's opinion – he'd organised a local *Charity Event* called Red Hair Day, and then later had had the gall to contribute £3000 on Bisko's behalf to the Newingsworth Children's Aid Fund – *also a Charity*. He'd then *brazenly denied that he'd sent the cheque*. The red-faced Personnel Director had actually *screamed* the Company Policy at him, *"BISKO'S DON'T DO CHARITY"*

He was, without doubt – a loser.

Derek felt bad and would have liked to help. If this case ever reached the Industrial Tribunal stage, he could make a story of it. Otherwise... the guy would remain a loser...

One loser and one part-loser, so far, but there was little question about Aunt Thelma – she was a *winner*.

Her brother had agreed to a family meeting. If she wanted to be part of a family again, it was obvious that this could be her one chance, her only chance – and so she grabbed it. She made peace with her twin brother and formed an immediate friendship with his dear wife, Muriel. Having met her niece, Sally, for the first time, she declared her to be a charming girl.

And the feelings were mutual. Sally now had a real live aunt, and couldn't understand why there should have been a problem in the first place. As for Derek, well inevitably, he was introduced by Muriel to Thelma as Sally's fiancé, *Sweaty*, and there was no chance of her knowing him as anything else after that...

After they'd met, Mrs Masterton was delighted to be informed, by Aunt Thelma herself, that she was going to be living next door to her. Sally and Derek were soon to be wed and would be moving. They'd landed lucky (although Derek suspected it had been more in the way of a bribe) and had been gifted a cottage on the outskirts of Newingsworth by Sally's doting parents as a wedding present, and they would be moving shortly to live there. Thelma would move in, as they moved out.

And another winner had been Derek's grandad. Getting back his much-loved bike had been wonderful. He was also greatly relieved that Gran had been putting less pressure on him to complete these ruddy crosswords, particularly now that Derek was away – he missed that help. He had a worry about his wife though. She was tending to be forgetful – about the crosswords and many other things – more regularly. He suspected she might be going scatty, batty, or bonkers – *before him...* so it looked like Derek's gran could be progressing in the direction of *loser...*

Several months had now passed since Muriel's 'short exciting adventure away from home' as she called her hostage spell. Sally had been amazed that her father and her mother were still living under the same roof. If Derek had done that to her, she'd have strangled him in his sleep, *guaranteed...* Strangely, and in contrast to what Sally had expected, her mother had become ultra supportive of her husband's new venture, the acting, and the time was fast approaching for him to prove how good he could be.

If asked, Derek would not have described Sally's father as a winner or a loser – his chosen word for that gentleman would have been a *CHANCER*. Derek had been an enormous help with publicity for the Slatterfoot Amateur Players. He'd carefully written articles about his future father-in-law, telling of the manner in which this *leading man* had prepared to become a *leading lady* in their forthcoming production of that hoary old chestnut of a play – Lady Windermere's Fan – articles which, of course, when printed, had to avoid becoming incriminating evidence.

Of course, in between time, normal newspaper routines still had to continue for Derek and he was pleased to have a chance to compose one of his 'good news stories' for the Gazette, based on a letter Sally received at the office...

It had come from the south of France and was signed by four young people who'd recently had their double wedding in Saint-Tropez. Maddie, Steve, Jane, and Michael had sent kind regards to Newingsworth, and enclosed a cheque for £100,000 to be paid to Newingsworth Retired Townspeople's Home, and a photograph of a happy foursome. They'd spent a very enjoyable 'holiday' in Newingsworth a few months ago, with a lovely lady called Muriel who lives there. They sent her love and kisses, and said she would know who they meant...

The aforementioned, Muriel, smiled when she read it. She was pleased it had all worked out nicely for them...

As the bond grew between the three female members of the Donaldson clan, Muriel, Aunt Thelma, and Sally, so also the relationship between Derek and his future father-in-law developed. *Developed?* Sort of like a noose tightening around a neck, was the feeling Derek had.

Derek became a valued member of the Slatterfoot Amateur Players – *reluctantly* he stressed. He had been cajoled into performing the task of prompter. Assisting Alexander to learn his lines had encouraged this, and then being dragged along to attend rehearsals with Alexander, and to meet the others, had been his downfall. They'd had no-one prompting – he was *landed* with it...

And then Alexander had sent Derek into a blind panic during the afternoon before that first performance. The phone call from Alexander clearly stated that he, the leading actor, could no longer go through with it. He'd taken cold feet, said he couldn't remember the lines, his female voice had left him, and that he was about to *end it all...* Derek's worry was not the manner by which Sally's dad was about to leave the world. Oh no...

Alexander had phoned all the other cast members beforehand. He'd explained that Derek knew all the lines and would be *taking over the leading role*.

Derek didn't...

He immediately shot over to the theatre and began to administer a mixture of alcohol and cough mixture, a large glassful, down the throat of the reluctant father-in-law-to-be. On the threat of a second drink of the mixture, Alexander gave in and said he'd do it after all, and then gave a wonderful performance.

Derek was mightily relieved.

It was now several months later and already Derek looked on himself as an old married man. He and Sally, now Mr and Mrs Toozlethwaite, were settled in their own cottage, the nearest neighbour being about half a mile away.

A well known fact had been proven this morning – women take a long time to get ready. Earlier today, Sally had spent ages getting dressed and applying her make-up. She had gone off eventually, on her own, to visit her mum and her Aunt Thelma. She hadn't left him much time to get ready – and it had taken him just as long as her... And he was meeting Alexander for lunch.

Gran and Grandad had taken to popping in to visit the young couple, just when the fancy took them. It would have been just the thing if they had appeared at the door after Sally had gone. They would have had heart attacks – for certain, and have delayed Derek even more by doing so.

Late Saturday morning and he was now, at long last, on his way into town, and having skipped breakfast he was starving, but as he sat in the taxi, he wished he'd taken more time to get prepared. He felt uncomfortable, as if he'd put on something back to front.

There had been one major achievement today – at long last, he'd created *his very own* storyline. Inspiration had suddenly come to him while getting ready, and this very morning, once he'd dressed, he'd had to rush to the computer to record his new ideas. They'd had to be recorded immediately. He knew how easily it had been in the past to lose an inspired thought. He had his new computer and he knew how to use it, and as he'd typed, he'd decided that he was going to *enjoy* the experience of learning all about his subject – he'd feel the effects for himself.

'Incognito...

What to wear had been a difficult decision – colour co-ordination had never been a strong point. Vertical stripes to fatten you up and horizontal to slim...? Or was it the other way round? Did it matter though? If it was someone else's clothes you were about to squeeze into, should it make the slightest bit of difference?

The choices had been made and the thirty-year-old was now walking confidently but casually towards the bar. This chosen skirt felt very short and very tight. When it had been put on, there had been no-one to ask the perennial question – does my butt look big in this? *But dressing in company would not have been correct, not for the first time, now would it? You had to be alone on that first occasion, surely...*

Choosing to be blonde had been a good start. Matching that with dark colours had been the next decision. The ear-rings had been difficult – so many to try...

Now, the shiny, black, high heels clicked sharply on the tiled flooring – mustn't slip and twist an ankle – that was an obvious danger with very high heels, of course, and hobbling along in pain would impress no-one. No sympathy wanted today, just admiring glances...

The table had been booked for one o'clock and nice timing had been achieved...

It had been a sleepless night. An attempt had been made to apply camouflage to the eye area but the eyes still felt bleary – and it was not a day to feel listless and out of sorts.

Sally was a tough taskmistress. She expected and demanded high standards...

It had been she who had arranged this meeting with the bank manager – our man on the inside, as she had described him, the man who would supply all the detail required to ensure nothing could possibly go wrong... Apparently this was someone she knew very well and his plan would be infallible.

Preparing for a bank robbery would require great care and attention to detail.

At least Sally's instructions had been clear about how they should find each other.

"Go to 'The Pelican's Perch' in Blythe Street and he'll be standing at the bar, at one o'clock, drinking a blue cocktail – with a cherry."

So here we are at the bar, but he hasn't arrived yet, obviously. The place is deserted except for a brunette in a stunning red dress sitting on a tall stool at the bar – nice legs... drinking a blue cocktail – with a cherry?

"Hello, Sweetie," said the strong manly voice, with a fluttering of eyelashes thrown in.

"I'm Thelma," he continued, "Are you are the fellow who likes to be called... Derek?"

Derek nodded, and tried to hide his surprise by checking that he'd no ladders in his tights...

It was another fella...

Sally hadn't explained this bit too well to him...'

He was happy with this first draft, but would Sally be pleased at the way he intended to develop her character. She was to be the tough and nasty lady organiser of the gang.

In real life he hoped that she would remain strong and supportive of him into the future, and believe in him, particularly when she found out how he would be doing the research for his book ...and would she have agreed with his choice of apparel, for the meal?

At least, she would have recognised the selection he'd made – *it was her clothes he had on...*

Sally wouldn't be back until about seven, so as long as he was home before her, she'd never know... well, not this evening at least, but she'd have to be told at some point. He was extremely glad that Mrs Masterton no longer lived next door...

He would have to make a clean breast of it to Sally ...then, as he sat in the taxi adjusting his bra stuffed with socks, he realised that perhaps a different phrase would be more appropriate...

He removed the little mirror from his handbag for the umpteenth time, gazing at his reflection, and checking his lipstick and teeth for smudges.

"*Relax, Sweaty,*" he told himself, "*...you've chosen the perfect shade of red...*"

Although, was the eyeliner perhaps overdone?

He giggled – imagine – coming out dressed like this...

Maybe he shouldn't have listened to Alexander... he could be very *persuasive*...

Now – should a bank robbery be suggested...?

A line would have to be drawn *somewhere*.

This was as far as *he* was going, thank you very much...

The Derek Series

Please... Call Me Derek

Derek travels from child to confused adult, from reporter for the local paper to any job available, doing everything he thinks he should, but doing it his way.

'Derek's In Trouble

As funny as ever and as unlucky as always, Derek is going through another unexpected crisis in his life.

A local reporter with the partner of his dreams, his life is all set to be perfect.

So, how will he explain his foray out in his wife's dress?

Then, there's the leggy lady intent on making a lasting impression ...on top of that, there are everyone else's problems to sort. Is his Gran, the secret Radio agony aunt, capable of helping anyone?

Derek's Revenge

Derek has not had much success getting his first great novel started - in fact, the research it requires has nearly cost him his marriage and ruined several pairs of his wife's tights. All he needs is a better topic, maybe he should be writing non-fiction, he is a journalist, after all... As is normal for Derek, things go pretty rapidly and hilariously downhill from there!

Derek's Good Relations

Relations and Relationships - poor Derek has far too many of both - he has a book to write - a mother he has only just met - a wife about to give birth and a poodle who hates him.

Life had been so different a year and a half ago.

Back then it had been a life before ET and Mom and a heap of other people interfering with his good intentions.

In Mac Black's fourth Derek book the plot thickens and Derek tries to be devious as he blunders from disaster to disaster making us laugh all the way!

Derek in Action

Derek to the Rescue - Derek has a CAUSE but, being Derek, he also has a host of misunderstandings to sort out, mistakes to rectify and a wife to mollify.

As a natural leader, he knows that beating the Railway Developers is down to him. As a natural disaster area, we know it is unlikely to go quite to plan.

In Mac Black's fifth and final Derek book the plot is stirred as poor gullible Derek tries his best and makes us laugh all the way to the end!

MacQuarrie Black

From the Author

I enjoy humour in all forms. In my life, I have had fun performing daft roles in amateur theatre and, at times have written and presented silly poetry – I loved hearing the sound of laughter. Now, I am having great pleasure in writing fiction in the hope of gaining smiles. This, I modestly claim, to be not bad for someone who can't tell a joke to save himself, but, changing my name has been a temptation. Instead of MAC BLACK I'd become CHAIDSUFF GREY – that way my fortune might come from people looking for erotic stories. Mine are MEANT for grown-ups and are only a LITTLE bit naughty in places.

If you would like to keep up with my latest news and the new series I am writing – please visit www.macblack.info